Paul felt a nudge of awareness.

He noted the changes time had wrought in Amy. From the freckle-faced pixie who had trailed him as a child, to the blushing, self-conscious teenager, she had become the woman before him now.

Amy had been cute as a child. Pretty as a teenager. But now she had become strikingly beautiful.

Paul regretted now that he hadn't bothered to stop and really notice Amy. All their lives he had taken her affection and adoration for granted. Had treated it lightly.

Yet always she had stayed faithful. Always she had had a purity, a sincerity, a solid, simple faith in God that had made Paul keep his distance.

But now…now, when it was too late…now, when she was pledged to another…

Now a powerful yearning seemed to draw him to Amy….

Books by Carolyne Aarsen

Love Inspired

Homecoming #24
Ever Faithful #33

CAROLYNE AARSEN

has been writing stories almost as long as she has been reading them, and has wanted to write a book for most of her life. When she could finally write "The End" on her first, she realized, to her dismay, that it wasn't. Three rewrites later turned it into a book that was finally marketable. What she learned along the way was to write a story that was true to what she believed and was the kind of book she liked to read.

Her writing stems from her life's experiences. Living in a tiny cabin with five children in remote British Columbia, opening their home to numerous foster children, helping her husband build the house they now live in, working with their cattle on their ranch in northern Alberta—all become fodder for yet more stories to come.

Carolyne hopes her writing will show that our Christian life is a growing, changing relationship with God and a constant fight with our own weakness. Thankfully, God keeps taking us back.

Ever Faithful
Carolyne Aarsen

Love Inspired

Published by Steeple Hill Books™

STEEPLE HILL BOOKS

Steeple
Hill™

ISBN 0-373-87033-7

EVER FAITHFUL

Copyright © 1998 by Carolyne Aarsen

Printed in U.S.A.

For the Word of the Lord is right and true,
He is faithful in all He does.
—*Psalm* 33:4

I'd like to dedicate this book to Loree Lough,
fellow writer and encourager, and, as always,
to my husband, Richard.

Chapter One

"How much longer will the grass hold out, little brother?" Amy's saddle creaked as she leaned forward, staring ruefully over the pasture.

Rick shrugged. "Couple of weeks, more if we get rain."

Amy Danyluk lifted a tangle of reddish hair from her neck and tucked it under her old cowboy hat. The sun's heat, warming her head, seemed to mock Rick's hope for rain. So did the rivulets of sweat running down her back. She pulled up the red bandanna hanging around the neck of a once-yellow T-shirt and wiped her neck with it, squinting at the cows in the distance.

From here they looked content as they moved slowly along, their calves kicking up their heels and running in circles. However the chewed-down areas close to the horses were a mute testimony to how little feed the cows had left. "I think we'll have to get the lower fields ready just in case we need to move them."

"The fence needs to get fixed before we do that." Rick pulled his hat off his head and wiped a trickle of sweat with his arm. "Whew, it's hot."

Amy nodded. "I was hoping we could work on it in the morning, while it's still cool."

"No can do, sis. I'm busy on Monday. I promised Jack I'd

help him in the garage until four.'' Rick rubbed the side of his nose and threw Amy an apologetic look. ''Sorry. I made the plans over a week ago.'' He pulled on Sandover's reins, turned his horse around and walked away.

''This is not the time of year to make other plans,'' Amy muttered. They had hay to haul and cut and bale again. The corrals needed work, and the old fence needed repairs. They had to cross fence their hayfield. She had to work all of this around her own job, as well as gardening and taking care of their father, Judd.

Amy swung her own horse, Misty, around and with a nudge, easily caught up to Rick. ''If you can get that tractor working on Tuesday we can haul the bales in a couple of days. I can get a day off next week and we can start on it then.''

''Speaking of hay, we'll need to buy more if we have to bring the cows down sooner,'' Rick commented. ''I had hoped to turn those pregnant heifers I bought into the lower pasture.''

''Hopefully we won't need to buy hay if we cross fence the hayfield. I still don't know why you bought fall calvers. They just don't work in our program.''

''It's a good way of making our cash flow more even. Besides, they were a terrific deal, for purebreds.''

''But cow prices are down. And a deal is only a deal—''

''If you can afford it,'' Rick intoned, his voice taking on that bored tone that told Amy he heard her but had stopped listening. He pushed his hat back on his head, his auburn hair darkened with sweat. ''I know it was a chance, Amy. But sometimes you have to take them.''

Amy sensed it was time to stop hammering. She wished she could let things roll off her back as easily, but she couldn't. She was the one who did the books, who knew exactly how far they were into their operating loan. She had been in charge since an accident with an auger had taken off half of her father's leg, ten years ago. She knew she had a tendency to fret, whereas Rick was more inclined to count on things working out in the end. ''Okay, Rick, I'll lay off. But I want you to help me out here, big-time.''

''How's that?''

"Start praying for rain," Amy said quietly.

Rick was spared the need to reply as Sandover pranced to one side. Amy drew her own horse back to fall behind him. Sandover was green broke and unpredictable. Amy didn't want Misty hit by a flying hoof.

"I'd watch his ears, Rick," Amy warned, watching as the horse tossed his head.

"He's just high-strung, glad to be out." Rick pulled Sandover's head around, and with another defiant shake of his head, the horse settled. Rick flashed his sister a triumphant grin over his shoulder. "See. All under control."

"I'm going to the Hendersons'. You coming?" Amy asked, ignoring him.

"What do you need to do there?"

Amy shrugged in reply. Rick didn't need to know, he would just tease her.

"Well?" Rick insisted.

"If you need to know, I want to borrow Elizabeth's hot rollers and pick up a pair of panty hose she bought for me."

Rick's head spun around faster than Sandover's. "Panty hose?" Rick's incredulous tone said much more than his words. "Rollers? You won't even know how to put those things in your hair."

Amy still said nothing.

"And since when do you care about how you look?"

"Since Tim and I started going out. You know that," Amy replied, wishing the flush would leave her cheeks. She didn't need to feel guilty. Her desire to look attractive was nothing to be embarrassed about, especially not in front of her little brother.

"C'mon, Amy. Your motto's always been 'death before makeup.' Your idea of dressing up for a date was to iron your T-shirt. Now you're going to wear panty hose and—" he put heavy emphasis on the word "—curl you hair. What's next? Lip gloss?"

"It's my engagement party. Why wouldn't I want to look my best?"

Rick drew alongside her, and she chanced a sidelong glance,

catching his quizzical look. "I don't think you're being straight with me, sis. The last time I saw you dressed up was—" He paused, his brow furrowed in thought. His expression brightened and he snapped his fingers. "I remember. Two years ago, you bought a dress and you curled your hair." He narrowed his eyes. "Two years ago. The last time Paul Henderson came home."

"Would you give me a break?" Amy said, angry at what he implied. "Like I said before, it's our engagement party. Tim's and mine. I bought a new dress for him. I'm curling my hair for him. Paul hasn't been around for years."

"And you haven't spent this much time on how you look in years."

"And every time he comes home," Amy continued, pretending not to hear, "he's got another girl on his arm."

"You can't compete, Amy," Rick said shortly. "He's way out of your league."

"Why are you even bringing this up?" Amy turned on her brother, angry and frustrated with the position he put her in. "I happen to be engaged. Tonight's our engagement party. Tim and I are making plans to get married. Paul hasn't been important to me for years." Amy swung Misty around and clucked angrily to her horse.

Misty broke into a gentle lope, the breeze cooling Amy's heated face.

Why did I overreact? Amy berated herself. Now he's going to think he's right.

Misty crested the hill, and Amy drew her to a halt. She glanced back over her shoulder. Sandover plodded slowly along, his head down, looking disarmingly submissive.

Amy turned back, a gentle sigh lifting her shoulders as her eyes took in the view. The valley lay below her, sun-warmed and restful, the sweep of the fawn-colored hills undulating away from her. Solitary stretches of pine trees lined their rims, sending delicate fingers of darker green down the hillsides.

She drew in a slow breath, as if drawing in the life-giving sustenance of the tangy air of the Cariboo. She knew there were other places in God's creation more spectacular, but she had been placed here, and here was where she belonged, as surely as the grass and as snugly as the rocks.

A soft, warm breeze teased her heated cheeks, and she turned her face to it as she lifted up a quick prayer, thanking God for Tim, friends and home. She shook her head, wondering at her brother. He still didn't believe that her childhood crush for Paul Henderson had slowly worn away with each year Paul stayed in Vancouver and each new girlfriend he brought home for his brief visits.

The thump of hooves behind her broke into her thoughts. She turned in time to see Sandover rear, his front hooves flashing out.

"Get off that miserable horse," Amy called out.

But Rick stayed on, a grin splitting his face at the challenge. Sandover bucked, shook his head and came to an abrupt halt. Rick exerted steady pressure on the horse's bridle, slowly pulling his head up. "Just go on ahead, Amy. I'll catch up," he called.

Amy hesitated, then, reassured that Rick indeed had the horse under control, turned and clucked to Misty. If she hurried she would be able to make it to the ranch, get what she needed and be out before Rick and Sandover reached the yard.

Misty hit her long trot, easily covering the ground on the way to the Hendersons' spread. They traveled a path well-worn over the years, toward a place Amy had considered her second home.

It was Elizabeth and Fred Henderson who had become her second parents when Rick and Amy's mother, Noreen, left Judd, ten years ago, one month before Judd's accident.

Elizabeth had dried Amy's tears both then and during each crisis after that. It was to Elizabeth that Amy at a tender-hearted age of twelve ran with stories of being picked on in school. Elizabeth was the one who shamed Judd into buying a prom dress for Amy and it was Elizabeth who taught Amy to pray, to trust in God for both the large and small things of her life. It was a good trade all the way around. Amy had no mother and a bitter father. And Elizabeth had three boys and no daughter.

And now she was going to open her home for Amy and Tim's engagement party, a job that would have been Noreen Danyluk's had she elected to stay with her family.

Amy rode into the yard and dismounted before Misty came to a complete stop. She pulled the reins over Misty's head and tied her loosely to a corral post. "Be back in a flash, girl," she murmured to her horse, stroking her neck. Misty blew as if in answer, and Amy turned and jogged up the walk to the verandah.

The door swung easily open and Amy stepped inside, unlacing her roper boots and kicking them off with the ease of many years of running in and out unannounced. "Anybody home?"

"The stuff is in the laundry room," called out a voice from the top of the stairs. "I'll be right there."

Amy walked down the hallway, ducking into a small room tucked under the stairs. A crumpled paper bag lay on the dryer and Amy peeked inside, checking the contents.

"How's my girl?"

Amy jumped, then glanced over her shoulder at Elizabeth Henderson. She leaned her small frame against the doorjamb, a smile crinkling up her face, brown from the sun. Her gray, short-cropped hair stuck up in all directions. Dust smeared the front of an old high school sweatshirt cast off from one of her sons. The knees of her blue jeans sported twin circles of grime.

Amy turned and gave Elizabeth a quick hug. "Where were you?" Straightening, Amy brushed a cobweb from her wrinkled cheek.

"I started cleaning up the spare room for Paul's latest girlfriend and ended up in the attic, hauling around all the old junk."

"When is Paul coming?"

"I expect both of them any minute." Elizabeth smiled as if in anticipation.

"Tracy, is it?"

Elizabeth shook her head, tucking her arm through Amy's as she led her back down the hall. "Stacy. They've been going out four months. A record for my eldest son. I think it's actually quite serious."

"It's about time he settles down."

"I know I shouldn't be impatient, but I'm looking forward to grandchildren and none of the boys are helping me out there. At least I know you won't disappoint me. It will be wonderful having you living down the road, a married woman." Elizabeth paused in the doorway to the kitchen. "Do you have time for a cup of tea?"

Amy shook her head regretfully, leaning down to look out of the window. Rick and Sandover were finally in the yard. He had pulled into the shade on the north side of the barn. Sandover pranced impatiently, throwing his head around. "I better not. Rick's horse is acting pretty rank today."

Elizabeth took Amy's bag while Amy pulled on her worn boots. Straightening she caught Elizabeth's bemused look.

"What?" she asked with a smile, taking the bag back.

"I'm proud of you, Amy. That's all. God has been good bringing you into our lives." Elizabeth reached out and lovingly tucked a wayward strand of hair behind her ear. "It will be fun having you and Tim living just down the road. And I'll be glad when you can finally quit that job at the grocery store."

"I'll be glad, too. But for now it pays a few bills and gives me money to save up for our wedding." Amy leaned over and gave Elizabeth a quick, one-armed hug as a feeling of love for this diminutive woman rushed through her. "I'm looking forward to introducing Tim to the aunts and uncles."

"And they're all dying to meet the man who has such an important place in your life. And who finally made you lose that crush you had on Paul."

Amy suppressed a sigh. It stood to reason that an occasion like an engagement party was a time to remember old boyfriends and crushes. "That was a long time ago, and I was a silly little girl."

"Not so silly." Elizabeth smiled, crossing her arms over the faded sweatshirt. "Every girl has to start somewhere."

"It just took me longer to quit, that's all." Amy pushed open the door, and they paused a moment on the verandah spinning out the farewell in the manner of old friends and family.

"God works things out in His own way." Elizabeth slanted

Amy an apologetic look. "Paul could never settle here, while Tim seems more than happy to." She sighed. "It's hard to admit that your oldest son needs to do the most growing up."

Amy shook her head, remembering Paul's various escapades. She could see them with a more critical eye, now that she had Tim to compare Paul to. "Paul has always been restless. As long as I can remember he had to drive the fastest, work the hardest, break what he could bend, and push what could be moved."

"He needs to find peace, and he won't the way he's living," Elizabeth said. "It's just a continuation of him haring around the countryside, looking for challenges and excitement. Only now he does it wearing a suit and using a cell phone."

Amy laughed at the image. It wasn't too hard to transpose the image of Paul Henderson—one arm out of the window of his pickup as he maneuvered his way through potholes and over rocks with a pretty girl clinging to him—with the image of a more civilized man, cell phone to his ear driving a car shaped like a bullet.

The roar of a vehicle winding down the valley broke the silence.

"I wouldn't be surprised if that's Paul now." Elizabeth stepped forward to squint at the plume of dust roiling behind a red sports car driven far too fast for the rough country roads of the Cariboo.

Amy frowned as the car came closer. "I thought you said he drove a Land Rover?"

"That's our Paul. Always buying and selling, changing vehicles as often as he changes girlfriends, looking for the perfect match." Elizabeth smiled, but Amy sensed a note of censure in her voice.

"If his new girlfriend and that car's a match, she'll be pretty classy," Amy commented, her eye on the sleek sports car.

The car made one more turn, flew into the yard, gravel churning as it came to a sudden stop.

The door flew open. At that same moment Rick cried out. From the lee of the barn, a startled Sandover exploded into the yard.

The gelding whirled, bugled a challenge and bucked. Rick held on, his face grim. Sandover arched his back, cleared the ground, and Rick flew through the air, landing on the ground with a sickening thud.

Amy felt her blood turn to ice in her veins as the horse reared above Rick, mane flying. Rick rolled out of the way of his flashing hooves. Sandover came crashing down, just missing Rick. The horse shook his head and reared again.

Amy willed her leaden feet to move, her arms to function. She dropped the bag she held, jumped off the verandah and ran.

Hands caught her from behind, voices called out warnings. Without looking to see who it was, she shook free, stumbling to where Rick lay. He peeked over his arm, flashed another grin at Amy and got up.

Amy felt relief sluice through her. A movement out of the corner of her eye caught her attention. Sandover reared again, his eyes wild, foam flecking his bridle.

"Move, Rick," she yelled, throwing her hat at the horse. Sandover shied away, spinning, then stopped to face her.

Amy kept herself between Rick and the horse, praying, watching. "Get going, Rick," she snapped, her eyes on Sandover.

Rick scrambled out of the way.

"Amy, you get away from that horse," she heard a familiar deep voice yell.

She couldn't. The horse was unpredictable, and she had to get him back into the corral.

Sandover threw his head, and Amy caught the reins as they whipped past her.

He reared and she let him go up, letting the reins slip through her hand. Then, using the brief moment of instability, when he was at his highest point, she moved over, pulling on his reins to turn his head. Again he went up. Again she pulled him in a circle, working him closer and closer as Sandover churned up the ground. Slowly the circle tightened. Then as quickly as it began, Sandover stopped, flanks heaving, head lowered.

Amy waited, ensuring his submission, slowly pulling his head around. Only then did she relax her hold on the reins.

Sweat ran in rivulets down her temples, between her shoulder blades. Anger and edgy fear coursed through her. The horse could easily have killed or badly injured either her or Rick. Pulling in a deep breath, she felt a tremor in her gut. Each time she had worked with this horse he brought her right to the limit before he gave in. But she couldn't indulge in histrionics right now. She had to get the horse into the corral and the tack off.

A dull throb made itself known in her left shoulder. She couldn't remember being struck by the horse. She clenched her teeth against the pain, pulling Sandover's head around to lead him to the corral. She ignored her trembling knees and the ache that grew worse with each movement as she tied Sandover to the top rail.

"Good job, Amy." A deep voice spoke from the other side of the fence, and Amy looked over her shoulder into eyes as blue as midsummer lake water.

Paul Henderson.

He stared back at her, his incredibly blue eyes crinkled up at the corners. A thin-lipped mouth turned up in a tight smile. He wore his hair longer than the last visit, dark streaks threading through the blond. His face had lengthened; his jawline seemed stronger.

"Hey, Paul," she replied, turning her eyes back to her hands as they unbuckled, loosened and tugged. Her fingers didn't want to cooperate.

Reaction, she reminded herself.

"You scared me, Amy." The words were spoken quietly, but Amy sensed a note of concern behind them that couldn't help but warm her. "Do you need any help?" he asked.

Amy glanced at him, looking past his familiar face to the unfamiliar clothes. A teal green silk shirt that looked as if it cost more than the saddle was tucked into gray pants that fell in well-tailored lines to leather loafers. She smiled ruefully. "Thanks, but I can manage."

She reached up to pull the saddle off. Pain wrenched through her arm, and she almost dropped it.

"Amy, are you okay?" Ignoring his expensive clothes, Paul sprang over the fence.

Amy stared fiercely at the saddle, concentrating on breathing through waves of pain that slowly eased.

"You're hurt," Paul said, his hands pulling hers away from the saddle.

Amy shook her head. But another hot stab shot through her arm. "I'm okay," she managed to say through clenched teeth.

"No, you're not." Paul reached out to touch her, and she pulled away.

"Yes, I am." She didn't want him touching her. She just wanted to go home.

Elizabeth wandered over, accompanied by a tall, slim girl. She wore a loose silk jacket in earth tones that hung artfully over a narrow skirt.

Amy caught a swift impression of soft brown eyes, delicate features and a flawless complexion. Gorgeous, of course. Paul never came home with the plain ones. Amy was suddenly extremely self-conscious of her dusty face and old clothes.

"Amy, I'd like to introduce you to Stacy." Elizabeth leaned over the fence, the beautiful woman standing beside her. "Stacy, this is Amy."

"Hello, Stacy." It would hurt to shake her hand so Amy only nodded. Flustered at what must seem a show of ill manners she turned to Rick. "You'll have to walk back with Sandover." She looked back at Elizabeth, Stacy and Paul. "I should get going. I'll see you all tonight." She kept her smile on her face as she mounted Misty and rode her out of the yard. Once out of sight, she allowed herself a grimace of pain. *Stubborn woman,* she reprimanded herself. *Too proud to ask for help.* She only hoped that no serious damage was done. She could ill afford to be laid up with a sore shoulder. She had too much work to do on the ranch.

Glancing backward she saw the Hendersons going back into the house and her brother starting on his long walk home.

She didn't feel sorry for him, but it was hard not to feel a

little sorry for herself. Somehow she had to get ready for a
party tonight, convince her father and Rick to come, and find
something else to wear. The sleeveless dress was out of the
question now.

Chapter Two

"And how are you really feeling?"

Amy almost jumped at the sound of Paul's voice behind her on the stairs. She had taken some time away from the party and the congratulations of Henderson aunts and uncles and found sanctuary in the stairwell. Paul lowered himself to the stair beside her and she scooted over to give him room.

"Where were you?" she asked, avoiding his question and his probing gaze.

"Checking out my old bedroom." He smiled at her and, reaching over, touched her shoulder again. "This afternoon that horse kicked you, didn't he?"

Amy shrugged, then winced. She knew from past experience she could never fool Paul.

"Yes, I don't know how it happened, but Sandover's hoof grazed my shoulder. It feels a little better now." Amy pulled a face. "But not much," she conceded. She turned to Paul who leaned his head against the wall beside him. His even features looked relaxed, his shapely mouth curved into a gentle smile. She remembered countless times she had lost herself in daydreams over his face, creating the eternal cliché. Young girl in love with older neighbor boy. But Paul always humored her, and in return to her love letters, would write his own back—

joking letters full of his terrible puns, reassuring her that someday her prince would come. In his way he gently broke it to
her that the prince wouldn't be him. He didn't intend on staying
around Williams Lake long enough to fill that role for her.

"What are you smiling about?" he prodded.

"Remembering old daydreams," she said turning her engagement ring on her finger. Her love for Tim gave her the
confidence and ability to look at Paul with new eyes. Her reaction to him this afternoon was more about the surprise of
seeing him than anything else, she had concluded.

"And what conclusion have you come to?"

"That you were right," she said. "You weren't the right
person for me. And I wasn't the right person for you. I see that
in each and every girlfriend you bring home."

"And what do you think of this one?"

"Hard to say. I haven't had a chance to really talk to her
yet."

"And I haven't met your Tim." He smiled back at her. "So
what's he like? Does he floss? Work out? Watch his cholesterol
level? Tell me how you met."

And Amy did. She had been arguing with her accounts manager when Tim Enders walked in. In a matter of minutes he
had soothed the ruffled feathers and managed to put together a
deal that worked for everyone. And then he had asked her out
for dinner.

"One date led to another and pretty soon we were horseback
riding, going for drives, fishing and, most important of all,"
she added with a conspiratorial grin, "sitting together in
church. And that pretty much sealed the engagement. It wasn't
official until the day we were up in the mountains for a hike."
Amy fell silent remembering the burst of sheer joy when he
asked her, the feeling of belonging to somebody who wanted
to share his life with her overwhelming her.

"He's a lucky guy."

"And I'm very blessed." Amy nodded, looking down at her
engagement ring once again. "I want to be a good and faithful
wife to him."

Silence hung between them punctuated by the sounds of

laughter coming from the living room below as both realized the import of her words.

"I know you will be, Amy. You are a person whose love is faithful and pure."

"Thanks." The compliment warmed her, creating a mood that seemed to settle their relationship onto a new and more comfortable plane. "And you're a good friend."

"One that hasn't been around much lately," he said with a rueful look.

"Well you're here now, and I'm glad you came. And now I'd like to find out how Stacy managed to snag a guy half the girls in the Cariboo were yearning after."

Paul laughed. "C'mon."

"If I take away the ones that were panting after Mark Andrews before he got married and ignore the ones who are engaged," Amy pursed her lips thoughtfully, "maybe not *quite* half."

Paul just shook his head.

"So," Amy continued, "is she the one?"

"I think so," Paul traced the crease of his pants, his look thoughtful.

Amy bit her lip, knowing her next question trod on shaky ground. "Which church does she go to?"

"None. But neither do I, so that's no problem."

Amy turned away, suddenly disappointed in her old hero. "That's too bad, Paul."

"You sound like my parents," he replied testily.

"I was hoping I sounded more like your sister."

"I thought you didn't like being called that."

Amy shook her head. "You're five years older than me. I'll always be younger. I'm hoping I will always be like a sister to you."

"You'll always be a sassy little redhead, that's what," Paul said, his smirk skipping over the serious tone of their previous conversation, creating an easy return to the give and take of their youth.

Amy glanced sidelong at him, her smile acknowledging the change in the tone of the conversation. Paul hadn't changed, but as she analyzed her new feelings for him, she realized with thankfulness that she had grown up.

"There you are." Stacy stood below them, smiling uncertainly up at both of them.

Paul got up and walked down to join her. "Just catching up with an old friend," he said easily, brushing a kiss across her soft cheek. "You never did get a proper introduction to Amy did you?" He looked up at Amy, who still sat on the stairs, a soft smile curving up delicate lips tinted with gloss. Her gleaming copper hair flowed over her shoulders, curling up at the bottom. Warm gray eyes fringed with dark lashes looked down at him with humor in them.

The tomboy he had always remembered looked feminine and incredibly appealing. To be sure, she still wore jeans and a shirt, but the jeans were black, the linen shirt was decorated with embroidery on the sleeves. It was a look that suited her as much as Stacy's soft flowing dress became her. He glanced at his girlfriend. He couldn't help but compare the two women. Stacy always looked elegant, composed, everything coordinated. But the Amy in front of him looked nothing like the dusty, bedraggled girl of this afternoon. He remembered again how easily she handled a horse that he would have walked a wide circle around.

"So are you going to introduce us or do I have to do it myself?" Amy asked, tilting her head to one side as she came down the stairs.

"Sorry." Paul mentally shook himself and drew Stacy closer. "Stacy Trottier, this is Amy Danyluk, neighbor, friend and the little sister I never had." He turned to Stacy who shifted her cup of coffee to one hand and reached out one well-manicured hand as he spoke.

"So what kind of work do you do in Vancouver?" Amy asked, shaking Stacy's hand.

"I work with computers." Stacy pulled her hand back.

"That's a pretty broad field." Amy laughed. "What kind of work?"

Stacy took a sip of her coffee looking at Amy over the rim of her cup. "I set up Web-sites and program computers."

"How do you do that?" Amy persisted, unintimidated by Stacy's terse replies.

"Do you know what an ISP is or an HTML editor?" she asked as if challenging Amy.

Amy raised her eyebrows with a smile, as if unashamed of her ignorance. "I don't have the first clue what you're talking about."

"Don't even start, Amy," Paul warned. "Stacy can talk about the 'Net until the cows come home, and you and I both know cows never do."

"I don't mind," Amy replied. "Someday I'd like to get a computer. I'm sure there's something on the Internet about cattle."

"There is," Stacy said, leaning forward. "You'll find information on things you can't even imagine."

"And a lot of things you can't imagine people would want to know," Paul added.

Stacy shrugged. "That comes with the freedom of expression inherent in the Web."

"I don't think Amy's particularly interested in the Internet anyhow. Why don't you ask her about her cows?" Paul continued. Once Stacy started on her favorite topic, she didn't easily stop. He knew Amy was only being courteous.

But neither paid him any attention. Amy asked Stacy another question. Amy was always polite, Paul thought. Always polite and always careful to make people feel good. For a moment he thought she would be put off by Stacy's abrupt attitude, but Amy acted as if she hadn't noticed.

Paul watched as she tilted her head to one side, trying to comprehend, interjecting with quiet questions. She nodded, as if she finally understood and then dropped her head back and laughed at something Stacy said.

Her hair slipped across her shoulder, her gray eyes sparkled. Paul couldn't keep his eyes off her. He watched her more than his own girlfriend. In fact, since the party started he had watched her, knowing where she stood and who she talked to and how much time she spent with Tim.

Not exactly the behavior of a man in love, he thought, criticizing himself wryly as he moved away from the bottom of the stairs and the two women, into the living room and the rest of his family.

His capriciousness seemed symptomatic of his life the past few years. What he had didn't satisfy him, so he looked to what he didn't have. As far as his relationship with Stacy was concerned, he had thought it would last longer than it had. It didn't help that their work always seemed to come between them and their relationship.

That's why he planned this trip home. He liked Stacy and knew he wouldn't find better. He wanted to make their relationship work. He didn't feel so empty when he was around her.

He worked his way through the family room, past the younger cousins who grumbled about homework and jobs. He dodged aunts who bustled about refilling coffee cups as they caught up on calamities and exulted over joys. He poured himself a coffee.

The house was full to bursting with family, friends and members of the church, and his harried mother was in her element. It had been a few years since Paul had been to a family get-together, and he hadn't realized until tonight what he'd missed.

He and Stacy entertained frequently and attended functions put on by their friends. But that's precisely what they were. Functions. Another tool used by those on the way up, to network, schmooze and gather information. He had enjoyed them, but each year created an increasing restlessness he couldn't pin down.

The past months had been especially hectic. He and his partner, Bruce DeVries, had successfully bid on an apartment block in Victoria and two more in Vancouver proper. That meant evenings and weekends taken up with verifying subcontractors' prices, meetings with engineers, organizing schedules, and all the while keeping the current projects flowing smoothly. It had just about fried him out.

This holiday had been in the works for a while. Plaintive calls from his mother and quiet requests from his father had been sandwiched between urgent faxes, whirlwind financing, cell phones ringing in his car and pagers going off on job sites.

Then his partner dropped the bomb. Bruce wanted to quit the business. He gave Paul first option to buy out his share. Paul felt as if he had come to an important point in his career. Buying Bruce out would give him the opportunity to expand the business in a way Bruce never wanted. He knew Henderson Contractors had the experience and reputation that would give them the edge in larger projects. It would mean bigger challenges and bigger returns.

Paul swirled the coffee in the bottom of his cup, frowning. It would also mean more work, hiring a couple of people to do the work Bruce did, more headaches and more stress.

He finished his coffee in one gulp and set the empty cup on a side table. Somehow none of these challenges held the allure it once would have. Lately he felt as if he ran harder and got nowhere. Always just out of his grasp was the happiness he kept thinking he would find with the right combination of changes in his life.

So when the invitation came for Amy's engagement, he took a chance, scheduled three weeks of holidays so he could think. Maybe in the open fields of his family's ranch he could find a way to fill the emptiness that grew with each increase in his net worth.

"So, how's the family entrepreneur?"

Paul jumped as his uncle Gordon slung a friendly arm over his nephew's shoulder, squeezing him. "You make that million you were always talking about?"

Paul grinned down at a smiling, bearded face, spectacles hanging as crookedly on his uncle's nose as the oversize sweater did over his narrow shoulders. "It depends if you want to talk to my banker or the tax accountant."

"Tax problems mean you're making money, my boy."

"I've never been able to render to Caesar what is Caesar's without a lot of pain."

"From the looks of that fancy car parked outside and that equally fancy girlfriend, I'd say you and Caesar are doing pretty good.'' Uncle Gordon dropped his arm and pushed uselessly at his glasses. ''You two going to get married?''

''Me and Caesar?''

''Oh, you're still pretty fast. I mean you and that girlfriend.''

Paul stifled another groan. It seemed everyone in his family, from the youngest cousin to his aged grandparents, felt it their right to pry and find out the level of his and Stacy's relationship. Trouble was, he thought, looking down at his favorite uncle, he didn't even know that himself.

''Maybe,'' was his noncommittal reply. If he said more, Stacy would find out before he had a chance to talk to her.

''Well I guess we'll find out when you send out wedding invitations. I hope we're going to be invited?''

''What do you mean?''

''We don't see too much of you these days. I'm just making sure you think of us when the time comes.''

Uncle Gordon's tone was jovial, but the words hit the guilty spot that his relatives always struck with unerring accuracy. Family could do the guilt thing so well, Paul thought, working up an answering grin for his uncle.

''I've been busy, yes...''

''Idle hands aren't good, either, but just don't forget about us while you're wheeling and dealing.'' His uncle clapped him on the back. ''You met Amy's guy yet?''

Paul shook his head. Throughout the evening, people pointed out Tim with a nudge and a smile, as if Paul should feel slighted. They hadn't officially met, however. ''I've heard a lot about him,'' he said instead.

''Tim's just the man for Amy. If anyone can help her turn that ranch around, he can.'' Uncle Gordon squinted up at Paul and, though his expression was kind, Paul could sense the slight note of censure in his voice. ''He's given her some good ideas and helped her out some.''

''Amy is a wonderful girl, Uncle Gordon,'' Paul conceded, not needing anyone else pointing out her good points. ''I'm glad that she's found someone good enough for her.''

''I've always liked her.'' Uncle Gordon looked past him. Then, with another pat on his nephew's back, he left to answer his wife's summons, leaving Paul to shake his head over his family's bluntness.

He glanced across the noisy room. People milled about, re-arranging the crowd. Finally he spotted Stacy. She had moved to the family room and was now cornered by his younger brother, Tyrell. Her short brown hair glistened, her expressive eyes crinkled as her mouth curved up in a smile. A response to some smart comment from Tyrell, Paul was sure.

With a proprietary grin, he sauntered over to claim her.

"Up for a game of pool?" His other brother, Derk, caught him by the arm as he passed.

Paul looked over to Stacy and Tyrell, now joined by his aunt Grace. He stopped, knowing exactly what she would be bringing up—each childhood prank, misdemeanor and his frequent brushes with the RCMP. He didn't feel like rehashing old crimes.

"If we can get the rug rats away from the table, I'm game." Paul followed Derk downstairs, shutting the door on the buzz of conversation, ensuring a break from further inquisitions from family. They were greeted by a louder burst of music as they reached the bottom of the stairs and the open recreation room dominated by a pool table.

"Shut that thing off," Derk shouted to nobody in particular. And of course nobody listened.

Grumbling, he walked over to the shelf stereo that practically shook and turned it off.

"That's my favorite song," cried a young girl sticking her head out of a bedroom.

"It isn't mine." Derk took a pool cue and handed one to Paul.

"But Derk, it's 'Jars of Clay,'" complained another, as if that explained everything.

"Well, I'm surprised they haven't shattered by now," he called back.

Paul laughed at the aggrieved look of his younger cousin and winked at her. "When we're done you can deafen yourselves again, Tiffany."

She looked back at him, frowning, then recognition dawned. "Oh, it's you, Paul."

"Oh, c'mon, it hasn't been that long," he complained, feeling her hesitation wounding him with a gentle pain.

She shrugged as if unable to spare the time to answer. Tiffany and another girl Paul didn't recognize ducked back into a bedroom, shutting the door behind them.

"It has been a while, big brother," Derk said, racking up the balls. "What was the last family do you came for?"

"Not you, too," Paul complained, chalking his cue. "You know I was up for Christa and George's wedding."

"Did you know they're having a real hard time toilet training their oldest child?"

"Right," Paul said dryly.

"Who did you bring to that?" Derk frowned, his eyes unfocused as if reaching far back in his memory. "Christine?"

Paul wrapped his hands around his cue, resting his chin on them, a wry smile twisting his lips. "Juanita."

"She the one with the black hair in those freaky triangle curls?"

"That was Jennifer. Juanita had short blond hair."

Derk bent over, squinting down his cue at the white ball. "Then who did you bring to Aunt Grace and Uncle Siebren's anniversary?"

Paul hesitated, realizing how bad this all sounded. "Pearl."

Derk reached back and with a quick movement broke the balls, sending them scattering over the table with a satisfying *snick.* "Where does Stacy fit in the lineup?"

Paul walked to the other side of the table, giving his brother room to shoot. "Why do you need to know?" he asked peevishly, disgruntled with the turn of the conversation.

Derk dropped another ball into the corner pocket. "Because Tyrell and I have a bet going to see if you hit ten women before Mom and Dad's fortieth wedding anniversary."

"That's sick." Paul shouldered his grinning brother aside and lined up his own ball. He gave it a vicious hit and the ball caromed off the side, missing the pocket completely. "I haven't gone out with ten girls, and you know it."

"No, you haven't," said Derk, thoughtfully leaning over and sinking another ball. "Stacy's only number eight."

"I don't keep track of the number of girlfriends. It's not gentlemanly." Paul stood back while his brother worked his way around the table, annoyed with the prim sound of his own words. He sounded like Aunty Triss.

"I would say going out with eight girls is not gentlemanly." Derk straightened and flashed his brother a grin, taking the sting out of his words.

Paul merely shrugged and took his turn, uncomfortable with his brother's comments, even though he knew they were made in fun.

"Don't look so glum, bro. I was just kidding." Derk elbowed Paul, causing him to miss a shot.

"Just for that I get two penalty shots."

"Take all the penalty shots you need. You are getting so beat, it's sad. All that carousing around Vancouver is taking the edge off your game."

Paul shot Derk a warning glance. Catching the hint, Derk changed the subject.

The door above the stairs opened again and their father, Fred Henderson, came down the stairs, accompanied by a tall, dark-haired young man. Paul recognized Amy's fiancé, Tim Enders.

Aunts and cousins had pointed out this wonderful man with indiscreet nudges and winks as if to show Paul he wasn't such a big deal in Amy's life. As if he didn't know that already.

"Can Tim and I join?" Fred asked.

Paul only shrugged. Derk nodded.

"Have you already met Tim?" Fred directed his question to Paul. Paul shook his head, reaching past his brother to shake Tim's hand, then stood back assessing him.

Tim's finely sculpted features were set off by dark wavy hair. He was the same height as Paul, almost the same breadth. Handsome if you like the sulky model look, thought Paul, knowing he was being judgmental. He blamed it on the mood his brother had put him in. All evening he had been hearing Tim's praises sung and his own shortcomings brought forward. And now he was faced with this paragon of virtue, and he didn't think he liked him very much even though he couldn't think why not.

They racked up the balls and soon were involved in an excruciatingly polite game of pool. Ten minutes into the game, the door opened again. This time a pair of slim, jeans-clad legs showed themselves at the top of the stairs, paused a moment, then Amy descended.

Paul watched as Amy looked around the room, her eyes flitting with disinterest over everyone there, including him. It wasn't hard to see the moment she spotted her fiancé. Her soft mouth parted in a gentle smile. She walked around the pool table to lean against Tim, gazing up at him with the same adoring look that once had been directed at him.

And Paul didn't like it.

"Are you sure you want to go home now?" Tim dug through the jumble of coats on the freezer. He pulled Amy's out and handed it to her.

Amy nodded, the pain in her shoulder making it difficult to ease the coat on. "I feel bad that Dad and Rick left early," she said. But that was only a small part of the reason. She felt like the day had started twenty-four hours ago, instead of eighteen. It had been an enjoyable evening, but tiring.

The porch door opened, and Elizabeth burst through it. "There you are!" she exclaimed, stopping short as she saw Amy putting on her coat. "You aren't leaving yet? Fred, tell her to stay awhile." Elizabeth turned to her husband, who only shook his head, winking at Amy in understanding.

"I'm tired, Mom. And my dad's already home." Amy smiled up at Elizabeth and Fred, reaching out to both of them. "I was just going to go looking for you to thank you for this evening. It was wonderful."

"I'm so glad we could do this for you, honey," Elizabeth drew Amy close and stroked her hair. Amy ignored the pain in her shoulder as she let herself be held, enjoying the security and familiarity. She straightened and stepped into Fred's open arms that clutched her too tightly.

"Sorry, honey," he apologized as he felt her wince. He loosened his hold, but didn't let her go. "We're so glad for you and Tim." He gave her one more careful squeeze, then reached past her to shake Tim's hand.

"Thank's for all you did for Amy and me tonight," he said as he stepped back. "I'm sorry my parents couldn't make it, but I enjoyed meeting the rest of the Henderson family."

The moment lengthened as Amy felt her love for these surrogate parents deepen and tears threaten. Finally Tim opened the door to the outside, breaking the atmosphere. "We should go, Amy."

They exchanged another round of quick goodbyes, and Tim and Amy stepped out into the soft night. The moon was a silver disk pressed against a black velvet sky scattered with handfuls of stars. Amy looked up and offered a quick prayer of thankfulness. How blessed she was to live here and to think that their children would be able to experience the same open spaces.

Tim opened his car door for Amy but didn't close it when she stepped in. Instead he looked down on her, his shoulders and head silhouetted against the moonlight. Amy felt his waiting and glanced upward.

"What is it?"

"You look beautiful...."

Amy smiled back, a gentle warmth suffusing her. His compliments still made her feel slightly uncomfortable, as if she expected some other, truly beautiful girl to step up from behind Amy and whisper her thanks to Tim.

"I just wondered," he continued, "why you didn't wear your dress tonight?"

Amy caught her bottom lip between her teeth. She had been careful all evening, not hugging him and staying on his right side. So far she had managed to keep her injury hidden from Tim. He hated it when she worked with the horses.

He waited. Quiet. Still. If Tim wanted her to tell him something, he only had to wait. Her own desire to fill the silence would draw out any secret she tried to hide.

But tonight she didn't feel like telling him and wouldn't get drawn in by his patience. She still had to load the dumb horse in an old truck with no tailgate and take him somewhere. If

Tim knew that, he would be after her to get someone to haul it for her, and she couldn't afford that.

"I spilled something on it when I was trying it on yesterday, and it was still wet when I came back from Kamloops," she said finally.

"Is it stained?"

"I don't think so." She smiled back up at him. "I'll have it clean for Sunday, don't worry."

Tim laughed and pushed shut the door, leaving Amy squirming with a mixture of guilt and annoyance. She *had* stained the dress, and it *was* still damp, but she could easily have worn it.

Except it wouldn't have hidden the purple and blue hoof-shaped bruise decorating her bare shoulder. And now she had spun an even tighter web by promising she would wear it on Sunday, three days from now.

Tim was too caught up in how she dressed, anyhow, she consoled herself. Until she met him, a shirt with buttons and pressed blue jeans was about as dressed up as she got during the week. Sundays, an old split riding skirt of her mothers did just fine. Anything else required too much care and maintenance.

"It's too bad you couldn't wear it tonight," Tim continued, getting in the car. "I love how it looks on you." He reached over and Amy braced herself for a hug, but thankfully he only brushed his lips across her cheek.

"Yah, it is too bad," she agreed, looking ahead, feeling guilty about the lie in spite of her justification.

They drove in silence until they reached Amy's house. A yellow glow spilled out of a downstairs window.

"Either your dad fell asleep reading, or he's waiting up for you," remarked Tim as they drove up the driveway.

"Probably asleep." Amy had begged him to stay at the party longer, but he pleaded exhaustion. Amy didn't know what from. His own chores were minimal, and when he was done, he spent the rest of the day in front of the television. Rick had been polite. He didn't mind the Henderson family, it was just Paul he disliked. Thankfully there were enough people there that he could avoid Paul most of the evening. But when Judd wanted to leave, Rick quickly volunteered to bring him home.

As they drove past the lit window, Amy swallowed her disappointment. She should have had two parents at the party tonight. If it wasn't for the fact that Tim's parents hadn't come, either, her resentment would have been even greater. At times like this she missed her mother all over again.

Tim pulled up in front of the porch, put the car in gear and opened his door. Amy waited for Tim to open hers, thankful for the courtesy. Her arm hurt more now than this afternoon and she dreaded the affectionate good-night she usually got from Tim.

Their footfalls on the gravelled walk were the only sounds in the darkness. They reached the house. Amy lifted her foot to take the first step up the stairs when Tim suddenly caught her by the shoulder, turned her around and almost dragged her into his arms.

She fell against him, unable to stop the soft cry of pain suddenly stifled by his lips.

He pulled her closer. Amy squeezed her eyes shut, fighting the urge to cry out, to push him away from the agony pulsing down her arm. She tried to turn, to find a better fit, when just as suddenly, Tim released her.

Amy took a step back to balance herself, supporting her right elbow.

"What's the matter, Amy?" Tim looked down at her, his eyes two dark smudges, his expression unreadable. "Why is it so hard to let me hold you? Why have you been avoiding me all night?"

Amy waited until the pain settled down to a dull throb, then looked up at him realizing where her half truths had taken her. "I'm sorry, Tim. I should have told you earlier." She looked away, guilt making her hesitate. "When I caught Sandover this afternoon, he must have hit me with a hoof. My shoulder's all bruised and swollen."

"And that's the real reason you're not wearing your dress?"

"I'm sorry," she whispered, still looking down at the ground.

"Why didn't you tell me?"

"I know you'd be angry."

"Amy, what kind of man do you take me for?" He reached over and caught her face in his hands, his thumbs gently forcing her to look up at him. He bent over and carefully brushed his lips against hers. "Please don't tell me you're afraid of me?"

Amy shook her head, realizing how ludicrous it all sounded. She knew now, facing Tim's gentle concern, that she had, as usual, underestimated him. "No, I'm not afraid of you. I guess I just don't want you to worry about me."

"Well, I do. And that's okay. I love you so much, and I don't like to imagine you working with that crazy horse. I wish you'd get rid of him." He gently drew her near, careful this time not to jostle her shoulder. "But what you told me isn't as bad as what I thought all evening."

"And what was that?"

Tim hesitated, a sigh lifting his chest. "I thought that Paul's return gave you second thoughts about us."

"Never think that, Tim," Amy pulled back to look up at Tim, her voice almost fierce. Amy clutched his shirt, disliking the turn of the conversation, afraid of his doubts. Doubts come before the engagement, not after. "I made a promise to you. I'm going to keep that promise."

Tim smiled and caught her hand in his. "I know, Amy. I'm sorry I doubted you." He fingered her ring, a frown creasing his forehead. "I've spent most of the night having Paul pointed out to me. To the Hendersons' credit, they all said I was better for you than Paul ever was." He looked into Amy's eyes and smiled. "But I was starting to wonder..." He hesitated. "You don't have to tell me if you don't want to, but what really went on between you and Paul?"

Amy felt her heart lurch. She shook her head, almost smiling at her own foolishness. "I never made a big secret of my crush on Paul. And that's all it ever was. A crush. To Paul I was just a pesky little girl who followed him and wrote notes to him." She looked up at him, willing him to believe her. "I've never meant anything to him, and in the past few years, I've realized that he's not the kind of man I want as my husband. He's had more girlfriends than you have even dreamed of, and he's lived a life that is far beyond what I seek in a husband.'' She smiled as she reached up to touch his smooth cheek. ''Our relationship is built on a communal faith in God. Something I think my parents missed out on.'' Her heart constricted as she thought of her mother. Her broken vows had created a heartache that Amy would never wish on any child. ''You wait and see, Tim Enders. I'll be a good and faithful wife to you. I will.'' Ignoring the pain in her shoulder, she pulled Tim's head down, sealing her vow with a kiss.

Chapter Three

Paul paused in the doorway of the kitchen. He had been on his way outside, but the sight of his mother at the sink stopped him. The morning sun shone on her short gray hair, neatly combed. The sleeves of her cream-colored jersey were pushed past her elbows and black stirrup pants cinched bare feet.

"Why don't you grab a towel and pitch in?" she said when she caught his reflection in the window in front of her.

"I haven't done dishes in years. When are you going to get a dishwasher?" Paul yawned as he ambled into the kitchen. He leaned over to plant a kiss on his mother's cheek. He grimaced at the dishes piled high on the counter, hooked a stool with his foot and dropped onto it. "I thought we did all the dishes last night."

Elizabeth shrugged, rinsed off a cup and set it on the drain tray. "I found these downstairs in the spare room."

"Well it wasn't us. Dad, Derk and I were playing pool with Amy's fiancé most of the time." Paul rolled up the sleeves of his flannel shirt and tugged the dish towel off his mother's shoulder.

"And what did you think of Amy's Tim?"

"Seems okay," Paul replied, keeping his tone non committal. "I have a hard time seeing him living on the ranch like he says he will."

Elizabeth frowned. "Why?"

"C'mon, Mom. Did you see what he wore last night?" Paul stuffed the tea towel in a glass and twisted it. "Looked like he was auditioning for a spot on a soap opera."

"Actually he was dressed a lot like you."

"This is the way to dress," he said. "Old, faded jeans." He tugged on the front of his shirt. "Old faded shirt. When in the country…"

"And it was their engagement party. Of course he'd be dressed nicely."

Paul heard the tone of censure in his mother's voice and it made him feel like a sulky teenager. But he pressed on. "That may be, but I still can't imagine him living at Danyluks'."

"He talks about doing it, so your imagination doesn't count for much." Elizabeth eased another batch of dishes in the sink.

"I hope he likes driving." Paul commented as he pulled another dish off the tray. He wondered why he cared how Tim felt about Amy and the ranch. *I could never stop being a big brother,* he thought, smiling. "When are they getting married?"

"Amy hasn't mentioned a specific date, although I think Tim would like it to be soon." Elizabeth glanced at him over her shoulder. "She wants to get some money together and get the house fixed up before they move in. She also wants to get a trailer on the yard for Rick and Judd."

"That would be a good idea. I can't imagine four people living in that house." Paul shrugged. "Doesn't sound like she's in any rush, though."

"I think she'd like to get married soon, but her pride is preventing that. Pride and a lot of work. Rick's a big help, but she still takes on most of the responsibility herself. I just wish she'd quit her job."

"She still working at that accountant's office?"

"She worked full-time up until four years ago—when Judd started getting worse. Now she just works part-time at the grocery store and tries to run the ranch on her days off."

"What's wrong with Judd?"

Elizabeth shrugged rinsing the cup in her hand. "He's become much quieter. He used to be so stubborn and ornery, but not lately. Amy's been pushing him to go to a doctor, but he refuses."

"I'm surprised Amy still manages to keep up her relationship with Tim."

"She and Tim spend many dates at home with Judd, keeping him entertained." Elizabeth set the last of the cups on the drain tray and dried her hands.

"Doesn't sound like such a bad way to spend a night." Paul rolled down his sleeves as he thought of all the running around he and Stacy did when they found time to spend together. Supper out, the theater, opera, the occasional movie. An evening at home sounded appealing. "But you haven't told me yet what *you* think of Amy's Tim," Paul teased as he finished drying the cups.

Elizabeth shrugged. "I like him very much. He's a sincere Christian, he has a good job and is well liked in the community. He's tall, good looking..."

"Sounds like you're talking about Dad's prize bull."

"Don't be flip," Elizabeth admonished. "He's worked at the bank for the past two years, so hasn't really been around that long."

"Long enough to make a move on Amy and propose to her."

"Paul," she warned.

He lifted his hands in mock surrender. "Sorry. I didn't know he meant that much to you, as well."

Elizabeth shot him a level look. "If I didn't know better, I'd say you're jealous."

Paul looked back at her, holding her gaze. "I guess I just have to get used to the idea that little Amy Danyluk is old enough to get married."

"She hasn't been 'little Amy Danyluk' for a long time now."

"She hasn't been chasing me around for a while, either."

"Aha, you *are* jealous," his mother cried, laughing at him.

Paul flicked the towel at her in reply. "I'll be able to dance at her wedding, Mom."

Elizabeth, her face suddenly thoughtful, drained the sink and rinsed the soap suds out.

"Where are you?" Paul asked, setting a stack of plates in the cupboard.

"Being a mother. Thinking about weddings." She looked up at Paul, her expression hopeful. "I guess I'm wondering if Dad and I will ever throw an engagement party for you."

Paul sighed and leaned back against the counter, wrapping and unwrapping the damp towel around his hands. "Maybe. Someday," he said with a noncommittal shrug.

"You've been saying that for the past three girlfriends." Elizabeth rescued the towel and hung it on the rack by the stove.

Paul blew out his breath and crossed his arms. He thought her lack of questions last night was due to a change in tactics, but he should have known she would corner him sooner or later. "I don't think marriage always has to come up when two people are dating."

"Then why are they dating?"

"Companionship, friendship..." The words sounded lame to him.

"Friends and companions you go fishing with. Girlfriends you kiss when you think your mother isn't looking." Elizabeth tapped him on the chest as she passed him.

Paul had to remind himself that he was almost thirty and hadn't needed to answer to his mother for close to twelve years. "Stacy and I understand each other..."

"I would hope so, you both speak English," his mother said with a laugh, leaning back against the counter beside him. "I know you're serious about her, this is the first girlfriend you've brought here for longer than a day."

Paul tapped his fingers against his arm, as he sought words to explain his and Stacy's relationship. "I want her to see where I came from, what made me who I am."

"And what did?"

Paul frowned.

"Made you who you are," his mother explained.

He looked ahead at the neat table in the large kitchen, now

pushed against the wall. Once it had been stretched out, sur-
rounded with chairs, now only four chairs were tucked under
it. He remembered many family meals around the table, times
of sharing and Bible reading and prayer. How many times had
he sat at this same table and looked out the window wishing
he was anywhere else but here, in this kitchen?

"I'm not even sure who I am these days, Mom," he replied
softly. "I'm making good money. I have lots of stuff. The
business is even more successful than I thought it would be. I
always thought I could quit when I got to the point I wanted
to, but I just keep on going and going. It doesn't really stop."

"The toughest thing about success is that you must remain
being a success," his mother quoted. "You don't quit. It lures
you on out of necessity or out of a desire to challenge yourself."

Paul laughed shortly. "You're right." He slipped his hands
into his pockets, studying the toes of his socks. "The only
problem is each time I finish something, each time I check my
bank balance, it still feels empty. I work and look forward to
what I can buy with what I make, but by the time I open what
I've bought, or park it, or moor it or whatever, it still isn't
really what I wanted." He frowned, hearing his thoughts spoken out loud for the first time in years. Any girlfriend he had
didn't understand. They usually liked the fancy condo, the fast
cars, dining out in fancy restaurants, the boat, the ski trips to
Whistler-Blackcomb. Any of his friends openly envied his success. None of them would understand that he sought more and
he hadn't found it in spending or experiencing.

"What you've wanted all your life isn't really what you
need."

Paul nodded. "I was just thinking that." He lifted his head
catching his mother's concerned look. "Did you know how
badly I wanted to get away from here? Did you know how
dissatisfied I was once, with this life-style? With going to
church? With living with people you've grown up with?"

"We knew." Elizabeth reached over and rubbed his arm.
"We didn't like it, but we had to let go. Just like we had to
let go of the other boys. Doesn't mean we have loved you any

less or prayed for you any less. Tyrell, Derk, they've each had to make their own choices, as well.''

"At least Derk is still close by."

Elizabeth nodded. "He comes up pretty regularly. Helps out when he can. I think he'd like to start up his own place. If not here, then somewhere in the Cariboo. We never planned on building up this place for our children to take over. Your father and I wanted each of you to figure out for yourself what you wanted.''

Paul pushed himself away from the counter, a wry grin curving his lips. "Trouble is, Mom, I still don't know." He had tried to articulate to his mother the hunger that clutched him these days, a desire for more than he had. He felt as if he expended a lot of energy and received nothing for it in return. Hence the trip back home, to his family, to his spiritual roots.

"Then it's a good thing you're here."

"I guess it's a beginning," he admitted.

Elizabeth pushed herself away from the counter and, reaching up, pulled his head down to hers. She pressed a kiss on his cheek and smiled up at him with eyes as blue as his own. "I just want you to remember that Dad and I love you, but more important, God loves you.''

"I know that, Mom," he whispered, pulling her into a fierce hug. "I just need some space and time."

"You've come to the right place for that."

Elizabeth hugged him back, and it felt so good.

The shrill ring of the phone broke the peace of the moment. Elizabeth pulled away and answered it. Paul leaned back again, a feeling of deep love for his mother filling him.

"Is Stacy up yet?" Elizabeth pressed the mouthpiece against her chest and turned to Paul. "It's some fellow named Jonathan. Says it's urgent." Elizabeth lifted her shoulders in a shrug. "Says the computer's down."

"I'm sure she is," he replied, feeling a twinge of annoyance with Stacy for giving her workers the ranch's number. They had promised each other an uninterrupted week at the ranch and whatever happened in Vancouver would be handled by their co-workers.

He ran upstairs and tapped on Stacy's door. "Are you up?"

"Come on in," Stacy called out.

Paul stepped into the brightly lit room, and his heart sank at the sight of his girlfriend sitting on the bed with papers scattered around her. He walked to her side and, picking up a file folder, playfully tapped her on the head.

"I thought we were on holidays?"

"Well—" she raised her eyebrows, flashing him a grin "—I was lying in bed this morning, trying to find a way to make one of my customer's program work more efficiently and had an inspiration."

"Jonathan will be glad to hear that."

"What do you mean?" Stacy asked, reaching for a paper covered with scribbling.

"He's on the phone."

"Now?"

"As we speak." Paul pushed some papers away and sat down on the bed.

"Why didn't you say so right away?" Stacy jumped up, but Paul caught her hand.

"Because I thought this holiday was to be a break for both of us. I wanted to take you riding this morning without your mind on the office back in the city." Paul ran his finger over her well-manicured ones, marveling at their softness. "I'm hoping you'll tell him to take a hike."

Stacy looked down at him, smiling lightly. Bending over, she brushed a kiss over his forehead then straightened. "A hike for Jonathan might be a bit of a stretch. He's not the athletic type. I'm sure it's some little problem I can fix over the phone."

Paul smiled and leaned back against the headboard of the bed, watching her trim figure as she left, appreciating how she looked in jeans as opposed to Ungaro or Ralph Lauren.

He dropped his head against the wall, as he thought of his conversation with his mother a few moments ago. He liked Stacy, maybe even loved her. They had a lot of fun together. She laughed at his terrible jokes and enjoyed the same movies and music. She gave him business ideas and helped him with his computers, something he hated working with.

She was the first girl he had gone out with that didn't bore him or talk about trivial things. He smiled as he remembered many deep discussions over economics and politics. Together they had saved British Columbia, Canada and North America many times.

He straightened, wondering what was taking her so long to return. He went downstairs to find her.

She was pacing around the kitchen, her hand worrying the phone cord, the receiver pressed against her head. She stopped, frowning at the floor. "It's so hard to say from over here. Sounds like some hacker got past their firewall. No I can't get on line from here. Doesn't sound like it would help anyhow. Can't you figure out what happened?" Stacy rolled her eyes and crossed the room once more, tethered by the telephone cord, fairly emanating frustration. "Okay, okay. I get the message. I'll come." She nodded impatiently. "I'll be there as soon as I can." With an angry click, she hung up the phone, turning to Paul. Her expression was apologetic. "I have to go back...."

"Stacy, don't go. Jonathan knew for the past month that you were leaving this week. Surely they can handle this small crisis." Paul walked across the room and caught her by the shoulders. "This is the only holiday you've taken for a long time."

Stacy nodded. "I know all that, Paul, but I won't be able to relax knowing a customer's system is down. It's not really a small crisis. We just started up, and we can't afford to lose any business. I can't leave customers waiting."

"What about a boyfriend?" Paul stroked her hair, his tone light, but his frustration just below the surface.

"I guess I'm hoping he'll understand." Stacy smiled up at him, but Paul wouldn't be cajoled.

For the past months he had eagerly anticipated showing Stacy the place where he grew up, the hills he wandered through as a child. He wanted to show her that part of himself. He had planned riding trips, picnics and long, leisurely drives. Now, with one phone call from Vancouver, it all disintegrated.

"Phone someone else to take care of it," he said, his voice clipped, hands resting on his hips.

"Paul, I'm the one who set up the system. I'm responsible for fixing the glitch." Stacy reached up and cupped his face with her hands. "I know how much you've looked forward to this. I'll try to come back as soon as it's fixed. You're going to be here another couple of weeks, aren't you?"

Paul couldn't help it. He pulled away. It had taken her months to arrange this particular holiday. He knew once she was back in the office another crisis would keep her there, then another and another.

Stacy tilted her head, taking a step towards him. "Paul please don't be like this. If it was Bruce who needed help, wouldn't you go?"

Paul looked down at her, trying to imagine the reverse situation and he knew he would have stayed. "When do you want to leave?" was all he said.

Stacy smiled her thanks. "Give me fifteen minutes."

Paul nodded and watched as she turned and ran back up the stairs to her bedroom. He glanced at his mother who frowned at the egg carton she had pulled out.

"I guess you won't be here for breakfast."

Paul shook his head. "We'll probably grab something along the way. Sorry."

"Doesn't matter, Paul. I was only going to make some bacon and eggs."

"With homemade bread and farm-fresh eggs." Paul sighed, thinking about the rubber food they would pick up from a drive-through. "I'll have to wait for that until tomorrow."

"You're coming back aren't you?"

Paul winked at his mother. "I'm only going to be in Vancouver long enough to drop Stacy off, kiss her goodbye and head back here."

He waited outside, leaning against his car. His eyes drifted over the hills, appreciating the emptiness of the country, the space that let you stretch your arms out. This was real, solid.

Stacy had tried to get him excited about staring at a computer screen, sending e-mail around the world with a click of a button, looking at things that moved on the screen, but he never picked up on her enthusiasm. He preferred dealing with people face-to-face. Cell phones, pagers, intercoms and fax machines were bad enough.

He sighed as he thought of the long drive down the Coquihalla and the even worse one through the oppressive bumper-to-bumper traffic of the heavily populated Fraser Valley. If he hurried he could be back here by late evening.

Stacy was even better than her word, and ten minutes later he stowed her elegant luggage in the trunk of the car. He started the engine while Stacy bid his mother a hurried goodbye and got in. The door barely clicked shut when Paul took off in a cloud of gravel and dust, disregarding the paint job of his car.

His impatience translated into speed and he barreled recklessly down the road, slowing only momentarily for an old one-ton truck lumbering down the road, a dilapidated plywood stock box on the back. He swerved around it, fishtailed, corrected and left it behind.

"I do want to get home in one piece, Paul," Stacy joked, glancing over her shoulder at the truck that shrank by the second.

Paul tried to stifle his impatience with his girlfriend, her job and the life-style that demanded constant work to maintain. With a self-deprecating shake of his head, he glanced at the speedometer and slowed down.

He flicked on the radio, hitting the CD player. Music instead of conversation filled the silence.

Stacy glanced at him, shrugged and pulled out her briefcase.

Paul knew he should try to be more communicative, but it would mean ignoring all that had passed between them, and he wasn't ready to do that.

It was going to be a long drive, but hopefully a peaceful return trip.

Amy clenched the steering wheel of the truck, her heart pounding. The fancy car flashed past her out of nowhere. Though it was almost obscured by the cloud of dust, it wasn't hard to identify the vehicle.

Paul Henderson's. Heading back home already.

Amy didn't understand her own disappointment. It shouldn't matter to her that he had left four days and two weeks earlier than planned. It was typical of Paul. Even Elizabeth had wondered if he could stay away from Vancouver for three weeks.

But she certainly hadn't expected his visit would be this protracted.

The old truck rocked as Sandover threw his weight over, trying to break free of the rope that tied his head to the front of the truck's box. Not for the first time Amy wished they had a stock trailer to move their horses around instead of this cumbersome one-ton truck with its home-made box. Two horses fit easily in it, but the truck had no shocks, and each bump in the road knocked the horses around which, in turn, rocked the truck.

She turned her attention to the road, preferring not to think about the rope that was the only thing keeping Sandover in a box with no back.

She had enough on her mind without having to cede any head space to this wild horse. In a couple of weeks the heifers Rick bought would come, and she and Rick needed to get the loading chutes and corrals ready. Fortunately she had enough materials. All she needed now was for her shoulder to heal quickly. A quick glance at her watch showed her that she was right on schedule. She had enough time to drop Sandover off at the auction market and get to work.

Another quick glance over her shoulder proved that Sandover had finally settled down. Amy relived the moment in the Hendersons' yard. It had scared her, and she realized she didn't need an animal around that was just going to cause trouble. She had to be ruthless.

The trip to town went peacefully. Amy dropped him off at the auction mart, then hurried back to the truck and her job at the grocery store.

Chapter Four

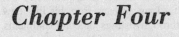

Clouds drifted in overnight, and Sunday morning Paul woke to a low gray sky. A slow, steady British Columbia rain drummed against his bedroom window. He turned his head and glanced at the face of the old metal clock beside him as it ticked off the seconds with a heavy, no-nonsense sound. Six in the morning. Church didn't start until ten o'clock.

His parents still slept, and he knew if he got up, he would wake them. Sunday was literally a day of rest for his family. He knew they wouldn't be up for an hour and a half.

He rolled onto his back and stared at the ceiling of his former bedroom. The fluorescent stars he stuck up there as a young boy still hung, forming the constellations—the Big Dipper, Orion, Cassiopeia. He remembered reading at night and shutting off the light just as his parents' feet hit the bottom stairs. They would come to tuck him in, and the still-glowing stars would betray him. How he devoured books then. The only thing he read regularly now were stock market reports and blueprints. Hardly the stuff of relaxation.

Paul flipped restlessly onto his side, wide awake. He wasn't used to lying in bed. In Vancouver once he woke up, he was out of bed and running.

You're here to relax, he reminded himself. It's Sunday, a day of rest.

He looked past the clock and noticed a book on the antique bedside table beside it. Reaching over, he turned it around to look at the cover.

A Bible. Trust his mother to lay not-so-gentle hints. Propping himself up on one elbow, he lay the book on the bed. May as well start relaxing now, he thought. Flipping it open, he glanced over words that hearkened to his youth. They were familiar and yet, after such a long absence from his life, new.

He paged through listings of commandments. Joshua's exploits, battles of the judges of Israel, Job's laments, all slid past his eyes. Paul turned the pages slowly, not really reading until he reached the Psalms.

"Blessed is the man who does not walk in the counsel of the wicked...his delight is in the law of the Lord. He is like a tree planted by streams of water." Paul laid his finger on the lines of the first Psalm and frowned lightly.

He certainly did not feel like a rooted tree, he felt more like the chaff the psalmist spoke of, blown by the wind. The past few years had been an ever-increasing whirl of business and pleasure. Speeding it up hadn't satisfied, it only left him dizzy.

Paul closed the Bible, uncomfortable with having his shortcomings laid in front of him each time he turned around. How many years had it been since he had gone to church? He planned on going with his parents this morning. That was always the deal when he came home.

But before this? Paul frowned. He didn't even know if there was a church close to the condo he lived in. He was sure he passed one each time he drove to work. Looking down at the Bible, he sighed. He had moved far from where he had grown up and what his parents had taught him.

And lately the emptiness of his own life showed him clearly that what he had tried to fill it with wasn't enough. He had fought coming home for too long because he knew it would mean looking at his life-style and reexamining what he had been working for. He knew he had some big changes to make in his life, but didn't know if he dared.

It was time to get to work and stop thinking so much.

His dad had a few chores to do before church. Paul could do them, instead of lying there going over ground that bore nothing.

And though he hadn't been to church in a while, he found himself looking forward to the gathering, the singing and the reminder of something greater than the stock market and government regulations.

The welcome rain that began on Sunday hung in the valley for the next two days. It kept Paul indoors working through the list of repairs his mother had tacked on the fridge, as well as the jobs his father had listed in his head.

The chores weren't onerous and gave Paul and his father a chance to catch up on each other's lives. Hours were spent hunkered over engines, hunched over tack as they worked. Paul shared his needs with his father. Fred reminded him of God's unconditional love that always called his children back. Paul listened, storing the information away, much like he did for any business decision. His relationship with God had been much like his awareness of gravity. It was there, no denying that, and it affected certain parts of a person's life, but he hadn't spent much time pondering it. Talking with his father gave him a glimpse of what was waiting for him, if he dared make a change in his life.

When the sun finally broke through the gray clouds, restlessness claimed Paul again. His dad had to run to town for parts, and Paul had no desire to park himself behind a windshield. He needed to be outside with the sun beating down on his back, sweat trickling between his shoulder blades.

Sasha, a buckskin mare, responded to his bribe of feed. He haltered her and got the tack ready. Thankfully Sasha possessed a patient nature because bridling and saddling her took longer than it should have. His hands fumbled with buckles and straps as he readjusted and tightened.

But when he dropped his hat on his head, pulling it low against the morning sun, and swung up into the saddle, a feeling

of familiarity took over. He drew the worn reins through his
bare hands, relishing the feel of soft, worn leather.

Sasha caught his mood and sidestepped as he drew the reins
in, holding her back until he got his other foot settled firmly in
the stirrup with the familiar and welcome creak of saddle
leather.

The mare snorted, shook her head and Paul let her go. In
minutes the trees of the yard dropped behind as he nudged her
into a gentle canter across open fields that beckoned and called.

Paul held the reins loosely in his hand, catching the rhythm
of the horse under him. An eagerness to take in the open spaces
of the country flowed through him. He felt as if he could move,
stretch out, as if the isolation gave him freedom to decide who
he chose to be.

Sasha's hooves pounded a steady beat up the gradual hills
as the sum warmed Paul's back and the soft breeze of the Cariboo
cooled his face. After a few miles Paul drew Sasha up.
She shook her head, the bridle jangling, and tried to take off
again.

"You're going to wear yourself out. Haven't you got enough
sense to see that?" Paul admonished, turning her in a circle as
she crab-walked. She blew, shook her head and tried to go
again. Paul turned her head, slowing her down. "Pace yourself,
Sasha," Paul said, repeating the words his father often spoke
to him. As the horse settled down, he smiled. Looking up, it
was as if some of what his parents spoke of hit a familiar place.

He too had been running, chasing.

Paul had chosen this time as a break, a time to ponder his
future. He knew he needed to slow down. He knew his life
wore him down. "Okay, Lord," he said, threading the reins
through one hand as he rested the other on his thigh. "What
am I supposed to be doing?" He gazed around the rolling hills
interspersed with ridges of pine, the hard blue sky painted with
wisps of white. But no answer blazed out of the sky, no words
appeared to tell him "buy" or "sell."

He took another breath, knowing that to some degree the
decision would have to be made by him alone. But for now he

was going to procrastinate. For now he was going to just enjoy being home and being a son again.

"It's been too long," he said softly, looking around. He sighed as if he was getting rid of stuff left over from the city, dropping the burdens of his daily work. It would wait. It would all wait. When he'd planned this holiday he'd wondered if he could stay away three weeks. Now he didn't know if three weeks home would be long enough.

He smiled, clucked to Sasha as they rode down a hill toward the road. It felt so good to be outside. God felt nearer already, out here in the open. The city was too much a testimony to man's self-confidence and self-reliance. But the rolling hills, solid trees and sparkling creeks of his home testified eloquently to their Maker. And Paul felt ready to listen.

Sasha meandered along the road for a bit as Paul reacquainted himself with the lay of the land, once as familiar to him as the curve of his mother's smile. They followed the road, and when it forked, Paul pulled Sasha's head to one side, turning her to the right.

The road traveled upward to the Danyluk ranch. Their spread was smaller than his parents'. Higher up, against the pines, hay land was too far from the river to irrigate properly, resulting in reduced crop and income. The number of cows the Danyluks' ran probably provided Rick, Judd and Amy with the bare essentials, but not much more. The Hendersons weathered tough times by selling hay to supplement their income when cattle prices were low. They also sent out many of the calves they raised to feeder lots, giving them a larger profit margin per animal.

The Danyluks couldn't afford to do that. This disparity had created hard feelings on Judd's side. Paul was always aware of that, but he and Amy shared a longer, albeit lopsided, acquaintance. He grinned as he remembered their changing relationship. Since she was a little girl of eight, she had followed him around. As he'd grown and found other girlfriends, she'd stayed faithful even though he hadn't encouraged her. Even as a young girl she'd had an aura of purity about her, a sincerity that had made him keep his distance. Her solid and simple faith in God had made him keep her at arm's length.

When he left for the city to find his fortune, she had slipped a note into his pocket declaring that she would never forget him and would love him forever. He'd given in and granted her a kiss, her first he was sure. He was nineteen, she was fifteen.

He came back periodically. Each visit realigned their relationship until she had changed from a quirky little sister into a friend and confidant. He suspected that she liked him for a few years after he left. She had never had a boyfriend. Until Tim.

And he had never seen her as other than a friend.

Until the engagement party.

Is that why you're visiting her now? To see if what you felt that night is any different now?

Paul shook his head, laughing at his own fancy. He was dropping by to see how she was doing, that was all. Just a big-brotherly visit to make sure she was all right.

Sasha's shod feet clopped carefully across the dilapidated wooden cattle guard as Paul rode up the Danyluks' driveway. The cattle guard badly needed repair, as did the barbed-wire fence that followed the rutted road. Closer to the house a pail leaned crookedly in the grass beside a fence post, the handles of the fencing pliers sticking out of it. It looked like someone had begun the boring task of tacking up and repairing the loose wires.

The door to the shop opened, and Rick stepped out, wiping his hands on a rag. Paul waved to him and got a curt nod in return.

"Welcome to the Cariboo," Paul muttered, as he drew his horse up to the house. He had never bothered trying to understand Rick's antagonism. He suspected Judd had a strong influence on it. Their feelings didn't run as strong as they used to, but there was always an underlying tension between the Henderson men and the Danyluks.

Paul dismounted, tied Sasha up and ran up the steps. He rapped on the door but heard no reply. Cariboo manners took over and he poked his head inside.

Amy sat by the table, talking on the phone, one elbow planted on the table in front of her. Her long hair hung loose, flowing over her shoulders, the light from the window beside her caressing it, gilding it with bronze highlights. Her arched eyebrows were pulled together in a frown over soft gray eyes.

Paul felt again a nudge of awareness. Again he noted the changes time had wrought—from the slightly freckle-faced pixie that trailed him as a child, to the self-conscious and awkward teenager who would blush, then turn around and hit him, to the woman who sat at the table now.

Her face had lengthened, her cheeks hollowed out, her hair slipped from a red to pale copper. She had been cute as a child, pretty as a teenager, but now had become strikingly beautiful.

Paul felt a moment's regret that he hadn't bothered, before this time, to stop and really notice her. All her life he had taken for granted her affection and adoration and had treated it lightly.

But now a yearning seemed to draw him to her. Maybe it was part of the need he felt to seek fulfillment from his past. Maybe he just needed to connect with one of the few friends who hadn't moved away; a friend who still had faith in a God he had taken for granted.

Or maybe his mother was right. Maybe he was jealous.

Amy tapped the pencil on the pad of paper in front of her, her expression frustrated. Judd hollered from the living room, summoning her.

Amy covered the mouthpiece of the phone. "Just wait a minute, Dad." Wincing, she stuck her left finger in her ear and hunched over as if to listen better.

"Not until next week? We figured on that part being in town this morning." Amy paused, glancing up. She saw Paul and blinked in surprise.

She didn't return Paul's smile and looked down instead.

Paul hesitated at her response, but stepped into the house anyhow. He noted with satisfaction that though the place looked decrepit on the outside, inside the house was tidy. The linoleum was worn beneath mismatched chairs, the cupboards had seen better days as had the scarred and worn table, but in spite of all that, the room was clean and neat.

Paul gave his hat a toss that landed it neatly on the rack beside the door. He pulled the bootjack out of its usual corner around the door and jerked his boots off.

"Well how much is it going to cost to have it delivered here? No, I need it right now." Amy listened to the reply. Her shoulders sagged and she winced. "I need to make some arrangements. I'll have to call you back." She dropped the phone on the hook and sat back, cradling her arm and frowning at Paul. "I thought you were gone."

Paul raised his eyebrows in surprise at her abrupt tone. "I've still got seventeen days left of my holiday," he replied evenly, trying to forget her earlier greeting, or lack thereof. He crossed the room and hooked his foot around a chair, drawing it close to the table.

"You passed me on Saturday, heading to the city."

Paul frowned at the tone of censure in her voice, wondering why she would be antagonistic toward him. Maybe Rick and Judd had finally convinced her what a wastrel he really was. Maybe, he thought with a small measure of disappointment, maybe she had changed in other ways as well. "I just drove Stacy back. She had an emergency at work. Didn't you see me in church on Sunday?"

Amy blinked her surprise. "No. But I didn't see your parents, either."

"We came late and ended up sitting in the balcony."

Amy nodded and reached up to rub her eyes with her fingertips. Sitting across from her, Paul noticed the weary droop to her eyes.

"Who were you talking to?" he asked, concerned.

"Case IH in Vancouver. I ordered a part for the tractor. It was supposed to be in this morning but it got sidetracked with another shipment from Prince George, and Rick needs it right away."

"Can't you go and pick it up?"

She fidgeted with a pencil and paper on the table in front of her.

Paul reached over and, as he had done so many times in the past, affectionately stroked an uncooperative strand of hair out of her face. Even as he did so, Paul caught himself. Once she would have waited eagerly for any sign of attention, but no longer. She belonged to another, and his rights to touch and console had been abrogated.

Amy pulled back, confirming his thoughts.

She doodled a moment, biting her lip, a faint blush staining her cheeks. "I can't because I don't have a truck. The fuel pump went this morning. It gave me trouble when I hauled Sandover to the auction mart on my way to work, but I thought it would last for a bit yet."

"Did you get a decent amount for the beast?"

"Enough. We got back what we paid for him so I'm happy."

"You don't sound happy."

Amy frowned. "I would have liked to keep him and work with him some more. He had a lot of potential."

"And a wicked kick," Paul added, touching the elbow of her sore arm.

"Amy," Judd called again from the living room.

"What?" Amy turned in her chair and winced with pain at the sudden movement.

"Nothing. If you're too busy yapping with Henderson, don't bother."

Amy rolled her eyes, got up and walked to the living room, supporting her sore arm. Paul decided to face Judd head-on and followed her.

Judd Danyluk lay stretched out in a worn recliner, a pair of crutches leaning against it. The bright afghan tucked over his legs served as a sharp contrast to the cracked vinyl and threadbare armrests. Paul had seldom been in this room. In the Cariboo most visiting was done with elbows propped on a kitchen table, nursing a cup of coffee or tea.

"What's the matter, Dad?" Amy's voice lost its impatient edge, her hand resting lightly on his.

Judd was rubbing his eyes, frowning. "I can't see real great. It's like everything's blurry."

"How's your heart feel? Are you having any pain going down your arm?"

"It's my eyes, Amy, not my heart." Judd glared up at her and blinked again. He shook his head and then frowned. "I don't know why I can't see so good."

"Does it hurt?"

Judd shook his head, looking around. "No. Just feels funny."

"You've got your regular checkup coming up, you can ask the doctor then."

"I suppose." Judd pushed himself up. "Oh, hello, Henderson." Judd acknowledged Paul's presence with a curt nod, then turned back to Amy. "Who were you talking to?"

"Case IH. I'm trying to straighten out a mix-up with parts." She crossed her arms, supporting her shoulder, and frowned as she looked down at her father. Paul had to smile at the sight. As long as he could remember Amy was almost as much a mother to Judd as daughter—bullying him into helping on the ranch, making him go outside, eat properly, get out and visit other people, reminding him to do his devotions.

"And you're not going to talk about canceling your doctor's appointment."

"I told you I would go." Judd glowered at her, and Amy stared back.

"You canceled the last two."

"I'll go."

"I know you will. I'm going to take you in," Amy said as she turned and left.

Paul watched as she carefully bent over to tie her boots, heavily favoring her sore shoulder. He wanted to go and help, but figured he wouldn't be welcomed. His ego was wounded at her offhand treatment. He didn't know what it was he wanted from her, but he did know it wasn't this casual attitude. Time for him to leave.

The phone rang again, and Amy straightened with a sigh.

"Do you want me to get it?" Paul offered.

She shook her head and strode over to the table. She picked up the phone, turning away from him and Judd.

Judd straightened his recliner and reached for a deck of cards beside him. "Have time for a game of crib?"

Paul didn't really want to. It was a strange turn of events. Amy, who always listened, who always had time to talk, obviously didn't want him here, whereas Judd, who could hardly speak a civil word to him, was inviting him to stay. The old guy must be mellowing, he thought. And Amy had outgrown him.

He turned back to Judd and pulled up a chair.

As Judd silently dealt the cards, Paul tried to ignore her as she spoke on the phone.

"You're going to buy a car?" she exclaimed to whoever was on the other end. "How in the world can you afford it?"

Paul picked up his cards and glanced up as the porch door opened. Rick entered the kitchen, frowning.

"I might be able to drive you. Rick's been working on our truck." Paul saw her glance hopefully at her brother who lifted his hands in resignation. "Nope. I don't have a vehicle," she said, frustration edging her voice. "It would work out great. I have a tractor part to pick up in Prince George, and I know I owe you big-time but I just can't. I'd drive the tractor if I could, but Rick's got it in pieces all over the garage floor."

Paul looked down at his cards, discarded two and tried to ignore Amy's obvious distress.

"I know, Shannon, I'm sorry. Yes, I'll let you know if anything changes. Take care." She hung up the phone with a loud click.

He looked up in time to see her sag against the counter, her lips tight, her eyes shut. She looked like she was in pain. He couldn't take it any longer. He set his cards down on the table and got up.

"You ain't quitting already?" Judd accused, turning to watch as Paul strode to the kitchen.

Paul stood in front of Amy, waiting for her to notice him. She finally opened her eyes. "You can use my car, Amy."

"No. Thanks, anyway." She straightened and moved to get past him.

He took a step to the side, blocking her passage. "Don't be

so stubborn. You can't do much work with that shoulder, you may as well go pick up that part, and this way I can help out Shannon as well. I owe her, too." Paul remembered with a sudden moment's regret, a date with Shannon Lawson over seven years ago. She had pestered him to take her to a local dance. When she got more serious than he intended the date to be, he talked Rick into taking her home. It had happened many years and a lot of girlfriends ago. She teased him about it each time he came home; her offhand treatment of the fiasco made him pass it off. But now, with too many comments from his family ringing in his ears, he felt as if he should somehow try to make up for it.

Amy bit her lip as if contemplating, glanced over at Rick, who looked as if he would sooner eat nails than allow her to accept Paul's offer. "No I don't think so...."

"It's easy to drive. I'll ride Sasha home, pick up the car and be back here in less time than it takes you to shower and change."

"Look Paul...I can't imagine taking that expensive car of yours around the yard, let alone all the way to Prince George."

"I'm sure a girl who learned how to double clutch in a one-ton beater before she had her learner's permit wouldn't be afraid to drive my little car," Paul insisted.

"That thing is worth more than our cows," spluttered Amy.

Paul could tell she was starting to give in and pressed his advantage. "I'm going to sell it anyhow. If you total it, I won't have to go through the trouble," he continued, grinning down at Amy.

"I don't drive that badly," she protested.

"So you are going to drive it."

She glanced up at him, a wry expression on her face. "I suppose..."

"I can take Shannon," Rick put in, his expression hopeful.

"No. You've got to check the cows. The last thing Paul needs is a heavy-footed guy like you driving his car." Amy ignored Rick's sputtering and looked back at Paul sighing in resignation. "I guess I'm going."

"Good." He took the phone from her before she changed her mind. "What's Shannon's number. I'll call her myself."

Amy gave it to him, and as he dialed, he kept his eye on her. Her face had more color than a few moments before, and she looked a little less tense. He hoped it was because of his offer.

Shannon picked up the phone with a terse "Hello."

"Hi, Shannon, it's Paul."

"Oh, you. The guy that sets all the Cariboo hearts aflutter."

"Not really," he said with a frown.

"Paul," her tone was disappointed. "Is that the best you can come up with? 'Not really.' Or are you afraid I might nag you into taking me out again?"

"No," Paul laughed, comforted by her breezy tone. "You've got better taste than that."

"Actually I do. I'm in love with a far more interesting guy than a mere businessman."

Paul grinned, leaning back against the table. He'd always liked Shannon. She was fun and straightforward. "So you think businessmen are boring?"

"No comment." Shannon laughed. "You didn't phone to listen to me pester you."

Paul grinned then decided it was time to get back to business. "Amy will pick you up about eleven o'clock. Does that work for you?"

"Anytime would be great. Thanks...."

"Take care," he said, hanging up the phone and turning to Amy who was still frowning.

"I wish you hadn't done that," Amy reprimanded him. "Rick will be gone, and you won't be able to get back home. Unless you walk."

"Well, I don't have a whole lot to do today, I can hang around here until Rick or you come back."

"In case anyone's noticed, I'm not gone yet," Rick put in, glowering at both of them.

"Then maybe you should get gone," Amy replied. "When you check the cows, keep an eye on the calves of 25B and 68C. They were looking a little peaked last time I checked them.

You might want to take some Liquamycin and scour boluses along, just in case.''

Rick nodded, watching Paul with narrowed eyes. He slapped his gloves against his legs once, turned and left.

Amy turned to Paul with an apologetic look. ''Sorry about that. Rick's just being Rick.''

Paul said nothing, aware that the statement didn't require an answer.

''I can't ask you to do all this,'' she said, trying once more.

''Amy, you're not asking me to do anything.'' He stifled his impatience with her insistence. ''I'm offering and this is your cue to give in and say 'Thanks Paul. Why don't you go and get the car and I'll be ready when you come.' Please stop making a big deal of this.''

''Okay, but if I hit something...''

''I checked the policy before I left Vancouver. I'm fully insured against wild horses, cows, pigs, chickens—the whole farmyard and a few others besides.'' He grinned at her and pushed himself away from the table. ''So I'll just put on my boots, and then I'm history.''

He gave in to an impulse and ran the back of his fingers over her cheek. ''See you later.'' He turned and left, whistling, feeling more cheerful than he had since he'd come here.

Chapter Five

"I'm glad Paul sweet-talked you into using his car," Shannon remarked as she slid into the sleek sports car, closed the door almost reverently and sniffed. "He never had a vehicle this nice when he lived here before." She looked over at Amy and grinned. "Too bad the man didn't come, too."

"He's taking care of my dad while I'm gone."

"Your dad's fine," snorted Shannon. "He doesn't need to be baby-sat." Shannon frowned. "Or would that be old-man-sat? I don't know."

Amy shook her head at her friend's bluntness as she carefully pulled into traffic. "Dad hasn't been too well lately. I'm glad Paul's staying."

"Me, too. It gives me a chance to drive in style instead of the Greyhound." Shannon stroked the leather of the seat, almost caressed the dashboard. "Very nice, indeed." She turned to Amy. "I was sorry I missed the man at your engagement party. He's been gone so long I've forgotten what he looked like."

"Like he stepped off the cover of *GQ*."

"Oh. Just like Tim."

"Tim doesn't dress anything like that," Amy protested.

"C'mon, Amy. I'm sure the man doesn't even own a pair of blue jeans."

Amy frowned. "Of course he does. When we went riding a few weeks back..."

"He wore chinos." Shannon patted her on the shoulder. "That's okay. It's about time someone elevated the dress code around here."

Amy shot her friend an exasperated glance. "I wish you wouldn't talk about Tim like you merely tolerate him. I know you like him."

"Tim's a wonderful guy. There's no doubt about that. I'm still having a hard time adjusting to the change in you."

"We've been going out for almost sixteen months."

"It doesn't seem that long. And now you're engaged." Shannon sighed wrinkling her nose at her friend. "Remember how we used to steal Paul's school pictures from Tyrell's room?"

"My dad was furious when he found them."

"I'll never understand why he disliked Paul so much," Shannon said with a frown. "My mom and dad thought my crush on him was funny. Though they did warn me about chasing him too hard. Poor guy, I'll never forget how relieved he was when he talked Rick into taking me home after our one date. I got over him pretty quick, after that."

Amy said nothing, her mind drifting back to the time when she and Shannon, giddy eleven-year-old girls, both madly in love with Paul Henderson, would follow him around. Both knew he was unattainable, and after a while, Shannon threw away all the pictures she and Amy had scammed from Tyrell and Derk, Paul's younger brothers. When Shannon wasn't looking, Amy fished them out.

"What did your dad have against Paul, anyhow?" Shannon continued, breaking into Amy's thoughts.

Amy shook her head. "He had a dislike of Hendersons period. He's always had a hard time with the fact that they have a more successful ranch. It isn't as bad as it used to be."

"Well I hope he won't chew Paul's head off while we're

gone.'' Shannon flipped down the visor, checking out her lipstick in the mirror. ''So how was the engagement party?''

''It was fun. I was sorry you couldn't make it.'' Amy stepped on the brakes at the highway, almost sending both of them through the dash.

''Whoa, girl. This isn't your one-ton,'' Shannon cried, bracing herself against the dashboard.

Amy blew out a sigh as she shifted back into first as a pickup behind her let out a blast on his horn. ''I knew this car would make me nervous.''

''I'll drive it.''

Amy shook her head. ''The way you drive? You'd have every Mountie from here to Prince George on your tail.''

''I've only had two speeding tickets.''

''In the past month.'' Amy eased the car out onto the highway, ignoring the impatient driver behind her. ''No wonder your boss won't let you use the truck.''

''Drew won't let me use the truck because he's stingy. I'll be so glad to be finished working for that man.''

''And then what?'' Amy glanced sidelong at Shannon. ''You always talk about quitting, but what else would you do?''

''Maybe I'll throw myself at Paul Henderson's feet again.''

''Trust me girl, Paul Henderson is a waste of time.''

''I know. But he's so good-looking and so rich. I mean, look at the kind of car he drives.'' Again Shannon ran a finger along the dashboard. ''Of course I could settle for Rick,'' she said quirking a grin at Amy.

''Rick's another hard one to pin down.''

''What do you mean?''

''It seems like we're always working on different projects with no time to sit and talk. I'll be at work and he'll be checking the cows. Or I'll be in the garden and he'll be running to town for parts. He's gone every evening to Jack Dilton's working on the truck. Not that I mind. I'm glad he likes working on the equipment. I just wish he'd be a little more enthusiastic about the other work. He's got to settle down and figure out what he wants sooner or later.''

"Maybe you should ask him what he wants?" Shannon suggested gently.

"I have, and he always shrugs and says he likes what he's doing."

"Push him."

Amy frowned. "What do you mean?" She threw her friend a sidelong glance. "Do you know something I don't know?"

"What? Other than the fact that your brother is quiet, shy and good-looking?" Shannon laughed. "Nope." She leaned back in the seat and stretched, changing the subject. "I really like this car, Amy. Paul didn't have it the last time he was up, did he?"

"No. I think he had a Land Rover then."

"When was that?"

"I think about two years ago."

"Oh, yes. He had that absolutely gorgeous blonde. What was her name?"

"Don't ask me. I can't keep up with Paul's girlfriends."

Shannon half turned, catching Amy by the shoulder. "You sound grouchy again. Don't tell me you're jealous of his girlfriends?"

"Of course not," Amy snapped, tired of people always bringing up her previous crush on Paul. "Paul's the last person any girl in her right mind would get serious about."

"You used to think he was the best."

"C'mon, Shannon." Amy glared at her friend, who winked playfully back.

"Maybe you still do? Just a little bit?"

Amy sighed.

"Teeny bit?" Shannon persisted. "You are looking confused."

"If I am it's not because of Paul." Amy couldn't seem to keep the defensive tone out of her voice.

"Why then?"

"You don't want to know."

"I'm your friend, Amy. I'll listen. We've got hours together."

Amy was silent a minute, trying to gather her thoughts, the

thrum of the engine the only noise in the car. "I don't know, Shanny," she said finally. "Things have been so out of sorts. Dad's been talking about Mom. The ranch has been keeping me busy. My work has, too. I can't do much with this shoulder—it hurts and it's getting me down. I've been trying to save up some money to fix up the house with, and every time I get somewhere, Rick needs some more tools or bearings machined or something that puts a dent into the savings." She paused, allowing herself a brief moment of self-pity. "I feel like everything's getting dumped on me at once. I feel like people, including my best friend—" she took a moment to throw a meaningful glance at Shannon "—are all watching me to see if I'll drop Tim and jump into Paul Henderson's arms."

Shannon had the grace to look ashamed. "Sorry. I was just teasing."

"Well so is everyone else 'just teasing.' And I'm a little tired of it."

"Time for a subject change. Tell me more about your wedding. Have you got a dress yet? Have you taken any time away from your precious ranch to make any plans?"

"And how's Vancouver?" Judd leaned forward as he cleaned up the cards and cribbage game.

"The company is expanding, and we're busier than ever." Paul took a quick sip from the coffee cup he held suspended above his spread knees. He hardly dared sit too far back in the decrepit chair that he had pulled closer to Judd's.

"You don't sound happy about it."

Paul tipped his cup back and forth, watching the brown liquid swirl around the bottom, as he contemplated his answer. "I've got some big decisions to make, that's all."

"What decisions?" Judd leaned back in his chair reaching for the remote control of the television. "Whether you should buy stocks or mutual funds?"

Paul carefully placed his cup on the coffee table, ignoring Judd's remark. "My partner wants me to buy him out."

Judd shook his head, a mocking tone in his voice. "And your business is making a profit. Tough decision."

Paul ignored his sarcasm. "It is, actually. It will mean more work." Paul tried to keep his own voice even. He hadn't come here to spend time with Judd, and only stayed as a favor to Amy.

"Since when is a Henderson afraid of work? Your dad is still expanding. I hear he's eyeing the Kincaid spread."

"He is."

"Still doesn't have enough land?"

Paul didn't want to get drawn into Judd's antagonism. As long as he could remember, Judd had borne an unspoken grudge against Paul's father, resenting his success. Between Rick and Judd, it surprised Paul that Amy still held on to her friendship with his family. "He's talking about selling our place and retiring at Kincaids'. It's a little closer to town and the house is smaller."

"He should buy this place." Judd looked around the room. "This would be small enough."

Paul didn't reply, knowing anything he said would be superfluous.

Judd leaned back and studied Paul. "You don't like me do you, Paul?"

Paul looked straight into Judd's eyes, wishing he could say how he really felt, yet unable to because of his friendship with Amy. "It's hard to like someone who keeps resenting my family and their success."

"Probably." Judd looked away from Paul as if considering his next comment. "And, yes, I have resented your dad's success. I worked my fingers to the bone on this place, got married and then my wife fools around...." He stared at the opposite wall, lost in another time. Then, with a shake, he looked back at Paul. "And your dad's business keeps on growing, his ranch just brings in more money. It's a little hard to take."

For Judd Danyluk, making an admission like that must have been like opening a vein, Paul thought. "I'm sure it would be," he conceded.

Judd glanced at the crutches leaning against the chair beside him. "I lost my wife, then I lost my leg, and trying to work this ranch has never made up for either."

Paul found himself at a loss for words. He had offered to stay with Judd only for Amy's sake, and now he found himself almost feeling sorry for the old man.

"Now Amy's getting married," Judd continued. "My little girl's growing up."

"At least you won't lose her," Paul replied.

"I suppose." Judd scratched his chin, shaking his head. Then with a shrug, he dismissed the topic. "And what about you? Are you planning on marrying that class act you brought to Amy's engagement party?"

"Stacy and I haven't fixed a date yet."

Judd snorted, pushing his chair upright with a creak. "You sound like Amy. She can't make up her mind when to get married, either."

"Why is that?" Paul wanted to hear Judd's opinion of the situation and maybe find out more about the man Amy had chosen.

"She says she needs time to get everything in order. Before Tim moves here."

"You don't sound too pleased about that. Don't you want Tim living here?"

"I don't mind the idea. But Amy's a stubborn perfectionist, and the ranch is a demanding taskmaster. She'll never get things the way she wants, and she'll just keep putting off the wedding." Judd looked at Paul, his eyes narrowed. "She has someone good, and she shouldn't lose him, thinking he'll wait until the time is right. I don't want him to resent this place like Noreen did."

Paul leaned forward, waiting. Judd had never been this forthcoming before, and never had he spoken of Noreen in other than disparaging tones.

Judd only shifted in his chair, and without another comment lifted the remote control and turned on the television.

He must have said too much, Paul thought tossing down the dregs of his coffee.

Canned laughter, forced and phony, filled the room and Paul got up. A picture of Tim and Amy that hung on the wall between the kitchen and living room caught his eye. He stepped closer, studying it. Amy looked tense as Tim hugged her close, her eyes too wide, her smile too bright, and Tim, well, as far as Paul could see, Tim looked a bit too smug.

Jealous.

He examined the feeling that suddenly clutched him. Definitely jealousy. He couldn't imagine Tim living here, either, he thought studying his face. Paul gave himself a mental shake. Amy had made her decision, and it wasn't up to him to judge or question.

He glanced over his shoulder at Judd, who sat frowning at the sitcom as it milked weary jokes and mocked life. He needed to get out.

He suddenly remembered the pail sitting by the fence post when he first drove into the yard. He could do some fencing until Amy came back. The thought put a smile on his face.

"I'm going out, Judd, do you need anything?"

Judd shook his head without looking up.

Paul shrugged, turned and walked out of the house. He'd be back in a while to check on Judd, meanwhile he could do something useful.

The fencing tools were exactly where Amy had left them. Hands on his hips, Paul surveyed the fence that ran along the driveway then took a turn to follow the tree line. Half of the wires had come loose, some posts held no wire at all. Amy and Rick had their work cut out for them, if she planned to get them stapled up before the cows came down from the summer pasture.

He looked back at the cattle yard. They had replaced some of the rotten boards with new ones that gleamed white beside the weathered gray of the old wood of the corrals. Beyond them, the barn's door hung at a crazy angle, held by a single hinge. Baled hay stood like forgotten boxes out in the fields. The Danyluks still used inefficient square bales which would have to be hauled by hand. But not by Amy. Her shoulder would put her out of commission for another week, minimum.

Paul turned back to the fence and hefted the fencing pliers. He eyed the leather gloves that lay on the ground beside the pail. Too small. He'd have to work without them. He smiled, remembering countless hours tacking up wire while a younger Amy kept up a stream of chatter, handing him staples, her own hands bare.

He carefully lifted a sharp staple from the bucket and pounded it into the shaky fence post, bemused at the raft of memories that accompanied this trip. The decision to buy out his partner, Bruce, seemed easy to make back in Vancouver, but now, his feelings weren't clear on the matter. Being home, even for these few days, shifted his perspective. Stacy was supposed to be here with him, experiencing this, and now she was in Vancouver.

And he didn't even miss her.

He gave a stubborn staple another whack, and it sank deep into the hardwood of the post. All four wires were now securely anchored. A sparrow sang somewhere off in the distance as he bent over to pick up the pail. He paused a moment, relishing the warm sun and the softness of the day. He pushed thoughts of Stacy and business to the back of his mind.

As he moved along the fence line, the long grass rustling as he passed, a feeling of completeness welled up in him. Like putting on an old pair of boots worn to the shape of your feet, he felt like he belonged.

Could he come back? Would he want to?

His questions brought him back to Stacy. With a soft sigh Paul moved on to the next section of fence. He didn't want to think about Stacy right now.

Amy opened the door to the bank, cool air rushing over her as she stepped inside. Even though she had spent most of the day in an air-conditioned car, it felt unnatural to be shivering in short sleeves inside and sweltering outside.

The drive to Prince George had gone quickly. Fortunately, she had met no RCMP on the highway. Paul's car didn't seem to care whether it went 110 kilometers per hour or 120. The extra speed gave her extra time. Enough extra time to stop on the way home and see Tim.

"Hi, Amy." The receptionist looked up with a smile.

"Tim's not busy, and he'll be glad to see you." She gestured with a pen towards his office.

Tim sat hunched over a desk, tie loosened and coat hanging over the back of his chair. As she watched through the open door, he rubbed his head with a pencil, his forehead creased. Amy felt a thankful lift of her heart at the sight of her handsome fiancé.

She tapped on the door. "Got a few thousand for a poor starving rancher?"

He looked up, startled. Then grinned widely as he came around the desk toward her. He reached behind her, closed the door and gave her a careful hug. "Aren't you a welcome sight?"

Amy leaned her good shoulder against him, inhaling the fragrance of his clean shirt, the faint hint of aftershave. "I missed you."

"That's good." Tim tipped her face up to his and dropped a quick kiss on her forehead, then stepped back, pulling up a chair for her. "What brings you to town?"

"I had to pick up a part from Prince George. Shannon needed a ride there to pick up a car she bought."

"The old truck actually made that long trip?" Tim grinned at her, returning to his own chair.

"C'mon. Matilda is perfectly capable of going cross Canada if she wants to." Amy wrinkled her nose at him, trying not to feel disappointed that he put the desk between them so quickly. "But I didn't have to. Paul Henderson loaned me his car."

Tim's eyebrows shot up. "The snappy red number that was parked in front of his mom and dad's? I'm surprised he trusted you with it."

Amy looked down at her hands, twisting her engagement ring around on her finger. She couldn't quite figure out why his comment bothered her. "I'm not that bad a driver," she said finally.

"Of course you're not. I didn't mean that." Tim pushed his pencil back and forth between his fingers. He looked up at her, his mouth crooked up in a half smile. "I'm sorry."

"No problem."

"So do you have to be back at the ranch right away?" Tim leaned back in his chair, twirling his pencil.

"I should. I've got dozens of things to do. I just thought I'd stop in and say hi. Paul is staying with my dad. I shouldn't leave him there too long. Dad isn't a big Henderson fan."

Tim nodded his head and gave his pencil another twirl, watching it as if thinking. "Do you have time to go out for supper?"

Amy hesitated.

Tim leaned forward. "What? You don't want to go out with me?"

"No, no," Amy shook her head. "It's not that. I have to take Paul's car back." She forced a smile, torn between Paul's generosity and the reality of her father's personality. "Besides, I'm not dressed to go out," she said, trying not to feel self-conscious about her faded blue jeans.

"So we go to Tony's. It's a casual place."

"I don't know if I should."

"Why don't you phone Paul and ask if you can have the car a little longer?" Tim turned his phone around and pushed it toward her.

Amy bit her lip, wondering at her own reluctance and Tim's insistence. She felt uncomfortable about both.

"We haven't seen each other for a while," he continued.

Amy knew he was right, and, taking a deep breath she punched a free line and hit the numbers. The phone rang a few times, then a deep voice answered the phone.

"Hi, Paul. How's my dad?" Amy twisted the cord around her finger. "Really? That's good. I was wondering if I can use the car a little longer. Tim wants to take me out for supper.... That's okay then...? Thanks. Home by twelve...? I know it's a weeknight. Don't worry, I'll be home earlier than that." Amy looked up at Tim and smiled. Tim looked back at her, his face impassive. Amy untwisted the cord and rubbed her hand over her pants, aware that maybe the phone conversation had gone on a little too long. "Thanks, Paul. I'll see you later."

She dropped the phone in the cradle meeting Tim's guarded look. "I guess that's all settled."

"Great." Tim glanced at his watch and got up. "I've got a few minutes of work left and then I'm done."

"I've got to run down to Dilton's garage. I'll meet you at Tony's."

Amy got up and picked up her purse. Tim waited for her, one hand on the open door. As she passed by him, she lifted her face for his customary peck on the cheek. Instead he pulled her close and kissed her full on the mouth. Amy stepped back, surprised, unconsciously glancing over her shoulder at the receptionist who stared at them, looking as shocked as Amy.

"See you later," he said with a tight smile.

Before supper, Amy made a promise to herself that she wouldn't think about the ranch or Rick or her father or any of the myriad tasks that loomed over her. She was just going to enjoy being with her handsome fiancé.

They settled into a table, going through familiar motions. Tim always rearranged his silverware and moved his glass. Amy watched him and smiled, thinking how wonderful it was going to be to see him across the breakfast table each morning, the supper table each evening.

"I think I'm going to like being married to you, Tim Enders," she said, touching his hand as he fussed with the cloth napkin.

"I think I'm going to like being married to you, too, Amy Danyluk." He returned her smile. "But we have one small problem."

Amy frowned. "What?"

He leaned forward with a teasing smile. "We haven't set a wedding date yet, so you're going to have to wait to be married to me until we pick one."

Amy looked down at her own napkin, pleating it carefully. It was easier to think about being married than the actual wedding. The cost scared her each time.

"Amy, my mom has been phoning constantly about making plans, and I can't even tell her what day."

"I guess because we're engaged, that would be a natural progression," she answered, returning his smile. "It's just that

Dad can't afford much right now. We'll need to get a mobile home on the yard for Dad and Rick. I don't want them in the house with us.''

"That's a relief,'' Tim laughed.

"But that's going to cost us money.''

"Why do you keep worrying about that?'' Tim grasped her hands, his brown eyes holding hers, his well-shaped lips quirked up in a grin. "I've told you before that Mom and Dad are willing to foot the bill for the wedding, and I'd sooner be humbly in debt to my parents and married, than proudly struggling to save money as a single man.''

Amy smiled at his apt description. Tim was his parents' only child, and she knew she shouldn't begrudge them their chance for a celebration in a style they were accustomed to. But if they paid for what the Danyluks' couldn't afford...that would mean they would pay for more than their share. "And living arrangements?''

Tim waved his hands as if dismissing that. "There are all kinds of ways around that.''

"Like what?'' Amy said with a frown.

Tim hesitated. "We could live in the trailer. Or even better, an apartment in town.'' He leaned forward suddenly, rubbing the wrinkle between her eyebrows. "You worry too much. Whatever we do is only temporary.''

"That's true.'' He was right. She did worry too much.

"In the meantime,'' he said, ignoring her and pulling out his pocket calendar, "we have a wedding date to set.'' He flipped it open. "So when do you think?''

"How about a year from now?'' she joked.

Tim stared at her, uncomprehending.

"Just kidding,'' she said, trying out a smile.

"I'm glad,'' he replied, relieved. "I was thinking closer to Christmas of this year.''

So soon. Amy's mind raced as she mentally flipped through the list of chores waiting to be done. Bales home, cross fencing to do, heifers coming, hay to bale, heifers due to calve, cows down from the summer pasture. Could she and Rick get it all done and still give her enough time to plan a wedding? "Can't we look at some time in the new year?" she offered hesitantly.

"I have a convention in Florida on the seventh of November. I was thinking we could make that part of our honeymoon."

Amy wrinkled her nose, trying to inject a light tone into a conversation that was beginning to sound distinctly business-like. "I don't know if I'm too keen on talking mutual funds and amortization on our honeymoon, Tim...."

"Well, it could save us money. My part of the trip is paid for." He leaned forward. "Besides, when would you get a chance to go to Florida again?"

"Next banker's convention?"

"Next one is in Vancouver."

Amy swallowed, trying to crush the beginnings of panic roiling in her stomach. She knew she should agree. They were engaged, getting married was the next step.

But so soon? the other part of her argued.

Tim waited for her answer, his face expectant.

I do care about him, she thought. What am I waiting for, anyhow? "Okay," she replied. "November sounds good to me."

Amy opened her purse and pulled out her date book resolutely flipping past the fully engaged month of October and turning to the almost equally full month of November. Hastily she scratched out "Equipment auction—Williams Lake" and penciled in "WEDDING" in capital letters, as if to remind herself.

"I'm glad we finally have that settled," Tim said, his smile relieved. "My mom wants us to come to Vancouver to visit the bridal registry. I tried to put her off because I was embarrassed that we hadn't even set a date. Now we can even order invitations."

Amy smiled, taking deep breaths, forcing herself to relax. She was glad to see Tim so excited, and in spite of her anxiety, his ebullience was catching.

It would all work out.

Chapter Six

$\sim$

The sun hung above the mountains cradling the Danyluk ranch when Amy turned into her driveway. It was still early evening. Tim wanted her to stay longer, but thoughts of Paul stuck at her home with her father cut short their time.

Amy drove Paul's car carefully up the drive, almost coming to a halt by the dilapidated cattle guard. She inched over it, wincing as the car bounced, almost praying it wouldn't slip into the ruts and bottom out. She didn't even want to imagine what a muffler for this fancy car would cost her. The fuel pump for the old truck had set her back enough, and Jack Dilton's carefully worded warning about their overdue account still hung over her.

Out of habit she glanced sidelong at the fence. Maybe tonight she might have time to fix it. She stepped on the brakes and stared. Wires stretched from one post to another, tight and even. How in the world...?

Puzzled, she drove to the house, parked the car and got out. From there she could see the entire fence line. Halfway down she saw Paul. It wasn't hard to miss the thick blond hair, the broad shoulders. He knelt down, the sound of his blows out of synch with his movements. Amy watched a moment, pleasure knifing through her at his unselfish act.

It wasn't right that he was working on their fence, she thought. She had to help.

She started jogging to the house, then quit. Her shoulder hurt too much. She could hardly wait until it started feeling better. It was a literal pain in the neck.

She stepped into the house, throwing her purse on the table. A note from Rick leaned against the bowl of fruit.

Took the tractor to Jack's. Will get Matilda running first thing in the morning.

Amy was relieved to know that their tractor was getting Rick's as well as Jack Dilton's expert attention. She wondered how much it was going to cost and she wondered why Rick didn't think he might need to help Paul with the fence.

Amy dropped the note and glanced at her father's empty recliner. He had gone to bed early again. When was his doctor's appointment? She glanced at the calendar. Not for a couple of weeks yet.

She walked carefully up the stairs to change, frustrated with her shoulder, wanting to hurry. The sight of Paul working while she'd been dallying in town made her feel guilty.

Ten minutes later, she stepped from the cool air of the house into the warmth outside.

As she walked across the yard, another pair of fencing pliers in hand, she squinted against the lowering sun to watch Paul nailing up the wires, his back bare. In spite of herself, her heart gave an unexpected thump at the sight.

Habit, she told herself as she walked down toward him. Eighteen years of hero worship hadn't faded as quickly as she had hoped. Besides, seeing Tim would have the same effect on her, she thought, even though she had never seen him shirtless.

She picked Paul's shirt off the ground, then glanced back over her shoulder at the yard and the green hills beyond them. The memories of the noise and traffic in Prince George made her shudder, but as her eyes drifted over the land, she felt tranquillity smooth away the tension of driving. She took a deep breath, inhaling the sun-warmed air of the Cariboo, undefinable yet so necessary for her.

She wished Tim would come out more often. She wanted so

badly for him to fall in love with the place she knew so well. After their honeymoon they would have time, she promised herself. Once they were living here, together.

With a soft smile she nodded and carried on down the fence line toward Paul.

"Hi there, city boy, get that straw out of your mouth," she called as she came closer. "You'll get worms."

Paul whirled around and smiled, working the offending piece of straw to the other side of his mouth. "That's just an old wives' tale to keep farm boys from looking cool."

"Well, then, put this back on. You look pretty cool already." She handed him his shirt.

"Like Frigidaire?" He asked as he slipped his hands into the sleeves and quickly snapped it up the front.

"How do you come up with these horrible comebacks?" Amy groaned. "I thought city living would have squeezed them out of you."

"Did you come to talk or badger me?" Paul grabbed another staple and pounded it in.

"I think I've always been good at both." Amy carefully bent over and slipped the gloves on. "So you can go home now. Dad looks like he's okay, and I can finish from here."

"I don't think so, miss," Paul replied, pulling a staple out of the pail with one hand as he took the pliers from her with the other. "I start what I finish and you're not supposed to work."

Amy turned a staple over in her gloved hands, feeling torn.

"Amy, you are thinking again. It's a habit you're going to have to set aside for a while. I'm here. I have time. I don't mind helping. For once in your life take what's offered."

Amy looked up at him, her head tilted to one side, her eyes meeting his bright blue ones. The pull toward him was almost tangible, and she looked away. It wouldn't be a good idea if he stayed and worked. *He's still too attractive and I've got too much of that silly little girl in me.* Then she looked at the row of loose wires that stretched away from her. *But it would sure help me out if I let him.*

She felt a light tap on her head. "Don't," he warned, "don't think so much."

She smiled, shrugged, then winced. "Okay, okay. I'm handing you the staples though."

"Of course," Paul returned with a grin. "We used to make an awesome fencing team. We can do it again." He saluted with his fencing pliers, bent over and whacked another staple in. "So, did you eat as fast as usual? Is that why you're home so early?"

Amy felt more comfortable with his usual banter. "No. Nor did I chew with my mouth open. I wanted to make sure I got home soon enough to return your car and rescue you from my father." She wrinkled her forehead at him. "So, I almost hate to ask, but how did it go?"

"He was okay. We played crib. He napped. I fixed the fence. We played crib. I made him supper. He went to bed and I fixed fence. Pretty routine."

"Very routine," Amy answered dryly, relieved at his easy tone. How Judd and Paul would interact had been on her mind most of the afternoon. What she had forgotten was how easy Paul was to have around and how amenable he could be when he desired. He bore no grudges, only an attitude of surprise that anyone should dislike him. She certainly didn't, in spite of all the disappointments she had felt over his lack of attention while growing up.

But even that, she mused as she sorted through the staples, was only a disappointment because of her expectations, not because of him. She picked a staple out of the bucket and handed it to him. He took it carefully, his fingers brushing hers as he did so. Their eyes met and held, his finger still touched hers and Amy felt as if someone had socked the breath out of her chest. With a swallow, she pulled back, fumbling as the bucket fell out of her hands with a clatter.

Blushing now, she dropped down, digging through the grass, picking up staples. Above her she heard Paul yank on a wire between the posts. "Can you step up the pace, lady?" he complained, his tone teasing. "Sun's asetting. Time's awastin'."

Amy took a breath and looked up at him, grinning. "You're

in the Cariboo now, city boy. You don't have to hustle while you wait," she commented, dropping the staples in the bucket, feeling even more the clumsy country girl. She was positive Stacy never dropped anything. Covering her embarrassment with bluster, she retorted, "I'm surprised you're not wearing your cell phone. How is your broker ever going to get hold of you?"

"Don't mock my broker. He gives me great advice."

"Buy low, sell high?"

"Better. He figures I can make a million in a couple of weeks. The only hitch is that I have to start with $900,000." Paul looked at her with a straight face. "He also told me that there are two ways to lose a million."

Amy dropped the last staples in with a grimace, wondering what he was going to tell her. "I hate to do this, but I'll bite."

Paul ticked them off on his fingers. "Betting horses is the quickest, and farming the most reliable."

"That guy is so smart, he's scary."

"That's why I don't spend a lot of time with him." Paul winked at her and picked up his pliers again. "What did you have for supper?"

"Just burgers."

"Saving money for your wedding?" he teased.

"Wasn't dressed for anything fancier." She couldn't keep the defensive tone out of her voice. It seemed to be the story of her life. Never dressed quite right, always scraping by.

"That shouldn't matter," he answered shortly. "You could walk through downtown Vancouver wearing thrift store clothes and still stop traffic."

Amy tossed him a sideways glance. "Compliments?"

He held her gaze, his own steady. "You're a beautiful girl, Amy Danyluk. Don't ever let anyone tell you different."

She stared at him a moment, then turned away, a faint blush warming her neck.

"And if you wipe that ketchup off your chin you'll look even better."

He ducked as she swung at him. He grinned at her, the mood

broken, then turned to look down the fence line. "How much of this fence needs to be fixed?"

She bit her lip. "Most of it."

"How in the world did your entire fence line get run down so quick?"

"Hardly quick," she countered. "Rick and I managed to keep the cows in the upper pasture long enough the past few years that we didn't need this field as much. We've been able to hay it most of the years. Unlike your family, we don't have access to lease land for summer pasture."

"And now the upper pasture is overgrazed and you need this one until winter," he finished for her.

"Actually that welcome rain a few days ago saved us. It was a real answer to prayer." She smiled a moment, then turned to Paul. "We need this one for the heifers that are coming. I'm hoping to cross fence it. They won't need all that land and we'll be able to hay the rest yet."

"Does Tim ever come and help?"

Amy shrugged carefully. "He's got a job. He's busy, too."

Paul nodded, and Amy ignored the skeptical lift of his brows. Too many times she had wished that Tim could come and help, but he always had other things he was busy with.

"Why didn't you ask my dad for help?" Paul asked. "He would've sent one of the boys over. Or better yet, you could have run your cows in our lease."

Amy said nothing.

"Amy?" Paul urged.

"I don't know," she sighed. "Dad never wanted to ask. Anytime I talked about it he flew off the handle and claimed we didn't need charity. I know it's been hard on him, not being able to work as much, but for my sake, I wish he wasn't so stubborn."

"Well, he talked quite civilly to me a few hours ago, and he hasn't tried to take the pliers away from me."

"He's mellowing," she said, smiling at him. "And I sure appreciate the help."

"Don't mention it." His tone became brisk. "Give that come-along a push, will you, please? We need to tighten the wire. If we want to get this fence fixed, we'd better get off Cariboo time and try some good, old downtown Vancouver hustle.'' He winked at her, and they worked in companionable silence until the settling darkness made it too difficult to see what they were doing.

They walked back to the garage in the cool of the gathering darkness, and as Amy glanced over her shoulder at the tight, even wires, a feeling of accomplishment washed over her. She hadn't done much work. Handed staples and tightened wire, that's all. But a large portion of another job was off her mind.

"Looks good, Paul.'' At the garage Amy took the pail from him and dropped her gloves in it. "Thanks for helping.''

Paul shrugged, rolling down the sleeves of his plaid shirt, grinning at her. "No problem. I enjoyed working with you.'' He leaned one hip against the frame of the open garage door, watching as she put away the tools, hanging up the pliers, setting the gloves aside, dropping the pail with a metallic clunk on the ground under the workbench. "I should come over tomorrow and clean this place out for you.''

"You've done enough.'' Amy stood up, brushing the dust from her jeans, one-handed. "This can wait for a winter day.'' She turned to him. "Do you want a cup of coffee before you head home?''

Paul shook his head, and Amy felt strangely disappointed.

"Thanks, anyway,'' he said, yawning as he pushed himself off from the door. "I think this city boy better head home.'' He looked out over the yard, his hands pressed at the small of his back while he stretched. "I'm tired, and I haven't worked this hard in years. It felt good, Punky.''

His use of her old nickname made her feel good inside.

They chatted, stretching out the accord that sprang up so quickly and easily between them. Their conversation continued as Amy walked Paul to his car.

"Did the car work okay for you?'' Paul asked leaning against the car, content to draw out the farewell.

"Well,'' Amy pressed her lips together, as if contemplating. "Her timing's a little off and the carb sounds like it could use some cleaning. Misfires going up hills....''

"That's not my car you're describing. That sounds like your tractor."

Amy sighed as reality intruded on the moment of peace. "Actually it is."

Paul grimaced in understanding. "That bad."

"Plus blow-by and a bad injector to boot. Scenario for a motor job."

"That's a pricey touch."

"Tell me." Amy blew her breath out. "Thankfully Rick's been working on it, and Jack's been helping. It will cost some, but not as much as if we took it into the garage. Which is a good thing. I've been chipping away at our charge account there but I don't seem to be making a lot of headway." She rotated her neck and winced as she moved her shoulder too far.

"Have you seen the doctor about that shoulder yet?"

"No. I've had to work the past week." She frowned at him. "Don't worry, Henderson, I'll go."

"And make sure you get Rick pitching bales when you haul your hay off the field." His expression was so much that of a protective older brother that Amy wondered how she could have felt anything other than sisterly feelings toward him.

"I can figure that one out."

Paul straightened. He reached over and carefully brushed some dirt off her cheek, his fingers warm against her cool skin. She looked up into eyes that glowed in the gathering dusk.

"Take care, Amy," he said softly, cupping her chin a moment. He let his hand drop to his side.

She swallowed and took a step back, her breath catching in her throat at his touch, the brief contact of their eyes. Her heart did a slow flip as her mind castigated her emotions. *Thought you were over him, you big sap.*

Paul waited a moment, then got in his car. She turned abruptly away, stalking to the house, determined not to give him another thought.

Her shower was brief—tricky to work up a lather in her hair with one aching shoulder, but it felt refreshing, nonetheless. She checked quickly on her father before she went to bed, and left the hallway light on for her brother.

She crawled into bed, clicked off the light and lay back, waiting for the mindlessness of sleep to drift over her.

But it wouldn't come. She carefully moved onto her back, as her mind replayed the events of a busy day. She turned her head, staring out of the window into the soft night outside.

Could Tim see the stars in town? Could he step outside in the quiet of the night when it seemed the entire world was enveloped in utter stillness? How would he like living out here where the silence pressed in?

Now that they had picked out a wedding day, she had more plans to make. She didn't like the idea of Tim's parents paying. She had some money of her own, but not nearly enough to put on a wedding. And the ranch always seemed to use up whatever extra she had. What was she expected to pay for and how much?

And what did he mean about living in an apartment in town? There was no way she could work the ranch and live in town. She must have misunderstood him.

Her mind flipped from the wedding to the trip to town, and her and Shannon's conversation. Shannon's enigmatic remark about Rick had slipped by her at the time, but she remembered it now. It was as if Shannon saw Rick in a different light than she had the past few years. Now that Amy thought about it, Rick seemed to be different around Shannon. Quieter, more self-conscious, and Shannon, too, became almost reserved. Which definitely was *not* like her. Shannon was more smart remarks and snappy comebacks. Even around Paul she always managed to keep up a flow of chatter that kept everyone laughing. Amy always envied Shannon her easy treatment of Paul even after what could have been an embarrassing situation.

In spite of herself, Amy remembered again the feelings of envy she felt when she found out Shannon and Paul were going out. The idea that her best friend was on a date with the man she loved had kept her up half the night even though she had no desire to be at a dance. Sure, Rick had taken Shannon home, but it had put a strain on their friendship for a couple of months. Until Shannon had confessed to Amy that she knew Paul had only taken her out on sufferance.

Amy shifted to her back, thinking about Paul. They had always gotten along, and with a smile she remembered their easy rapport this afternoon. It was as if their relationship was realigning, finding a better fit. She remembered his easy grin, their banter.

His hand drifting down her cheek, cupping her chin.

Amy rolled over, restless. She didn't want to remember how warm his hand felt and how it gave her a tiny shiver.

There were too many times she would have swooned if he'd even looked at her as he had tonight. She liked where she was now: engaged and in love with another man, a man who had chased her, instead of the other way around. How many times had her mother admonished her about chasing Paul? About making a fool of herself over him?

Amy thought of Noreen. Despite the years of separation, her mother's voice would come to her in bits and pieces. Why hadn't Amy or Rick heard anything from her? Did she not care? Why did she leave?

Finally, unable to still her mind, she reached over and clicked on her bedside light, pulling her Bible off the table beside her bed. Should have done this from the start, she thought.

She pushed herself up, turning to Psalm 112. "Blessed is the man who fears the Lord, who finds great delight in his commands. Good will come to him who is generous and lends freely.... He will have no fear of bad news, his heart is steadfast, trusting in the Lord."

Amy leaned her head against the wall behind her bed, staring sightlessly up at the ceiling. "No fear of bad news." Her bank statement was due to come in the mail, and in spite of the words of the Psalm she was afraid. The ranch had been dipping too much into their operating loan lately, something she didn't really want to talk to Rick about. She disliked bringing up their financial situation for fear he would think he had to go out and work. For now they were stumbling along, waiting to sell their calves in the fall, hoping for higher prices. If Rick worked fulltime, as well, Amy knew the ranch would suffer.

She knew she had to trust that God would take care of her and her family. It seemed the harder she worked, though, the tighter the net of difficulties wove itself around her. She struggled often with truly letting go of her problems. Wrong as it was, it seemed more responsible to fret and worry over them herself.

"Please help me trust," she prayed, reaching out to God, craving the comfort that she knew only He could give. "Please give me strength to take care of Dad, to do my own work, to encourage Rick." Her prayer continued as she held each of her family up to the Lord. She hesitated a moment toward the end, thinking of her mother, once again struggling with forgiveness. Things would have been so much easier if her mother were still here. But in the end, she prayed for her mother, as well, wherever she might be.

Amy gently laid her Bible on the nightstand, hesitating. With a quick movement she pulled open the top drawer and reached inside. The picture was buried beneath other books and papers. Amy pulled it out and propped it on her stomach, leaning back to study the old wedding picture of her parents.

Amy traced her mother's face, drawing on other memories to give the two-dimensional portrait life. She remembered her mother, tired, fretting, whenever Amy preferred to help her father with the baling instead of Noreen with the laundry. Amy recalled the countless times she would come in from doing chores to find her mother, elbows leaning on the counter, staring out of the window.

What made you leave us, Mom? Amy asked the picture. What could we have done to make you stay? I'm planning a wedding, Mom. I wish you could help me. I don't know what I'm supposed to do or where to start. Amy rubbed the glass with a corner of her bedsheet, polishing it. With a restrained sigh, she slipped the picture back into the drawer as more questions tossed about her mind.

How much of her mother was in her? Those who remembered Noreen said Amy got her delicate features from her mother, her stubborn personality from her father. Yet her gray eyes were the same shade as Judd's, her hair the same reddish tinge. So how much of her mother's spirit did she inherit?

Amy snapped off the light.

She was thinking too much again. Just as Paul had warned her not to.

She lay back, letting God's peace ease her worries, letting His comfort and love enfold her. Her eyes drifted shut, and sleep finally overcame the worries of the day.

Chapter Seven

"**D**oes Mom ever get people mixed up?" Paul commented as he and his father walked up the church steps together. Ahead of them, Elizabeth chatted briefly with everyone she met, commiserating with one person, smiling in congratulations with another.

"I've never seen it happen." Fred smiled as they stepped inside the church. "And if it ever did, she could manage to convince the people that, yes, their daughter *did* have her appendix out last week."

He followed his father into the sanctuary of the church, familiar sounds and even familiar smells bringing back memories of three boisterous boys and two harried parents. How often had he and his brothers followed his parents down this carpeted aisle? How many Sundays had they spent sitting in these same pews, behind the same people every week? It felt as if time had turned back.

But as he followed his father, reality intruded. He noticed for the first time the slight stoop to his father's shoulders, his mother's limp.

They were getting older and still working. Not one of their three sons had remained behind to take over the ranch. Instead, his father made do with hired hands and seasonal workers. Paul could see the day his father would be unable to do even this, and Paul wouldn't even have this to come back to. The thought hurt.

His mother paused to talk to someone else, and in that moment he glanced to where the Danyluks always sat. He saw Amy slipping into the pew beside Tim, her long hair loose and flowing over her narrow shoulders. She leaned toward Tim, and he bent his dark head over hers. He smiled at what she said and, slipping an arm about her, drew her close.

Paul felt a thorn of jealousy stab him. Perhaps that's what made him touch her shoulder as he walked past on the way to his parents' pew.

She tilted her head up, and her automatic smile froze in place. Paul hesitated as he saw her smile disappear. She nodded at him, then turned back to Tim.

He regretted his impulse, and as he settled into place beside his parents he wondered anew at the transition of his feelings towards Amy.

As he looked around the church he realized other parts of him had changed, as well. If not changed, he amended, then reverted back to his youth. Last Sunday they had come late and slipped into the back of the church. Today it felt more like home.

They sat in the same pew he had as a child, when he would spend services counting ceiling tiles, counting how many people wore glasses, how many ladies wore hats, calculating how long candles would burn during Advent services, and all the ways children spent time when their mind wasn't on the service.

The minister came in, the congregation rose, and when the voices were raised in song, Paul knew that today, much like last week, he wouldn't be counting anything. A thirst for God had touched him last week, and as he spent time with his parents it intensified. As the service continued, Paul felt as if he caught a glimpse of where his wanderings of the past years were finally leading.

Back here. Back home.

After the sermon, the organist began the offertory, and in

the lull Paul looked back and caught Amy's eyes. He didn't look away. Neither did she as the moment stretched and held.

Paul felt a deep feeling of accord and belonging course through him. This time, this place in God's house, holding Amy's gaze. It fit, they belonged.

She blinked and suddenly looked away, breaking the moment.

But as Paul looked ahead, he couldn't shake the feeling that the Lord had shown him something important.

"What do you figure brought Henderson into church today?" Rick stretched his leg out with a grimace as they sat in their living room.

Amy shrugged as she stepped over him to pour another cup of coffee for Tim.

"Hopefully the same thing that brought you," Tim said quietly to Rick.

Amy slanted him a grateful smile, thankful for his unexpected defense of Paul.

Rick frowned. "I doubt that. Paul Henderson never does anything unless it has something to do with money or girls."

"I don't know why you dislike Paul so much. He never did anything to you," Amy admonished. "You're starting to sound like Dad." She glanced over at her father, who only frowned at her.

Rick said nothing, merely took another cookie and bit into it.

Amy dropped down beside Tim, the soft material of her cream-colored dress puddling in a silky heap around her knees. It was the dress she was to have worn to their engagement party. She finally dared wear it today, albeit with a thin silk top underneath it to hide her still-purple upper arm. Tim's compliment still warmed her and made the cost of the dress worth the sacrifice.

"And how was church?" Judd asked.

"Pastor DeJonge gave a really good sermon on trusting in God." Amy cradled her hands around her warm mug, wishing her father would come to church himself. "I know that's something I needed to hear right now."

"Did you mention my prayer request?" Judd leaned back, tapping his fingers on his crutches.

Amy hesitated. Rick rolled his eyes. Amy looked at Tim who quirked her an encouraging smile.

"Tim and I thought it best if I mentioned it to Pastor DeJonge before church. We asked him to remember Mom in his private prayers," she said quietly, clutching the cup tighter. It was Tim's idea. He didn't think it necessary to bring it up another Sunday. Amy knew he was bothered by Judd's unexpected, rekindled interest in a woman who had not been a part of anyone's life for the past ten years. A woman who, as Tim pointed out, had been unfaithful and whose lack of contact only seemed to reinforce her lack of remorse.

Judd just nodded.

"Why are you thinking about her now, Dad?" Rick asked angrily. "She's gone. She hasn't called. She doesn't care. I'm surprised you do."

"Amy's getting married. I wish there was some way we could tell her." He clutched his crutches, and Amy exchanged glances with Tim. "I know—" Judd hesitated "—I know I haven't talked much about her but..." He paused as if he wanted to say more. "I think she needs our prayers," he said with finality.

Amy said nothing, still unused to the change in her father. In all the years since he lost his leg, he seemed to blame all the twists and turns of his life on Noreen. He still didn't want to come to church, but for him to be talking now about asking for prayer requests was as unusual as expecting Paul Henderson to settle down in the valley.

"Those heifers are coming tomorrow."

Rick's voice broke into her thoughts, and she turned to him. "Tomorrow?" she repeated.

"In the afternoon. The trucker called yesterday when you and dad were out in the garden. I forgot to tell you. He has to do a run to Prince George and will pick them up on his way back and be here around seven in the evening."

"I thought they were coming on Wednesday? We have to get the hay bales out of the fields yet and put up that fence." Amy breathed deeply, trying to slow a small beat of panic.

Rick shook his head. "I thought so, too. But that's what he told me. The truck's fixed so I can head into town for some more parts for the tractor in the morning. I'll be back after lunch so that will give us enough time to get everything together for them."

"But we've got to get the rest of the hay out of there."

"There's only twenty heifers. They won't bother the bales. We can get the bales hauled on Tuesday."

"I'm working Tuesday."

"So we do them Wednesday." Rick shrugged while Amy fought down a groan.

"What about cross fencing? We can't leave them to run around the whole hay field before we get a second cut."

"I thought about that already. We can get some of the electric fencing wire. It's cheaper than fencing."

But we already have all the stuff for a barbed wire fence, thought Amy, and we'd have to buy electric fencing material. She didn't want to look at Tim who knew exactly where their bank account sat.

"Well," she said with an uncharacteristic shrug, "I guess we'll have to figure that out when the time comes."

She pushed thoughts of the ranch aside for the rest of the morning and by the time she walked Tim to his car Sunday's peace had pervaded her thoughts.

"Have you had a chance to think about making a trip out to Vancouver?" Tim held Amy's hand in his own as they walked down to his car.

"Not a lot."

Tim stopped, pulling her other hand into his and looking down at her engagement ring. In the bright sun it winked back at both of them, sending out bright shafts of color.

"We shouldn't wait too long, Amy. Some of Mom's friends have already been asking about gift ideas, and it's high time you go looking for a dress."

"I've got the heifers coming tomorrow." Here we go again,

thought Amy with dismay. Work seemed to always intrude on Sunday. She knew God's grace permeated through the week, but she always took seriously the admonition to keep one day as a day of rest for her own spiritual well-being as well as physical.

"And the bales to haul and a hundred of other jobs," Tim interrupted. "I know you're busy, but we do have a wedding to plan."

Amy bit her lip, thinking. "I suppose we could make it this weekend. The heifers should be settled in by then. I need to work on Tuesday then haul a few bales home with the truck on Wednesday. The garden needs weeding. Dad can take care of that. And I still have to figure out what to do about fencing off the hay field." She paused then blurted out, "Can you help me out with some of the jobs? I'll have time to leave then."

Tim shrugged carefully. "I doubt it. I'm pretty sure I'm booked up this week. Besides what do I know about sorting cows or fencing?"

Amy nodded curtly, remembering Paul's question when he was helping her fence. She never paid much attention to Tim's lack of interest in the ranch. She knew he wasn't the ranching type, but it would be nice if he would contribute a little more than just financial advice.

"I'm sure Rick can take care of things while you're gone," Tim continued.

"You're right. I'm too much of a control person I guess." Rick never did things exactly the way she wanted, but she knew that one of her weaknesses was a desire to have everything done right.

"No you're not," Tim laughed, stroking her cheek. He turned back to his date book. "I'd like to leave Friday, can you get time off of work then?"

Amy nodded as she watched his well-manicured fingers neatly marking out a Friday, seeing her day of fencing disappear with one stroke of his pen. "I'll ask Elizabeth if she could stop by and make sure the men are eating properly," she replied quietly, swallowing down a feeling of trepidation at the thought of all the work she and Rick needed to do. It would work out, she reassured herself, she had to learn to let go.

Tim snapped the book closed, clicked his pen and slipped both of them inside his suit coat pocket.

"I'll phone my mother, then. She can make plans for those four days."

"It's not going to take that long is it?" As soon as the question left her lips, she wished she could take it back.

Tim shoved his hands in his pants pocket and looked away, sighing.

Contrite, Amy reached out and laid a hand on his shoulder. "Sorry, Tim. I didn't mean it to come out like that."

He looked back at her and shaking his head lightly, bent down to give her a quick kiss on her lips.

"Nothing to be sorry about. It might not take that long at all."

"It doesn't matter. I'll make arrangements for four days. That will give us plenty of time," she answered.

"I'd like to come over on Wednesday," he continued. "Our invitations are ready Tuesday and we'll need to address them."

"Which ones did you get? The cream or the pale blue ones?" Amy asked, remembering the long discussion at the printer in town.

"Neither. I called my mother and she thought either of them might be too plain. So we ordered the first ones we looked at. The one's you thought were too expensive."

Amy stifled her annoyance with him. "But..."

Tim touched a finger to her lips. "Mom and Dad were only too glad to pay for them. So I wanted to get something they would be happy with."

Amy opened her mouth to voice her objections, but guilt over her seeming reluctance to spend the weekend with him made her stop. That and the fact that his parents were paying for them. It shouldn't matter anyhow. They were only invitations. "I'll be ready with my address book and my pen," she joked, trying to work up some enthusiasm for the project.

"See you then." Tim gave her a hug and a quick kiss and got in his car.

Amy watched him drive away, feeling confused. If they had waited, like she had planned, she could have paid for a few more things herself.

She tried not to let it bother her. His parents had far more money than she and her father did. It was a simple fact.

She looked over her shoulder at the house. It wasn't big and it wasn't fancy. She knew if she had time and some extra cash it would be a lot of fun to fix up. But for now, maybe a mobile home for her and Tim would be the best solution. Rick and Judd could live in the house and then, when she had time, she could work on the house.

She smiled, thinking of future plans.

Hugging herself, she turned, her eyes following the horizon, listening to the quiet. In spite of the worries and cares, she loved living where her eyes could follow the pattern of a hawk circling in an empty sky, where she could whisper a soft prayer and feel God right there beside her.

Tim would love it here; she knew it.

With a satisfied smile she turned and walked back to the house.

Paul drew his horse to a halt on the lip of the rim. Sasha shook her head impatiently, the bridle clanking. At a soft word from Paul she dropped her head, and blew a breath through her nose.

Below them a rolling cloud of dust trailed a cattle truck heading up the valley. The roar of its engines reverberated along the hills as it geared down.

Paul leaned forward in the saddle, pushing the brim of his hat up to see better. The truck slowed and turned, heading for Danyluks' place.

Must be the heifers Amy had talked about. He clicked to his horse, nudging her with his boot heels. They followed the rim of the valley, staying in the cooler air of the pines.

The truck would have a climb once it took the fork in the road. Paul could reach the Danyluks at the same time.

Paul pulled in just as the truck was trying to turn around on the tight yard. Amy's horse, Misty, stood saddled and tied up by the verandah, munching on the same overgrown flower bed his own horse had been nibbling on a few days ago. As Paul dismounted he saw Amy directing the truck.

Or attempting to.

Amy had never been very good with hand signals. She couldn't seem to translate the direction the truck should move into hand movements and always got her left and right confused. Now she stood where the trucker could see her, but her hands constantly changed direction. It reminded him of the time she was teaching herself sign language. She would make a mistake then wave her hands as if erasing the previous movements, just as she did now.

Air brakes whooshed, the engine snarled as the huge truck lumbered backward, dropped his rear wheel into a mud hole and stopped. The heifers bawled, their hooves clanging against the metal sides in protest at the rocking motion. As Paul crossed the yard, the perplexed face of the trucker looked to him for help.

Paul knew Amy wouldn't like it if he took over, but also knew it would take far too long if he left it up to her.

He walked to the cab of the truck and pulled himself up onto the step. In a few moments he told the trucker where he had to end up. He walked back to the loading ramp and, ignoring Amy's crossed arms and thinned lips, he nudged her over. He nodded at the trucker and signaled for him to go ahead. Paul jerked his thumb to the left, then a few quick movements of his hands got the truck going backward, corrected him, and by the time Paul put his hands up for the trucker to stop, the back door was perfectly aligned with the top of the ramp.

He still hadn't dared look at Amy, who was now at the bottom of the ramp, opening the gate, closing another and climbing over the fence to get out of the way. The heifers sent up a steady ear-splitting bawl, and as soon as the doors opened they were crowding past each other in their eagerness to get out.

Paul watched, laughing as two heifers, stuck in the opening struggled, until the more stubborn one made it out. Soon they were all unloaded, and the gates on the liner clanged shut with a hollow echo. Amy signed the manifest slip and spoke to the driver about payment. They agreed on a check, mailed to his place of business. The driver waved at Paul, then climbed back into the cab. The truck's engine roared, the trailer swayed as the truck bounced over the ruts in the driveway and then roared down the road, shifting gears halfway down the valley.

Paul waited for Amy, unsure of his reception. She had looked plenty ticked off when he'd first walked over. But she only grinned as she passed him and clambered over the fence.

All is forgiven, I guess, he thought as he followed her. He watched her move through the herd of bawling heifers. She checked them over with a critical eye. They milled about, raising dust, bellowing. A bawling animal jostled her, but she just took a few casual steps back to regain her balance, unfazed by their erratic movements. A smile softened her mouth.

Paul enjoyed watching her. He couldn't imagine her in any other setting. She belonged here as much as the mountains behind her.

Amy nudged a recalcitrant heifer over. Her hair had fallen loose from her ponytail and it slid over her shoulders, obscuring her face in a red-gold mass. It caught the sun, glints of light dancing as she pushed it back.

She's beautiful. That thought drifted featherlight into his consciousness, floating for a moment until he caught and examined it.

All the years they'd been growing up, he'd called her cute. Her unique-colored hair, soft gray eyes and delicate features had made many male heads turn.

But now...now he saw before him a grown woman who carried herself with confidence, who had matured through her own trials.

Her beauty lay not only in her features, her striking coloring. With Amy her beauty was also a beauty of character, a Godly woman who put her needs behind the needs of others, loyal to her family and her faith. Something he had been both aware of and afraid of all his life.

Where he had become more restless, she had become more settled. She had grown and changed and matured, and now their lives were going in separate directions.

Or were they?

He recalled that brief moment of accord he had felt with her in church and the time they'd spent working and shook his head. He couldn't dwell on any feelings he had for her. He had no right. She was engaged to another man. He had his own problems to work out, and he knew it would only be selfishness on his part if he were to allow his feelings to continue in the direction they had gone the past few days.

But he couldn't seem to keep his eyes off her, couldn't keep the smile off his face as he watched her.

She came close, her grin a white slash in a dusty face. "Aren't they beautiful?"

"If you can call eleven-hundred-pound critters beautiful, I guess they are. They look like Simmental."

"Purebred." She glanced back at them with another smile. "As ticked as I was at Rick for buying them, I think they'll do us really well when they calve. I might even get a couple of herd-sires that I can run with our other cows."

"So what do you have to do with them now?" he asked as she climbed up on the fence beside him.

"They'll need booster shots, ear tags and possibly Ivomec." She rubbed her shoulder carefully, frowning.

"And how come your esteemed brother isn't here to help?" Paul couldn't help ask.

Amy shook her head. "We thought they were coming tonight. At least that's what the dispatcher told us. The trucker said he didn't have to make his first pickup and came straight here. Rick was going to be here after lunch."

"And now he's not."

"That's okay. They can stay in the corral until he comes home."

"There's not much room for them."

"They'll be okay."

"Why don't I help you? I've got time." Amy frowned, and Paul tapped her on the forehead again. "Thinking again are we, my little control freak?"

"I'm not," she protested.

"No. You aren't a control freak. But you seem to have a

hard time accepting my help.'' He slipped an arm around her waist and tugged her backward off the top of the fence, ignoring her protests. She clutched his arms and laughed. ''Go get all the stuff you need,'' he said sternly, reluctantly letting go of her. ''I'll be waiting.''

''Okay. I'll go,'' she said. She turned and jogged to the house, her hair streaming behind her, catching the sun like a beacon.

Paul sighed and turned back to the heifers. He had better keep his head on straight and his feelings in check or he was going to cause even more problems. It hadn't taken him long to forget Stacy. Nor did he seem able to remember that Amy herself was engaged.

Amy came out a few minutes later, holding a box. She took out a book holding records of their cows, and they marked the new tags with the next set of numbers.

Amy loaded syringes while Paul cut five animals out of the herd and worked them into the handling chute. Soon they had a system going and group by group the animals were given their shots, an ear tag, doused with a surface dewormer and sent out to a holding pen.

''That's the last of them,'' Paul called out as he opened the head gate of the handling chute and Amy chased them out. He walked through them once more looking them over. They were a nice size, good markings. He wondered how it would work out having them calving in the fall, but he was sure Amy would handle that in her usual efficient way.

''Got some warm water here, Paul,'' Amy called out from the other side of the fence.

He vaulted over, watching as she splashed water on her dusty face and washed her hands.

''Man, it's hot today,'' she groused as she stepped back, rebraiding her hair while he washed up.

The water felt good. He had forgotten how grimy a person could get, working with cattle in the summertime. Their hooves worked the ground into powder in no time.

''Supposed to get even hotter by Wednesday,'' Paul mumbled, as he toweled off his head.

Amy groaned. "I'm glad I'm working tomorrow. I'll have to haul hay Wednesday and figure out how to keep these new animals from ranging all over the hay field."

"Use that temporary electric fence. It's effective over a long distance and your hayfield isn't that far from your power pole."

Amy only shrugged and Paul guessed. They didn't have any and she couldn't afford it.

"Dad has some he hasn't used," Paul offered. "In fact I think he even has one that is solar powered. You wouldn't need to run a wire or rig up a connection. Completely self-contained."

"Thanks, but..."

"What's with the 'but'?" Paul hung up the towel on the fence and snapped up his cuffs and dropped his hat on his head again. "He's not using it. It works well. You can use it. This is not a problem, Amy." He picked up the pail and held it up with a grin. "Say you'll do it, or I'll dump this water on you."

"Yah, right, Paul. Like you'd do it," she said drily.

"Honey," Paul said, his voice taking on a silky tone. "Don't tempt me."

Amy looked at him as if sizing him up. She slowly shook her head, took one step forward and quickly reached for the pail. She slopped some water on him before he managed to pull it out of her reach.

"Sorry, Paul," she said laughing. She held her hands out in a conciliatory gesture as he advanced on her. "I'm sorry, Paul. Really I am."

"Easy to say, brat," he said plucking his wet shirt away from his chest. "You're in trouble now." He hefted the pail, still half-full of water.

Amy giggled, took one step backward, then turned and ran.

Ignored the warning signals that clamored to be heard, he ran after her.

She made it past the fence and ducked around the barn, laughing. Paul ran after her and made it around the corner. Too late he saw her there. All it took was a quick flip on her part.

He sucked in his breath as the now-cool water hit his chest a second time. Amy turned to escape as Paul reached out to grab her arm, dropping the now-empty pail. She twisted away, but their momentum pulled them down. They tumbled in a rambunctious heap on the grass. Amy laughed helplessly as she fell down beside him.

His hat fell off. Her hair fell across his face. Paul reached out and pushed it away just as her hand came up.

Their fingers meshed, their eyes caught, and Paul had the curious sensation of time slowing, the world tipping and falling away, leaving only the two of them suspended in space.

She lay next to him, unable or simply unwilling to pull away from his hand, the thrumming of her heart keeping time with his. It had nothing to do with running.

She grew suddenly serious, her expression intent. Paul felt drawn into her eyes, the gentle gray of skies before a welcome rain, soft, spiky lashes framing them.

Her quick breath fanned his cheek lightly.

Paul slowly released her fingers, let his own drift through her sun-warmed hair, his callused fingers catching the back of her neck.

Her throat moved as she swallowed.

"Please Paul..." she whispered.

Paul blinked at the sound of her voice, feeling reality intrude. He knew he should move away from her but wasn't ready to. Not yet. It felt so right to be close to her like this.

"Don't do this to me, Paul," she pleaded.

He drew in a ragged breath, let himself touch her face lightly, allowed his fingers to run down her cheek.

She clambered to her feet, her face averted from his, her hands scraping her hair back into some semblance of order. Paul watched her as he got up, feeling guilty, but more than that, strangely bereft. "Amy," he said, hesitating. He reached out and touched her shoulder tentatively. She pulled away.

"I want you to go now," she said, her voice a choked sound. She kept her back to him, her arms clasped tightly around her midriff, her fingers clutching her shirt. It smote his heart to see her looking so forlorn.

He reached down, picking up his hat and absently brushing

the grass from it. He was loath to leave her like this but didn't know how to bridge the gap that now seemed to yawn between them, as he tried to deal with his own shaken emotions.

In their brief moment of contact, he'd felt his whole world realign.

"If you need anything…" He dropped his hat on his head, feeling like he'd run a mile instead of across Danyluks' corrals, and drew in a steadying breath. "I'll send Larry down with the fence. He knows how to use it." It would be best for both of them if he didn't come anymore. In a few more days Vancouver and Stacy would be the reality of his life again.

She still stood, turned away from him.

"Make sure Rick pitches all the bales," he said quietly.

And then he left.

Amy clutched her waist, her head bent. She couldn't resist a hesitant glance over her shoulder at Paul's retreating figure. He walked slowly, his shoulders hunched, his hands in his pockets. Every step seemed to take something precious away from her.

She shivered in the warm air, rubbing her arms. As she did, her ring caught on her shirt. She lifted her hand, turning the stone to catch the sun.

The symbol of her promise to Tim mocked her.

Amy covered her face with her hands. She was no better than her mother!

You didn't do anything wrong!

You wanted him to kiss you.

You stopped him. Nothing happened.

Then why are you feeling so guilty?

Her thoughts slammed back and forth, accusing and reassuring.

Amy pressed her elbows to her side, her fingertips to her eyes. "Please, Lord, forgive me, please help me stay true…" Amy lifted her eyes to the mountains which had always been a symbol to her of God's majesty, power and faithfulness. "Help me, Lord, help me stay true," she repeated.

The purple ridge wavered in her vision as hot tears pooled in her eyes.

On Wednesday morning one of Fred Henderson's hired hands, Larry, brought the electric fence over. He informed Amy that he had been told to stay and help haul hay. He wasn't needed that day at the Henderson place.

Rick didn't argue, and Amy didn't have the energy. So Amy drove the truck, and Larry and Rick loaded the hay onto the wagon. It was a hot, tiring job and even with the extra help, the only part they got cleaned off was the field where the heifers would pasture. The fence was erected and activated, and Larry left.

Tim came over as he'd promised, to make plans for the weekend in Vancouver. He was going to pick her up after work on Thursday evening, returning home Monday afternoon. Amy hoped she would be able to stay that long in Vancouver. She hoped her father would be okay that long without her. She hoped Rick would have enough sense to stay at home and watch over the new heifers, making sure the fence worked.

Tim had brought the invitations. Amy didn't like the design. It was too elegant, too expensive, but because Mr. and Mrs. Enders paid for them, she kept her objections to herself and added her small list to Tim's ever-increasing one. By the time she was done hers, she was so tired she fell asleep, head burrowed in her arms on the kitchen table.

Tim finished the job alone.

Chapter Eight

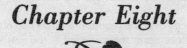

"I still say we don't need to shop at the mall for chinaware." Tim's mother stepped out of the car, continuing the discussion Amy thought ended when they pulled into the entrance ramp to the mall parkade. "If it's dishes you want, why go to a department store?"

"Don't be a snob, Mother," Tim admonished, winking at Amy. "I'm sure we'll find something here that Amy and I both like."

"As long as the china doesn't have matching wall clocks, I might be happy." Delia pursed her lips in derision, tucking her eelskin leather purse under her arm. "You know I detest malls."

She sniffed as Tim held the door to the walkway that took them inside.

They stepped from quiet into busyness. The usual rush of noise and people enveloped them, and Amy had to hustle to keep pace with Tim and Mrs. Enders.

She felt overwhelmed by decisions. This was the third store they had visited in their search for the perfect china pattern for dishes for their future home. She hoped Tim wouldn't want to do the furniture shopping his mother had spoken of the night before. Her head ached, and her feet ached, and all she wanted to do was go home.

But she followed her future mother-in-law and her future husband and nodded and smiled and tried to work up enthusiasm for the difference between Mikasa and Noritake and a host of others, when she would have been perfectly happy with Corelle.

They found the china section. Tim marched to one end, Amy to another while Mrs. Enders cast her critical eye over the crystal.

Amy glanced over the beautiful settings laid out to their best advantage. Once again she marveled at the vast selection, different in each store. Under the bright lights, the plates dazzled and shone, almost mocking her life-style. She couldn't imagine any of these beautiful dishes sitting on the cracked surface of the kitchen table at the ranch. It was hard enough imagining matched dishes, period.

"What about this one, Amy?" Tim called out to her. With a gentle sigh she walked over, making up her mind to agree with anything he chose. The money for the dishes would ultimately come out of his wallet, after all. None of the people from home would bother to check out the registry, instead they would simply ask her or Elizabeth Henderson what she needed.

"I like this." Tim pointed out a set of cream-colored dishes with a delicate patterning of brown vines and pale peach roses around the edge. "Plain enough for you and elegant enough for me."

"They're beautiful, Tim." Amy hesitantly reached out and touched the plates. The gold rim sparkled in the bright, artificial light.

"You always say that, and each time I sense a 'but' in your voice."

"I guess I just have a hard time imagining chili or macaroni and cheese on all these gorgeous dishes."

"C'mon, Amy, I know you can cook better than that," Tim teased.

"I can when I have the time."

"You'll have lots of time, once we're married."

"I suppose when I quit my job, I will," Amy commented. "But with those extra heifers—"

"What's a heifer?" his mother asked, as she bustled up to where Amy and Tim stood.

"Young cow that hasn't calved yet," Tim said.

Mrs. Enders nodded. "I forgot." She smiled at Amy. "Tim is always throwing these ranching terms at me. I can't keep them all straight." She turned back to Tim. "So have you decided?"

Tim pointed out the dishes they had picked out, and Mrs. Enders nodded. "They're very nice."

But to Amy her tone implied something different. Tim and his mother conferred with the sales clerk and made all the arrangements. Amy was glad that decision was made and looked forward to getting back to his parents' place.

She had forgotten about the trip back. Tim cut expertly in and out of traffic as they headed toward the Lion's Gate Bridge. He wanted to take the scenic route to show Amy the bridge. She spent most of the trip clutching the dashboard as cars cut in front of them and huge trucks lumbered past. There was no way she could live in this, she thought, breathing a sigh of relief when they finally pulled up in front of his parents' home.

Thankfully Tim vetoed dining out and, over his mother's objections, ordered in pizza. Once the meal was over, Amy gathered up the boxes and plates and carried them into the kitchen. Mrs. Enders took them from her with a smile and loaded the dishes into the dishwasher. Amy looked around the kitchen, appreciating the clean lines of the cabinets, done up in blond oak. "You have a very lovely home," she said to Delia Enders.

Delia looked up from her work. "Why thank you, Amy." She finished loading the dishes and wiped her hands on a towel that lay on the counter. "We've renovated it a number of times, and I think I'm happy with it now."

"I've been making some changes on the exterior of our house on the ranch, but with the wedding coming up, the rest will have to wait awhile." Amy sat carefully down on a stool across the counter from Tim's mother.

Delia crossed her arms and leaned back against the counter, nodding. "I understand that you plan to live on the ranch after you're married."

"Yes. I'm looking forward to having Tim around all the time. He's been so busy we don't always have the time to do any work on it together, or go riding."

"Hard to imagine our Tim on a horse," Delia smiled. "He has changed a lot since he met you."

Amy shrugged, puzzled as to whether Delia saw this as a positive or a negative. "He likes riding."

"How long are you going to be living on the ranch?"

"In our present house?"

"No. I mean on the ranch, in Williams Lake."

"I don't understand what you mean."

Delia waved her hands delicately. "Tim is a very bright young man with a lot of potential and ambition." She smiled deprecatingly at Amy. "I know I sound exactly like a mother, but his father and I are very proud of him. He has a brilliant future in banking." Delia tapped a manicured finger on her lips as if pondering her next statement.

Amy frowned, a vague sense of unease curling inside of her, trying to find a place to settle, sensing where Delia was headed. "Tim is quite happy in Williams Lake. I don't expect much from life. When Tim and I are married, I will have all I want."

"And Tim. Will staying in Williams Lake give him everything he wants?" Delia spoke carefully. "You have to think about his future."

Amy was spared the necessity of answering that question when Tim poked his head through the kitchen door. "There you are." Tim smiled when he saw them.

Probably thinks we're having a cozy mother-daughter chat, thought Amy.

"I've got the movie in the VCR. Everybody ready to watch?" he asked.

Amy slid off the stool, thankful for the diversion. She didn't look back at Delia Enders and settled into the couch, letting the movie and its pointless plot take her away from Vancouver and the not-so-veiled hints of her future mother-in-law.

When the movie was over, Tim's mother pleaded exhaustion and left. Tim's father followed suit and they were finally left to themselves.

Amy kicked her shoes off, dropped on the couch and leaned her head back against its buttery soft leather. This family room was the least formal room of the house, and her favorite. Wood paneling softened the high walls, complemented by the cream-colored carpet. But even in its homeyness, it exuded a gentle reminder of wealth.

She sighed as she looked through the floor-to-ceiling windows across the Burard Inlet. The Enderses' home on the north shore afforded a scintillating view of downtown Vancouver across the bay. Clusters of light shone from the high-rises that rose from the waterfront, their reflections shimmering in the water of the harbor. Even the location announced that money lived here.

"I've always loved this view," murmured Tim as he pulled Amy's head on his shoulder, wrapping his arms around her.

"It is beautiful," Amy conceded, watching the lights of the slow-moving ships as they headed out to unknown destinations, envying them their direction—away from the city. She had thought she would be able to enjoy their time in the city, but by this afternoon, after only two days, she yearned for the smell of grass, trees and open spaces. And she wished Tim wouldn't act so demonstrative. It wasn't his style, and it made her feel uncomfortable.

"You were pretty quiet over supper."

"I don't shop well."

"Well that bodes well for our future. I won't have to worry about you draining our bank account." He pulled back, soft brown eyes traveling over her face. "And what are you frowning about now, my girl?"

Amy held his concerned gaze a moment, then drew back. "I was thinking about shopping and dishes...and living in our house." She looked around at the obvious wealth of the Enderses' home. She turned to Tim. "Will you mind? Will it matter that our house is small and plain and needs improvement?"

Tim twined his hand through hers, fingering her engagement

ring. "I want to live with you, Amy. That's all that matters to me. I don't think it should matter to either of us where we live as long as we can be together."

"I know you'll love it on the ranch—the wide-open spaces. Once we're married, we can go riding in the evenings, and I can show you how beautiful it really is out there."

Tim smiled at her. "I'm sure none of it is as beautiful as how you look right here, right now."

"And what's that supposed to get you?" Amy teased.

"A kiss?"

She complied, feeling content. Life was good. And once she and Tim were home, even better.

"Maybe we should use the hitching post this time, eh, girl?" Paul tied up his horse and looked out over Danyluks' yard.

He knew Amy and Tim had left yesterday, so he figured it would be safe to come this evening. After their little episode in the hay field, he thought it best if he steered clear of her. But he couldn't resist stopping by to see how Judd and Rick were making out, even if they weren't his biggest fans. He did it for Amy's sake.

The kitchen door was open, and Paul stepped inside. Rick sat by the kitchen table playing solitaire.

"Hi, Rick."

Rick glanced up, nodded and turned back to his cards.

"Where's Judd?" Paul glanced around the living room, but Judd was gone.

"He was tired and went to bed early." Rick laid out another card, frowning at them.

"How are the new heifers doing?"

Rick slowly turned over another card and nodded again. "Did Amy phone you to come and check on me?" he asked, his voice tinged with the habitual anger he seemed to show to Paul.

"No. I thought I would stop by myself." He walked to the cupboard and opened it. "Mind if I make myself some coffee?"

"Go ahead." Rick put down the cards and turned to the radio.

Paul put the kettle on to boil and studied the toes of his scuffed boots as he waited. "I thought I would come by tomorrow and we can finish hauling the hay."

"Amy didn't say anything about you helping," Rick said as he spun the dial on the old radio.

"She didn't ask, I volunteered. I'm heading back to Vancouver in a couple of days, I'd like to get a few things done for her before I leave," Paul continued, stifling his impatience with Rick's truculence. "I also noticed a couple of the calving pens are coming apart. We could get them done by Saturday."

"I'll get them done," Rick grunted, listening intently to the radio, reddish brows meeting over his nose in a frown.

"Will you have time?"

"I might not." Rick turned off the radio and looked over his shoulder at Paul. "But I do what I can, Henderson, and I don't really need any help."

Paul sat at the table across from Rick, and leaning his elbows on it, took a careful sip of the steaming coffee, studying Rick over the rim of his cup, wondering why he was bothering with a young man who didn't really want him here. "How's the tractor coming?"

"Just about done."

They said nothing. Paul sipped his coffee, Rick shuffled the cards and laid them out.

"What brings you here, anyway, Henderson?"

"Just wanted to see if you needed any help."

"That's not what I meant." Rick carefully laid a black queen on a red king and looked up at him. "What brings you back to the Cariboo? Don't *you* have any work to do?"

"I'm here to make some business decisions." Paul knew that wasn't the real reason, but he knew he didn't want to share his spiritual struggle with someone who didn't particularly care for him.

"Not to put the hustle on the local girls?" Rick smirked at him.

"Hardly. I have a girlfriend already."

Rick laughed, a harsh sound. "That doesn't seem to stop you from staring at Amy in church, or stopping by whenever you can."

Paul was quiet, realizing anything he said would either be construed as a lie or as an evasion. Because he knew he was guilty of what Rick accused him of.

"I want you to leave Amy alone," Rick continued. "Each time you come here you've got a different girlfriend. And each time you leave, Amy's down in the dumps."

Paul's heart clenched at Rick's words, guilt washing over him. It hurt him to think that he had unknowingly hurt her.

"What's wrong with Amy, Paul?" Rick dropped all pretense of playing cards. He held Paul's gaze, hard and steady, his own gray eyes so much like Amy's. "She's twice the woman any of the picture-perfect girls you bring here are."

"I know that, Rick." Paul spoke quietly, thinking that he did care more for Amy than Rick could know. He sipped his coffee, trying to find the right words, frustrated that a man who didn't like him was forcing an admission about something so close to his heart and so much on his mind the past few days. "Amy has always been an example to me of what people should be like. Loyal, caring and hardworking. She has a strong faith in God that shames many of us and a purity that shames me." Paul looked down again, surprised himself at the words that flowed from him. He couldn't seem to stop them. It was as if he needed to tell someone, anyone, how he truly felt about this girl, no he amended, woman, that had taken far too much of his thoughts the past few weeks.

"Amy is probably one of the best people I know. I think I've cared for her all my life. But I also know her. I know she needs to live here, I know she couldn't live in the places I wanted to be." Paul took a sip of coffee, remembering a young man who always looked to be anywhere but the Cariboo. And a young girl who couldn't live anywhere else. "I thought I couldn't stay here or settle down with one person. And as it turns out, I was wise to keep my distance. Amy is engaged to a good Christian man with a solid future. Someone who wants to stay here with her. I don't know what I want for myself, but

I do know what I want for Amy. And that's a loving husband who cares for her and who can share her faith. I wouldn't hurt her intentionally. I want you to believe that.''

"I don't know what to believe about you, Paul. I just want to make sure you don't do to her what you did to Shannon.''

Paul frowned, trying to catch up to Rick's sudden change in the conversation. "What have I done to Shannon?''

A flush crept up Rick's neck and he looked up, shaking his head. "You can't remember? You can't remember taking her out and then making me take her home?''

Paul remembered. "That was a long time ago, Rick. We're both a lot older now, and I don't think it bothers her anymore.''

"No? Why does she flirt with you every time you talk to her?''

Paul couldn't help it. He laughed. "That's a joke, and we both know it.'' Paul leaned his chair back. It creaked as it balanced on two legs. Paul studied Rick, wondering what his problem was and why he should care about Amy's friend. A girl three years older than he was.

"Well, I don't think it's very funny.''

Paul pursed his lips as pieces suddenly fell into place. "Why do you care what Shannon and I joke about?''

Rick threw him an irritated glance, then laid out another solitaire hand.

And Paul understood. "You love her yourself, don't you, Rick?''

Rick's back became rigid; he slapped down a few more cards. The only sound in the room was the snick of cards being pulled out of the deck. Rick glared up at Paul, looked down again. Then, suddenly, the anger left Rick like stale air escaping a balloon. He shuffled the cards aimlessly then put them down. "I've loved her from before the time I took her home for you.''

"And been angry with me since, I imagine,'' Paul said drily. "Does Shannon know?''

"I don't dare tell her. I've always been Amy's little brother. She's at least three years older than me. I've got nothing to give her.'' Rick chewed his lip, much as Amy did when she was disturbed.

In spite of his earlier antagonism, Paul felt suddenly sorry for Rick, surprised at how frail the male ego could be. Paul sipped his coffee as he searched for the right words to encourage this uncertain young man.

"You underestimate yourself, Rick," he said finally. "You're good-looking, strong, mature when you want to be, and you don't think you've got something Shannon would want? You've got yourself, your health, two good hands a brain and this ranch."

Rick almost snorted. "Trouble is I don't want the ranch."

"What do you want?"

Rick clasped his hands together on the table, spinning his thumbs around each other, his fingernails stained with grease. "I've been working with Jack Dilton the past few months. Just a few jobs he wasn't getting done during working hours. He has offered me a job. I think I'm going to take it."

"Does Amy know about this?" Paul pulled one hand over his face, callused hands rasping over his stubbled chin. How was Amy going to react to that particular piece of news? She had always counted on Rick's help.

"I don't know. I was going to tell her after her engagement party, but then she hurt her shoulder. I couldn't tell her then."

"So why did you buy the heifers?"

"I thought I was interested, and the ranch needed to look at increasing its income." He looked up at Paul. "I wasn't trying to lead her on. I really thought I could do it. But when Jack offered me this job, I knew what I wanted to do more."

"What will happen to the ranch if you leave?" Paul asked.

Rick pressed he thumbs together, his lips pursed. "That's what else was holding me back from telling her. Unless she makes some changes, she can't really take care of it on her own." He blew out his breath. "We'll need a new baler, one that can make round bales. She'll need to refence some of the pastures so that we can rotate it better and run more stock. It can be done, but it will take money, and until things pick up, she won't be able to afford all of that."

"Will Tim help her out?"

Rick shrugged. "I'm actually surprised he's even moving out

here. I have a hard time picturing him living in this house. But he says he's going to. Must really love my sister, I guess."

"Amy's not a hard person to make concessions for," agreed Paul.

Rick directed him a sharp look. "You really do care for her."

"Yes, I do. But I don't deserve her."

Rick twirled his thumbs some more, the confessions of the past few minutes creating a silence that now felt comfortable instead of seething. "So what are *you* going to do?"

"Go back to Vancouver...figure out what I have to do with my business and my relationship with God." Paul tossed back the last of his coffee and got up. "Probably give Tim and Amy's wedding a miss."

"She'll be disappointed," Rick said.

Paul laughed shortly. "I doubt it. She doesn't need me messing up her emotions." He washed the cup as he glanced around the kitchen. He tried to imagine Tim in his crisp business suit sitting down to breakfast, while Amy scuttled about in her blue jeans and old baggy sweater, frying eggs, making coffee, listening to the stock market report on the radio.

It wouldn't meld. Instead a stronger image superimposed itself on the little scene—Amy and himself, sitting together at the table, discussing the work for the day. Paul gave his head a shake.

Rick tilted his head to one side, a sad smile curving his lips. "You surprise me, Henderson."

"Well if I surprise you, maybe Shannon will, too." Paul walked across the kitchen, his booted footsteps echoing in the silence. He plucked his coat off the rack beside the door and shrugged it on. He turned back to Rick, grasping the front panels of the coat with his hands. "Tell Amy what you told me. Tell her that ranching isn't what you want to do, tell her about Jack's offer. And while you're making all of these startling revelations, let Shannon know how you feel. You might be surprised at her reaction."

Paul buttoned the coat, turned, and left Rick staring sightlessly out of the window with his chin propped in his hand.

Chapter Nine

"Where are we supposed to meet Rick?" Judd asked as he settled into the truck, puffing. The walk from the doctor's clinic to the truck wore him out.

"Jack Dilton's garage," Amy groused as she pushed the truck into gear, hoping it wouldn't roll back down the hill she had parked on. "He wouldn't say why, and I didn't feel like asking."

Judd tapped his fingers on his crutches, staring at his daughter.

"What?" she asked peevishly when she noticed.

"You've been grouchy ever since you got back from Vancouver. You and Tim have a fight?"

"Of course not. I've just got a lot on my mind lately." She pulled into an empty spot in front of Jack's garage and turned off the truck. "The hay needs to be baled, I need to get the garden produce canned and frozen, Rick keeps taking off on me, and this wedding—" She bit back the last comment.

"What about it?"

Amy chewed her lip as she stared ahead, wondering if her father would understand. "Mrs. Enders wants this wedding picture-perfect. It's turning out to be a lot more work than I had anticipated."

"Just get through it, girl." Judd looked thoughtful, then, with a rueful laugh, opened his door. "You're right. The wedding isn't as important as the marriage. Just do a good job of that." He worked his way out of the truck, fitted his crutches under his arms and clumped up to the door of Jack's garage.

Amy followed, bemused at her father's advice. The breakdown of his own marriage made his comments all the more poignant.

They entered Jack's garage, and the familiar smell of oil, grease and dirt filled Amy's nostrils. A clipboard holding an assortment of papers marked with grimy fingerprints hung by a ragged string beside the cash register. Filters of all shapes and heights marched along a shelf behind the counter. Belts hung from the ceiling arranged in order of size. Beyond the swinging doors Amy heard the intermittent sound of a pneumatic drill and the clang of wrenches dropping on cement. An engine fired up. A voice called over the noise.

The doors swooshed open and Rick entered the shop, wiping his hand on a greasy cloth, clothed in a blue coverall. When he saw Amy, he smiled sheepishly. "I was just talking to...uh...Jack." He pointed his chin over his shoulder in the direction of the shop.

"Did you ask him about finding a new motor for the tractor?"

Rick nodded, looking backward as if waiting. The door opened again, and Jack came in. "Hello Judd, Amy. I won't shake your hands, mine are too dirty." He grinned at them holding up his hands. He turned to Rick. "I think I found out what I need to know. All that's left is...when can we enroll you in school?"

Amy's mouth dropped open. "Enroll...school?"

Rick licked his lips but avoided catching Amy's eye. "I've made a deal with Jack. He'll get a motor in for the tractor, put it in and get it running."

"Sounds good," Amy said, her heart beginning to thump hard. She knew there was more.

"I've got a low-boy unit booked to pick up your tractor first thing in the morning and Rick will pick up the motor later on in the day and get it in.''

''And what will this cost?''

Rick twisted the rag he held, glanced at Jack then back at Amy. ''I'm going to be helping here for a few months. Part of those wages will go to pay off the bill. Then I'm going to be apprenticing for my heavy-duty mechanic's ticket.'' Rick wiped his hands again, as if intent on getting each piece of grime from under his fingernails. ''I've tried to work on the ranch, but I just can't.'' He looked up, his expression pleading. ''The ranch will never make enough money for two families, and I don't like the work enough to want to expand. This way I can work for Jack and pay off our bill.''

Amy felt her breath leave her as his words registered. Events from the past few months superimposed themselves over her confusion and anger. Rick's reluctance to get truly involved, how he always managed to find time to work on the equipment, but not to help with the actual workings of the ranch. In many and varied ways he had been trying to tell her this, but she hadn't seen. Too many things on my mind, she thought, rubbing her temple with one finger. She wished she could find the words of encouragement Rick seemed to be waiting for.

''I guess this isn't such a surprise,'' Judd said, leaning forward on his crutches. ''You were always fooling with engines and equipment on the ranch.''

Rick looked eagerly to his father and nodded. ''It's the only thing I really enjoyed doing.''

''Your son has been here every week helping me where he could,'' Jack said with a laugh. ''I think he'll make a good apprentice. I can use him as a regular mechanic for now, and we're hoping to get him booked into trade school come January.''

Amy listened to the conversation, feeling separate from reality. She should have known. She should have seen it coming. I guess I didn't want to, she thought, leaning against the counter.

Rick tossed an expectant glance her way, and she worked up an encouraging smile. His excitement was plain. He showed more spirit about living with permanent grease under his fingernails than he ever had riding in the hills to check cattle.

Help me to be happy about his plans, Amy prayed, *help me to let go of what I want and put Rick's needs first.* She sighed and glanced sidelong at her father.

Judd leaned heavily on his crutches, yawning. The doctor's visit had worn him out, and Amy was glad for the excuse to leave.

"Congratulations, Rick," Amy said with a mighty effort to inject a note of enthusiasm into her voice. "You'll have to tell me more later. Dad needs to go home." And so do I, she added to herself. Rick's sudden news had drained her. "Will you be home for supper?"

Rick shook his head slowly, a blush staining his cheeks. "Actually, I'm going to Shannon's for supper."

Amy blinked. Why not? One more surprise—other hints and comments she had missed that she should have caught had she not been so involved in her own problems. She worked up a smile, nodded at Jack and left the garage.

She opened the door for Judd and helped him into the truck. As she walked around to the driver's side, she swallowed down a feeling of panic. She couldn't think about this yet.

She got into the truck, started it and turned it around, deliberately blanking out the past half hour, preferring to concentrate on work—moving the cows down to the lower pasture and the work she hoped Rick would do to get the baler ready for the second cut of hay.

Further than that, she couldn't plan.

"Our last night with our boy home, Mother." Fred smiled at Elizabeth as he pushed himself back from the table. He leaned back in his chair, his thumbs hooked in his belt loops.

To Paul it was a familiar sight. Kingdoms may rise and fall, rain might keep the hay from getting baled, cows may have trouble calving, but his parents always found time to sit back after supper, have devotions and take stock.

When all the kids were home, everyone took part. The talk could be serious or light, soft or loud. It didn't matter. There was always a sense of communion and security, like a benediction on the doings of the day.

Paul stretched, lifting his feet to an empty chair and contemplated the toes of his thick, gray socks. They were an old pair of his father's, more comfortable and practical than the silk socks he usually wore.

"Are you still going out for one last ride?" Fred cradled his cup of tea on his stomach, watching the steam rise through half-closed eyes.

"The moon is out tonight. It might be my last chance for a while."

"I'm so glad you could stay longer this visit. We've had so much catching up to do." Elizabeth pushed her plate away and leaned her elbows on the table as she sipped her tea. "I hope it won't be as long again," she hinted.

Paul shook his head. "Doubtful, Mom. I might be coming up more often on weekends."

"Work isn't going to keep you too busy?" his mother pressed.

"Not anymore. As it is, I'm not too eager to go back."

"Not even to Stacy?" Elizabeth asked, lifting a questioning eyebrow.

Paul traced the damp circle his mug left behind on the plastic cover of the table. "I've got some decisions to make about that."

"And did you get the space and time we talked about when you first came home?"

Paul nodded, his eyes still on the table in front of him. "I did. Except I feel more mixed-up than before."

"Why?" his mother's question gently prodded.

"I'm not as eager to go back as I thought. I feel like I've got unfinished business here."

"Amy for instance?"

Paul jerked his head up; his eyes caught and held his mother's knowing ones. "Considering the fact that her wedding invitation is on the living room mantel, I highly doubt it."

"Maybe," his mother said. She took a breath to speak again but was interrupted by her husband.

"What about your work, Paul? Are you going to buy out your partner?"

Paul shot Fred a grateful look. Trust his dad to sidetrack his mother when she was on the scent. Besides, he knew he'd far sooner talk about his business than his feelings for a girl who was going to be married. A girl he truly cared for. "I don't know," he replied.

Fred cleared his throat and, glancing at Elizabeth, leaned forward. "Your mother and I were talking. If you want to, we can easily work you back into the ranch. Derk had mentioned that he might want to come back. It could work out quite well." He paused, his work-roughened hands toying with his mug. "I don't want to put any pressure on you, just give you another option. Kincaid up the valley is talking about selling out...we could expand."

Paul took his father's hand in his own and reached over for his mother's, his heart swelling with love at his father's offer. "I don't know if I've told you enough how much I love you both," he said, his voice choked with emotion. They smiled at each other as the moment stretched out, companionable, comfortable. "I don't know what the next few weeks will bring. I can't make a proper decision now, here."

"Have you prayed about it?"

His father's question was quiet but it drove straight into Paul's heart. "I guess that's part of the reason I came home."

"To pray or to ask us to?" His mother squeezed his hand in return.

"Both," was his simple reply.

"Well," said his father. "Let's start."

With gentle smiles they bowed their heads and, for the first time in years, the three hearts were united with singleness of purpose.

Sasha acted feisty and was not content with a lazy walk around the Henderson ranch, so Paul let her out onto the road, holding her to a slow canter. The moon hung like a tipped silver bowl in the sky, its subdued gray light lending an otherworldly quality to the landscape. Hollows became secretive, hills, elusive.

God's presence seemed to rise up from His creation. Paul felt a moment of regret mingled with thankfulness; regret that it had taken him this long to come back, thankfulness that God's ever-faithful love was still available in spite of wrong decisions of the past.

And now...

He thought of Stacy and pulled Sasha to a halt with a gentle tug on the reins.

I know what I have to do, Lord, he prayed, his eyes wandering over the darkening landscape. *I know Stacy doesn't think she needs You and I pray that she might. But I also know we'll never love each other the way we should. I only ask that You help me do what's right for everyone.*

Paul drew in a deep breath as he finished, staring sightlessly over the indigo horizon. A faint orange glow, a remnant of the setting sun, edged the hills. He turned in the saddle. Behind him all was dark. The days were getting shorter, and soon fall, then winter would be here. And where would he be?

Sasha sidestepped, drawing his attention back to her. Paul let her walk, his thoughts returning to Stacy, feeling regret at what he saw as the inevitable breakup of another relationship. But he knew he wanted what his parents had as a married couple. A relationship built on a joint faith in the Lord. He knew he shouldn't settle for less.

And then what? Paul blew out his breath as he considered that question. He wanted Amy. It was that simple, and he knew he had to face that, as well.

He didn't deserve to even think about her. His past escapades did not recommend him to her. As he had said to Rick, he had always seen her faith as an example, and now it was a barrier. He could never deserve her love.

But did Tim? Paul tried to shake that thought away. Tim had goals. Amy always said they were going to live on the ranch once they were married, yet Rick didn't think so. Paul had no right to intrude on Amy's life now. She was settled and had her future mapped out and it didn't include an old flame.

She still cares for you. Hard as he tried, he couldn't forget that moment in the cattle yard. He'd held her close and it had felt so right. Their eyes had met and it was as if they'd both come home—home to a place they both belonged.

Sasha stopped abruptly, and Paul looked up, momentarily disoriented. His mind had wandered and so had his horse.

He looked around, finally able to place himself. A few more steps would take him to the bluff overlooking Danyluks'. They had come this direction so many times the past few weeks, Sasha must have assumed that tonight they were headed there again.

Pausing, Paul looked over the yard now lit by their yard light and pulled the reins in to turn Sasha around. Better that he stay away from here. Especially in his frame of mind.

As he did, however, he caught sight of a slight figure running through the light toward the barn. A light flicked on, and a golden glow shone through the windows. Paul leaned forward, the saddle creaking, his hands resting on the pommel.

What would Amy be doing in the barns this late in the evening? Surely she didn't have a heifer calving already. He was sure they weren't due for a few more weeks.

Curiosity drove Paul to nudge Sasha in the flanks, and the mare slowly picked her way down the hill to the yard. At the barn Paul dismounted, loosely tying the reins to the post.

He watched as Amy's figure created a fleeting silhouette against the window as she moved back and forth past it. She was alone.

A smart man would mount up again and ride out of here, he thought. But tomorrow he would be in Vancouver and, if all went according to her plans, the next time he saw Amy she would be Mrs. Enders, not Miss Danyluk.

But Paul didn't feel very smart tonight. He stepped inside.

Amy fought with a square bale of straw, dragging it into a pen. With a jerk she pulled the top twine off. She grabbed the bottom one and flipped the bale over with practiced ease. The straw spilled out in slices that she kicked around, dust rising up in the cone of light. Her movements were quick, hard, as if agitated.

"Need any help?" His question pierced the rustling quiet.

Amy whirled around, her hand clutching her heart. Then her shoulders sagged as she took a deep breath, blinked once then swung away from him, her loose hair sliding over her shoulder. "You scared the living daylights out of me," she accused.

"Sorry." Paul moved away, hurt by her lack of greeting. He squatted down, picking up a piece of straw. Sticking it in his mouth, he searched for something to say, a reason he should be here. "How was Vancouver?"

"Busy."

"You got yourself all registered, your stuff all picked out?"

"Yes." Amy shrugged, spreading straw with the toe of her boot.

She wanted him to go, Paul thought, but perversely he wasn't ready to leave. It was as if an uncertainty hung between them, and he wanted it settled before he went.

"Calving already?" Paul worked the straw to the other side of his mouth, his hands dangling between his knees.

"Not for another month. I'm just getting the pens ready. Our milk cow is due to freshen."

"And what did the doctor say about your dad yesterday?"

Amy said nothing, only gave the straw another kick.

"He kept his appointment, didn't he?"

"I took him in," she replied, her voice tight.

Paul chewed thoughtfully on the straw, watching Amy. She looked as tightly wound as a rodeo saddle bronc waiting for the gate to open. "What's wrong, Amy?"

She stopped moving the straw around, her hands slipping into her pockets, her gaze fixed on her dusty boots.

"Nothing," she said decisively.

Paul got up, concerned with her reticence, the brevity of her replies. "Amy." He touched her shoulder, and as he did so he caught the glint of tears in the corner of her eye. "Tell me what's wrong?"

She hugged herself, looking upward, blinking carefully. She took a slow breath that caught on the end. "You're leaving tomorrow, Paul. What's happening in my life won't matter in a few days."

"That's not true." He curled his hand around the soft curve of her shoulder, her words cutting him. "I've always cared about what happens to you." *Too much,* he thought.

He watched her silent struggle, arms crossed tightly over her stomach, hands clutching her waist. Something twisted inside him, deep and low, as she dropped her head and took one shaky breath. Then another. In the half-light her eyes glittered with unshed tears. Then, as he waited, one coursed down the curve of her cheek.

Paul could bear her silent pain no longer. He could no more stop himself from drawing her in his arms than he could stop the sun's descent each evening.

For a moment she tensed, her elbows clamped to her midriff, her fists pressed against her mouth.

"It's okay, I'm here. You don't have to be so tough, so strong." Paul stroked her rigid back, pulling her closer.

A shudder rippled through her tense body, then another, and suddenly she drooped against him, her hands clutching his shirt, her hot forehead pressed to his cool throat. A sob slipped out, then another and soon her tears flowed freely, her cries muffled against his chest.

"It's not fair," she cried, pulling on his shirt.

"What isn't?" Paul prompted, cupping her head with his large hand, stroking her neck with gentle fingers.

"Life, everything." Amy twisted his shirt. "The doctor phoned me this afternoon. I had to take Dad to the hospital right away." She paused a moment, drawing in an unsteady breath. "They figure he's diabetic. His blood sugar was so high they were scared he was going to go into a coma." She sniffled again and wiped her nose against the back of her hand, then palmed tears from her dusty cheeks. More streamed down to take their place.

She tried to pull away from Paul, but he still held her, sensing her need for comfort. She carried so much, he thought, looking down at her slight figure. Those slim shoulders bore so much.

"I know there are worse things...the doctor said it was a matter of getting Dad's blood sugar balanced." She sniffed again. "I'm just tired. Rick got a job at Jack's, and Tim's mom..." She stopped there, her words muffled against his shirt.

Paul rocked her gently, stroking her back, her soft hair. A feeling of protectiveness surged through him and he held her closer still, arms wrapped right around her.

After a time her tears subsided, yet she stayed in the comforting circle of his arms. Paul laid his head on her warm one, enjoying far too much the feel of her in his arms. It was wrong. He knew that. He was leaving tomorrow, his own future uncertain. He had no right to hold her so close, to take Tim's place as comforter.

Then why isn't Tim here?

Paul remembered other times—taking Amy to the hospital, caring for Judd when she went to Prince George, helping her with the fencing.

Why was Tim never around when Amy needed him?

He closed his eyes as if to banish the treacherous thought. But slowly another rose to take its place, this one more insidious than the last.

I want to be here for her. Not just now, but forever.

His mind raced ahead, imagining himself supporting, helping, loving. He buried his face in the silky mass of her hair as a wave of pure longing washed over him. Tim wasn't right for Amy, just as Stacy wasn't right for him. But how could he tell Amy that, now, with his arms around her and Tim's ring on her finger?

Amy was the one, however, who finally straightened. "Paul," she whispered, her voice hoarse. "Paul, you have to let me go."

"Why?" He inhaled the delicate scent of her, overlaid with the earthy smell of straw dust. He wasn't ready to let reality intrude on the haven he had created for himself and Amy for a few precious moments. But he knew he must.

He lifted his head, and as their eyes met, his breath seemed to catch midway in his chest. Once again he felt that indefinable pull of attraction that drew them together. This time he didn't fight it or stop to question.

He ignored the sudden flare of panic that ignited Amy's eyes.

He shut off the warning in his head and with a fierce tenderness, lowered his mouth to hers.

As he touched the warmth of her lips, her resistance melted as snow beneath spring rain. For a moment they clung, their lips moving softly against each other, fighting what they knew, pushing aside what waited for each of them. It wasn't enough, it could never be enough.

Then Amy pressed her hands against his chest, breaking the moment.

But Paul wasn't finished. He tilted his head slightly as he kissed her damp cheek, the soft hair at her temple, her eyelids. She stood as if waiting for him to finish and finally pulled away. As he stepped back, he let his eyes drift over her familiar and beloved face. A lump gathered in his throat.

He had cared for this girl all her life, and now it was too late.

"I wish I could say I'm sorry," he said, his own voice hoarse from emotion. "But I'm not."

He wasn't sorry for kissing her, but he was sorry for the confusion his kiss had created. A confusion that mirrored his own.

"I know it's not fair to tell you now, Amy," he said, the words coming out of that deep place he had hidden them, knowing he didn't deserve to receive anything from her. "You've got another man's ring on your finger. But I love you." He laughed shortly, looking down. 'It was selfish of me to tell you, but I had to."

He fell silent as he saw the import of what he said register on Amy. She closed her eyes as if to shut him out.

"I think you had better go back to your girlfriend, Paul Henderson, and stop playing games with me."

Her words cut him deeply, reminding him of previous commitments. He nodded as if agreeing.

"I'm not playing games with you, Amy. You've always been someone very important to me. I've realized too late how important." He waited, but she still stood firm. "I'll be praying for you, Amy." He touched the side of her cheek with his lips, and she flinched. Then he turned and left.

*   *   *

"Mr. Onyschuk on line four, Paul."

The tinny sound of the intercom on the desk behind him interrupted Paul's contemplation of the streets below. He turned his head from the rain-smeared glass of his fifteenth-floor office window and glanced back at a phone that blinked like a Christmas tree.

"And please put those other two callers out of their misery," Rhonda, his secretary, added plaintively.

Paul allowed a wry grin to lift one corner of his mouth. He tugged on his burgundy silk tie, an excellent complement to his navy blue, double-breasted suit, and wished that he had stopped by his condo to change after his meeting this morning. He usually favored more casual wear, but he and Bruce had to schmooze, and in the corporate world of Vancouver, schmoozing required suits.

Shouldering himself away from the window with the rain sheeting down it, he turned to face the inevitable.

Mr. Onyschuk probably wanted more information on the last set of blueprints Paul had sent out with one of the underlings in the office. Line one was Allied Concrete's sales rep—some guy named Wade or Wayne, who had been trying all week to connect with him.

Line three was Stacy.

He waggled his fingers over the desk trying to choose. And the winner was...line one.

"Hello, Wayne. Paul Henderson... Sorry, Wade. What have you got for me?" As he listened to the all-too-familiar sales pitch on servicing, delivery promises, quality control, payment options, Paul doodled absentmindedly. It didn't seem to matter what product the salesmen were selling—re-bar, cement forms, cranes, heavy equipment, paper or personalized pens, the pitch sounded the same as the others, the deal the best in town. And Paul was growing weary of being told that everyone was looking out for his best interests.

In this business, everyone looked out for themselves.

"Thank you for all that, Wade," Paul said as soon as he could. "Tell you what. Send me your brochure and card with some price lists, and I'll talk to my partner. Talk to you soon."

Paul waited a moment until he was sure Wade or Wayne had hung up before he hit...

"Mr. Onyschuk. How are you today?" Paul chatted and doodled, trying to ignore the flashing light beside line three. Mr. Onyschuk's problem took little time to straighten up and Paul hung up, leaving line three still sending out its mute plea.

Last week, over salmon linguini, he had officially put an end to his and Stacy's relationship. She had called each day since. Today he didn't feel like doing yet another postmortem on their situation.

Nor did he feel like sitting in the office going over the numbers on the last three projects Henderson Contractors had done for B.C. Transit. They'd made money, but Bruce didn't trust the cost analysis and wanted Paul to verify it before they took on another project for them.

But Paul didn't want to sit over a calculator in a stuffy office "verifying." Nor did he want to head out to the Upper Narrows to check on their newest work site and make sure all the subtrades were on schedule. It seemed pointless to keep going, hobbling from job to job—one partner wanting to sell out and another partner that couldn't commit himself.

With a frustrated sigh he pushed his chair around. The rain obscured his view of the mountains and distorted his view of the bay below them. When work was behind schedule, the weather concerned him, but otherwise he wasn't the one that got wet when cranes were moving and cement trucks were rolling in. He had spent his time pouring cement, perched on scaffolds and I beams. He and Bruce had worked their way to this office above it all.

And now?

Now all he could think of was soft gray eyes, hair that caught the sun and soft lips that could curve in laughter and just as quickly thin in frustration.

Paul leaned back, lacing his hands behind his head, slipping into the reverie that often caught him these days. He wondered how Amy was managing, if things were falling into place like Amy had so often reassured him—and herself—they would. He wondered if she thought about him as much as he thought about her, and he wondered if she had second thoughts about Tim.

And as he so often had, he prayed for her, for himself, for all the things that tangled themselves around her life. He prayed for her happiness. And that was all he could pray for.

He glanced over his shoulder at the telephone. The solitary light no longer blinked on its console. He felt guilty relief wash over him. He had talked to Stacy enough. With each phone call, she became more bitter, and the last time he spoke to her, she had thrown out accusations about his attraction for Amy. He wondered how she noticed—she had only been around for a day.

And his time away from her had shown him quite clearly that it would not have worked between them, even though she refused to see that.

He couldn't explain to her that his visit home had filled a need even as it had created a deeper one. He had renewed his relationship with his Lord and his family. But now he wanted to go back home, to the mountains, to Amy.

Paul plowed a hand through his hair as he reminded himself once more that Amy was engaged.

And what could he offer her in return? What was his life now? Busyness and running around. But what alternative did he have? If he went back to the ranch, would he be content to live there if Amy wasn't there? Could he be happy living in the Cariboo with Amy and Tim as next-door neighbors?

Could he convince her that Tim wasn't the man for her?

Paul dragged his hands over his face. He couldn't do that to her. She loved Tim, didn't she?

Then why did it feel so right to have her in your arms? When he had kissed her, just before he left the valley, it had felt so right. It was like a homecoming, like finding some lost part of himself.

"Paul, are you talking to your mother today?" Rhonda's voice cut into his troubled thoughts.

Pivoting in his chair he hit the button of the intercom before he picked up the phone. "How does she sound?"

"Work with me here, Paul," Rhonda sighed. "I only fib to

callers during your nap and when you have a very important meeting with the minister of transportation.''

"Put her through."

"Thank you very much."

"Minus the sarcasm."

Rhonda said nothing, and Paul hit the button. "Hi, Mom. How's things with my favorite girl?"

"Don't even start with that smarmy Vancouver chitchat."

"That's what I like about you, Mom. Cut to the chase." He leaned back in his chair, ready to connect with home.

"I dislike fake cheerfulness, you know that."

"So what momentous occasion made you decide to reach out and touch?"

"Just wanted to connect."

"Okay. Let's connect." Paul turned around facing the window. "How's things at the ranch?"

"Good. We got the cows down from the leased land and the hay is all hauled home. Prices are up. We should do quite well this year."

"And..." He hesitated, his previous thought too close to the surface for him to be able to adopt a completely casual tone. "How are things with Amy?"

"Judd went home for a while. Then Amy found him unconscious in his bedroom and she had to take him back to the hospital. Did you know he has diabetes?"

"Amy told me." Paul leaned back, pinching the bridge of his nose between his thumb and forefinger. He wished he could be there. "How's she doing?"

"You know Amy. Strong and independent—on the outside. She quit her job. It was getting too much." Elizabeth sighed. "Rick's working at Jack's now and he likes it."

"So what is Amy going to do now?"

"I don't know. She still comes over, but she doesn't talk much these days. She seems so troubled. Pray for her, okay?" Elizabeth asked.

"Every day." And night and morning, he thought, and whenever she crossed his mind. Which was often.

"And how are things with you?"

Paul was hoping she would skip that part of the phone call. "Got another contract from Speers and Lovell. They want us to build a mall in Surrey and another in Langley. We're bidding on a couple of high-rise apartments...."

"It's been two weeks since you broke up with Stacy," his mother interrupted. "You still okay with that?"

"I'm still glad I did it, yes."

"And are you going to buy out your partner?"

"I don't know." He looked out the window again at the dismal weather beyond, suddenly realizing how less depressing a rainy day felt looking out of the windows of his parents' house than from his office or condo.

"Have you thought about your father's offer to become partner in the ranch?"

"Constantly."

"Good." She sighed, a light sound. "I'm still sorry about you and Stacy, but I'm glad that you found out now instead of after you got married. It was the right choice, you'll see it in time."

"I see it already."

"So now what?"

Paul pulled his hand over his face and inhaled deeply. "I'm not sure I want to tell you." He paused, his hand still covering his eyes. "But I'm in love with Amy."

Silence greeted this remark.

"I know it sounds bizarre and the timing is terrible..."

"Doesn't sound bizarre and doesn't surprise me. I think you've always cared for Amy, but didn't dare raise yourself to her standard."

Good, old Mom, Paul thought. Not afraid to call things as she saw them.

"Be careful with her," his mother continued. "She has her own burdens to bear, and lately she carries them poorly."

"And is Tim around to help her?"

Another pause. "I'm not going to defend or accuse. Amy has to make her own decisions about what she needs."

"If it's any comfort to you, right now her needs are more important to me than my own personal satisfaction."

"You're a good man, Paul Henderson."

"Thanks, Mom. I've had good teachers."

They exchanged a few pleasantries, spinning down to the end of the conversation and the final goodbye.

Paul dropped the handset in the cradle, a wry smile curving his lips. He sat back, wondering, thinking. He offered up a prayer for Judd...and for Amy.

Then jumped as the door burst open.

"Couldn't you make a less dramatic entrance?" he grumbled as Rhonda dumped a pile of mail on his desk—letters to be signed, papers to initial, topped off with the morning paper.

"I'd like to see you try to open that behemoth you call a door a little less dramatically with all this stuff in your hands." Rhonda set his coffee beside the phone. "Also got a very abrupt call from Les Visser. He was way too busy to be put on hold. He told me he wants to meet with you to talk about the buyout."

"I'm too busy."

"No, you're not."

"If he calls again, Rhonda, I'm busy." Paul smiled up at his secretary, who looked over her half glasses, a smirk curving her bright red lips.

She shrugged. "Okay. Busy," she replied. "Better to bury yourself here, I guess."

Paul narrowed his eyes. He knew she meant something else, but she only smiled back at him.

"Rhonda, I pay you to talk for me, not at me." He pointed at the newspaper. "You've read this already," he said accusingly.

"I always do, you know that. I always read the announcements to make sure no one I know died."

He reached for it, but she slapped her hand on it, stopping him.

"No comics until you've signed these letters and told me what to do with all this other stuff."

Paul pulled his pen out of his pocket and clicked the top, glancing at Rhonda as he did so. She stood back, her hands pushed into the pockets of a loud plaid blazer that almost, but not quite, clashed with the auburn shade of hair that Paul was sure hid a number of gray hairs. "Have I ever told you what a bully you are?"

"Frequently." She gestured toward the papers, her hand still in her pocket.

He signed the letters with quick, impatient strokes, pushing them across the desk to her as he finished with each. He flipped through the letters she had opened, making notations only she understood. She gathered up the papers, her nails flashing bright red against the cream-colored parchment of Henderson Contracting's stationery.

"I'm going out for lunch," she said, shuffling the papers into a neat pile. "When I come back are you 'not in' for anyone else? Besides Stacy and Les Visser, of course."

"Actually, I think I'll be checking the site at the Upper Narrows. I haven't been there for a week."

"You can't keep avoiding her."

"I broke off the relationship face-to-face. What's to avoid?" Paul looked up in time to see Rhonda staring down at him, her head tilted to one side, her glasses in her hand.

"Have you told her exactly why?"

He and Rhonda had a good working relationship, but she, like most personal secretaries over time, was also privy to much of his personal life. He leaned back, twirling his pen in his fingers. "Incompatibility would probably be the biggest reason. I told her that."

Rhonda flashed him a sarcastic grin. "Wouldn't have anything to do with someone named—" Rhonda leaned sideways, looking down at the pad of paper Paul had totally obscured with doodles "—Amy?"

Paul frowned, flipping the pad of paper over.

"Don't need to be self-conscious around me, boss." Rhonda smiled, straightening. "You've been out of it since your little holiday. I suspected something happened there that eclipsed the importance of the buyout."

Paul balanced the pen between his fingers, watching it intently. Rhonda merely waited. He glowered at her over the pen but she sat down, stretching her legs out in front of her, crossing them at the ankle.

"I can wait," was all she said.

"I don't want to talk about it."

"Of course you do. Every man in love wants to talk about his girl, how wonderful she is, how she makes him feel. It beats doodling her name all over every spare piece of paper on your desk." Rhonda grinned. "Besides, that's what secretaries are for."

Paul caught his lower lip between his teeth and began writing on the pad again. Rhonda bided her time.

"How long have you and Dexter been married?" he finally asked.

"Twenty-seven years."

"Wow." He glanced once again at her colored hair teased to a mound above her grinning face.

"Yeah, these days I guess it's a 'wow' kind of thing."

"When you first met your husband, what made him different from other guys you dated? How did you know?"

"That he was the one?" A slow smile teased her mouth. "We fit. We could talk together about everything. We laughed together. We wanted to be around each other, needed to be together all the time." Rhonda winked at him. "My knees went weak when he kissed me." She pursed her lips. "There's no set formula you can plug a person in and say 'this fits, this is the one.' You just know."

"How about Dexter? How did he know?"

"I had to convince him. But it didn't take much."

"I don't think Stacy could convince me anymore."

"That's because she was more of a habit than a girlfriend. You seemed to have a need to prove that you could settle down with one girl after all the women you've been squiring around. Stacy fit the bill. But she didn't fill the need." Rhonda stood up and smiled gently down at Paul. "You know, since you've come back you've been even more restless than before you left. If you really want some advice..." She paused as if waiting for his usual sarcastic comment. But he couldn't give it and remained quiet. She continued. "The past year has been wearing you down.'' She gestured to the paperwork on his desk. ''This business, this city, your girlfriends—they've all been taking little bites out of you, eating you alive. Since you've started going to church you've talked more about waiting on the Lord. Well, I think He's given you a little shove.''

Rhonda picked up the letters and handed him the paper. ''Check out the announcement section.'' And with that cryptic comment, she left.

Chapter Ten

Paul snapped open the paper to the announcements section.

Tim and Amy's name jumped out at him.

Rhonda had kindly taken the time to circle the announcement of their wedding with blue highlighter. When Paul finished reading the formal language and double-checking the names, he leaned back in his chair, dragging his hands over his face.

The hard evidence lay in front of him, spelled out in black-and-white...and blue. It was there for all of Vancouver, and whoever else might be interested, to see. A sense of dread flowed through him. She couldn't marry Tim.

He turned to the phone and without hesitating, dialed Danyluks' number. Amy answered it on the second ring.

"Danyluks' residence."

The heaviness in her voice reverberated through the line.

He paused, feeling like a gauche teenager who called a girl on a dare and then couldn't talk. What was he going to say? Tell her straight-out she couldn't marry Tim?

"Hello? Is someone there?"

Paul shook his head and forged ahead onto safer ground. "Hi, Amy, it's me, Paul. I heard about your dad. How's he doing?"

"Not well..."

Her voice trailed off, and Paul heard her sigh. It hurt to be so far away from her. "I just wanted to call and let you know I've been praying for you," he said, wishing he could be there, holding her and comforting her.

"Thank you," she said quietly. "That's good to know."

"I've been going to church again—renewing an old acquaintance with the Lord." He pulled the newspaper toward him, folded open to her and Tim's picture. He traced her features with a shaking hand. "I wanted to tell someone else besides my family." *And I needed to tell you,* he thought.

"I'm glad for you, Paul." The genuine happiness in her voice gave him a shot of encouragement. He felt a rush of love for this girl who, in her own troubles, could be happy for someone else.

They were both quiet a moment.

"I wish I could be there, Amy," he said suddenly. "I want to hold you like I did in the barn, I want to tell you how I feel." *I want to talk you out of marrying Tim Enders.*

"Paul, don't..."

"Amy, I meant what I said." He took a breath and finally dared speak the words. "I love you. I'm not finished with this."

"You have to be...."

"I know I'm years too late," he cut in, not wanting to listen to her denials. "I shouldn't even tell you, but I can't keep it to myself."

There was no sound from the other end. Then finally she asked, "And what about Stacy?"

"I broke up with her as soon as I came back to Vancouver." Paul grasped the receiver, her question a sign of hope. "I want to talk to you. I'm going to drive up on Sunday."

"It's not going to make any difference, Paul."

He felt a clutch of dread at the practical tone of her voice. Then he remembered how she clung to him that night in the barn. He wasn't going to let her dismiss him that easily just because she had to prove herself more faithful than her mother. "Amy, we have to talk. I didn't have the right when Stacy was still between us..."

"And what about Tim?"

"That's what I want to talk to you about."

Amy said nothing, and Paul leaned his elbows on the desk, the receiver pressed tightly to his ear as he waited.

She hung up.

Amy dropped the nails she just finished sorting into their respective cans and pushed them back onto the shelves in the shed. The rain had forced her inside the past few days. She didn't feel like cleaning up the house so she came here, working on jobs she had been putting off for a couple of years.

It was ironic that she quit her job to help care for her father only to have him spend much of his time in the hospital. Yesterday he had recovered from another extreme insulin reaction, and this afternoon the nurses said his blood sugar was unreasonably high. Amy wondered if he was ever going to get his sugar levels balanced so he could come home.

"Amy," Shannon's voice called across the yard, reaching her in the shed. "Phone for you."

Shannon had come yesterday, bored with being by herself. She was in between jobs and stayed to help on the ranch. When Amy saw Rick and Shannon together, she suspected that there were ulterior motives to the visit. She didn't mind, although it took a little getting used to, to see her younger brother flirting with her friend and seeing her friend blush when he did so.

Shannon called again, and Amy paused, wondering if she should ignore Shannon or take the chance it wasn't Paul. He called twice yesterday and once again this morning. If he thought persistence and charm would wear her down, he was wrong.

"Are you coming, Amy?" Shannon was getting impatient. Might be someone else, Amy reassured herself. She took a quick breath, but it didn't seem to help her thundering heart or her clammy palms. Fear or anticipation? She only knew that after Paul's phone call this morning, it took half an hour for her heart to return to normal, for the knots in her stomach to loosen. With a shake of her head, she decided to face the inevitable.

She ran across the yard, avoiding puddles, her shirt getting soaked with rain. She ducked into the porch and brushed droplets of water off her hair.

"Who is it, Shannon?" she asked brusquely, as she entered the kitchen.

Shannon shrugged, her one hand over the mouthpiece of the phone. "She's not a sales lady, but she won't give her name or leave a message. I'm sure she phoned once before, but wouldn't leave a message. She sounds like she really wants to talk to you."

With a puzzled look Amy took the phone.

"Hello?"

"Amy, is that you?"

"Yes." Amy frowned.

"I read about your engagement in the Vancouver paper..." The woman hesitated.

Amy tried to match a face to the voice. It had a familiar tone and cadence. Perhaps one of Tim's mother's friends? An old friend from school?

The woman continued. "I really didn't know if I should contact you..." Again the hesitation.

"Who is this?" Amy finally asked, unable to place the voice.

"Amy, honey... It's Noreen, your mother."

Amy dropped onto the nearest chair. Her heart slammed into her throat, pounding in earnest now. "My mother... How?" she stuttered, trying to pull her scattered thoughts. "What do you want?"

Shannon raised her eyebrows, questioning, but Amy shook her head. Shannon, bless her heart, took the hint.

"I read the announcement of your wedding in the newspaper. I just wanted to...to congratulate you."

Ten years had passed since that heartbreaking day her mother left. It took only seconds, however, for the pain to return.

"Why call now, after all this time?" Amy took a steadying breath, surprised at the bitterness and anger that so quickly took place of the confusion. She bit her lip, tempted to hang up. Yet she felt irresistibly drawn to this person who had left so long ago that her face was a shadow, her voice an echo from the past.

"I'm sorry.... I was afraid of this."

But Amy couldn't sustain her anger. This was her mother. Her father was in the hospital. Her own emotions were unstable. "Don't hang up, please." Amy rubbed her forehead as if to draw out the words that had been brewing so long, imagined conversations that ranged through all her emotions. "Where are you calling from?"

"Vancouver. I moved here a year ago from Toronto."

So that's where you've been, thought Amy. In her mind Noreen had remained a shadowy figure that had left and slowly faded out, a slow death that had occurred in an unknown place. And all along it had been Toronto.

"Where do you work? What do you do?"

Do you miss us? Do you think about us? Did you cry? Did you care? It's been ten years. Why didn't you ever write, call, let us know? These questions stayed below the polite surface, bubbling, brewing, unable to be poured through the sterile medium of the telephone.

"I work as an editor for a travel magazine." Noreen was quiet a moment. "Amy, I don't want to talk about me. It's a boring subject. How are *you* doing?"

Amy closed her eyes. What should she say, which part of her life did Noreen want to know about? How to explain to this stranger the events that had rearranged her life in the past few weeks. Judd, Rick, Tim...Paul.

"I'm fine." She settled for the inane. "Things are busy on the ranch."

"They must be, if you're planning a wedding." A short laugh. "I know I don't have the right to ask, but how's your father?"

"He's in the hospital."

Trembling silence hung between them, taut with tension, fraught with more questions that couldn't be voiced.

"How..."

"He's got diabetes."

"Is it serious?" Noreen asked hesitantly.

"They can't seem to get his blood sugar levels down. Once they do, he can come home." Amy felt torn in two. The anger that had burned so hot each time she thought of her mother's leaving still smouldered, still demanded reparation and resented giving out any information.

And yet...

This was her mother. In Amy's childhood, Noreen's voice had greeted Amy as she came home, had followed her out of the house as she ran out for one last quick horseback ride before bed. Noreen's hands pulled blankets over her at night, smoothed hair from her face.

"Would it be possible to see you sometime?"

"I don't know. Things are kind of busy here right now."

"I see."

The line was quiet a moment and Amy waited, unable to speak.

"Amy, when you see your father, can you give him my greetings?"

More quiet. Amy relented. "If you want to see him, he's at the hospital in Williams Lake."

"I don't know if I'm ready to see him, but thanks for telling me." Noreen paused and in that space Amy knew she should extend another invitation. But she couldn't.

The strain of balancing her emotions became too much. "I've got to go," Amy said. "Thanks for calling." The comment sounded fatuous, and Amy hung up before she heard her mother's reply.

She stared at the phone, fingering the receiver still warm from her hands, as emotions swirled, elusive and difficult to define.

"Who was that?" Shannon parked herself across from Amy at the table, pushing a cup of tea at her, her face puzzled.

"My mother." Amy's laugh was a bitter sound. "Phoning me now—after all this time."

"Better late than never," Shannon replied hesitantly.

"I suppose." Amy sipped her tea, replaying her conversation in her mind, trying to imagine what her mother might look like now.

"Where does she live? What does she do?"

Amy felt her anger begin to rise, to supersede the confusion of her other emotions as she tried to imagine her mother living in the city. The place she ran to after she left them. "She's a travel editor. Nice, fancy job."

"Why did she phone?"

"To congratulate me on my wedding." Amy took a deep breath, remembering her wish of many evenings ago, when she wanted her own mother to help her plan her wedding. "She asked about Dad, but she won't go see him. She left because he was too old, and now he's older yet."

"How much difference is there in their ages?"

"About twenty years, I guess. Dad was forty-two when they got married, she was twenty. He turned fifty-five when she cheated on him. We never did know who she ran off with. Dad never said. All that matters to me is that she broke a vow, a promise she made in front of God."

The phone rang again, its shrill sound jolting Amy.

"I'll get it." Shannon pulled the phone toward her. "Danyluk residence. Who's calling please?" Shannon nodded, covered the mouthpiece and mouthed the words "It's Paul."

Amy shook her head, vehemently. The last thing she wanted was to listen to Paul, not now.

"I'm sorry she can't come to the phone right now." Shannon listened and pulled a face. "Of course I'm trying to cover up for her. Give her a break, it's been a tough week." Another pause, another face. "I don't know when Tim was here last. He's got a job, too." Shannon listened, her eyes growing wide. She shot Amy a surprised glance. "Okay, I'll give her the message. Yes, I'll do it just like you said. Goodbye." She dropped the phone into its cradle and stared at it a moment. Then she looked up at Amy. "I'm supposed to tell you, and I quote, so don't get mad at me okay? 'Tell Amy I love her dearly and I'm coming up on Sunday to do something about it.' End of quote."

Amy dropped her head into her hands, frustration and excitement warring within her. Her heart was going double time and her cheeks burned.

"Why is the man of your childhood dreams suddenly phon-

ing an engaged woman, declaring undying love?'' She caught
Amy's hands, pulling them gently away from her face.

"Oh, Shannon, I'm so mixed-up." She sighed, closing her
eyes, her heart pounding in earnest. "I feel like everything is
happening at the same time, like I'm juggling five balls and if
I don't watch them they'll all come down at once."

"I think you need a break," Shannon said.

Amy laughed shortly. "I think I do, too, but when and
where? Dad's in the hospital, the hay needs to be cut, Rick's
got this job..." She withdrew her hands and twisted them together.

"And Paul is phoning," Shannon added softly.

"Yes. Paul." Amy sighed heavily. "He's suddenly decided
he's in love with me. And isn't that convenient. I'm marrying
Tim in a few months, and Paul thinks maybe he should get one
more kick at Amy's heart before she does that." She rose to
her feet. "Does he think I'll just fall into his arms? Does he
really think I'm that gullible? I love Tim and Tim loves me.
We made a promise to each other. And Paul—" she paced
around the kitchen, as if trying to convince herself "—Paul
couldn't stay in one place if he was nailed down. He couldn't
stay faithful to a girl if he was tied to her." Amy stopped,
shoving her hands into her pockets. "Tim's a good man, Shannon. He loves me and he loves the Lord. What I feel for Paul
is just leftovers from a childhood crush and...and..."

"And what, Amy?" Shannon smiled sympathetically at her.

Amy stared at Shannon, shaking her head slowly. "There's
no 'and.' Things have gone too far to back away. I'm marrying
Tim."

She walked slowly to the door, rubbing her head as if to
erase all the events and thoughts of the past few weeks. "I've
got to go for a ride. Can you manage while I'm gone?"

Shannon flapped her hands. "Go already. Saddle up your
horse and head off into the sunset. When Rick comes back from
work, I'll help him with the calves."

"Thanks, Shanny." Amy flashed her a tired smile then
turned and trudged out of the house.

When she got to the pasture, her horse was too far away,

and she didn't have the energy to run after it. Instead, she climbed the corral fence and looked out at the mountains, trying to sort out the tangle of her life.

It was as if all the threads she thought she had such a firm hold on were slowly slipping out of her grasp and she couldn't pull them back together again.

Rick had been working steadily at Dilton's garage. His income gave them some financial breathing space, but it also meant that Amy had to take care of the purebred heifers and their own herd of commercial cows on her own. Though she had quit her job, there was always some other chore to do.

Or she had to spend time at the hospital learning how to take care of her father's diabetes. There was a diet to follow, food had to be measured and weighed, insulin adjusted according to blood tests that had to be taken three to four times a day. She didn't have time to think further than the next day.

And now Paul was pestering her.

His last visit left her emotionally drained. His last kiss still tingled on her lips. His words still rang through her mind. And now he boldly delivered his message to Shannon as if challenging Amy.

And Tim. Kind, solid Tim. She knew how much he loved her, what he would do for her. They shared their faith, they shared a dream.

And her mother...

Amy braced herself on the fence, her hands digging into the rough planks. Noreen couldn't live out here, she thought, taking in the undulating hills, their shades of buckskin and brown shading off to deep purple against the blue sky. Noreen couldn't see the beauty here, couldn't be a faithful wife, couldn't keep the promises she made.

All her hectic thoughts slowed as a coldness clutched Amy's heart.

Broken promises.

Amy turned her ring over on her finger, watching sparkles of white, green, pink and blue shoot out from the diamond that was a concrete symbol of the promises she and Tim had made to each other.

And what had Paul offered her? Only words. He had known all his life how Amy felt about him. And what had he done? Treated her like a little sister while he ran around with numerous other girls. Paul had spent most of his life running around, always wanting more. Each time he came back, he had another girl, someone else he had made promises to.

Paul couldn't keep his word. He had broken up with Stacy and they were practically engaged. He couldn't stay in the Cariboo, either. He still lived in Vancouver.

But Tim.

Tim was good, honorable and kind. He loved the Lord, and he loved *her*. He had offered her a solid relationship, himself and his life. And she had accepted. Yet she considered breaking her promise to Tim for a nebulous emotion for a childhood hero. She truly was no better than her mother.

Amy caught her breath. The thought almost shattered her.

Drawing in a deep breath, Amy turned her face heavenward, the heat on her face a penance as she pleaded for forgiveness and prayed for strength.

She prayed to be faithful to Tim, prayed to stop wanting things for herself, prayed to keep her promises.

Her feelings for Paul belonged to another, younger part of her life. It was time to put away childish things.

Slowly, the tension eased out of her. A breeze cooled her heated cheeks. It was as if God's hand rested lightly on her, consoling, reassuring.

She took a steadying breath, gazing about her at the beauty of the land that was solid and endured. She prayed her love would be the same.

"So Paul, I hate to push, but have you decided what kind of deal you want to cut?" Bruce took a long pull of his cigarette. His suit jacket hung crookedly on the chair behind him, his tie was knotted at half-mast on a shirt unbuttoned at the neck. His stomach, once firm and tight from packing cement forms around, was heavier, hanging over a leather belt that held up pants a few sizes larger. His black hair was cut close to his head, a far cry from the in-your-face ponytail he had favored for many years, a few threads of silver glinting in the overhead lights.

The sun's evening glow bathed the office. Rhonda and the other staff had left two hours ago.

Paul spent the afternoon at their latest project trying to get excited about being under budget and ahead of schedule. He and Bruce got together, as they usually did at the end of each week to go over their scheduling and new jobs coming up.

Tonight they had bigger things on their minds.

Bruce took another drag off his cigarette and, in deference to Paul who had quit a year ago, spewed the smoke out of the side of his mouth.

As if that makes a whole lot of difference, Paul thought, watching the smoke drift lazily toward him, anyway. With a sigh of resignation, he hunched forward tapping his pencil on the papers in front of him, looking at them but not really reading.

In spite of their weekly meetings, he felt as if he hadn't really talked to Bruce the past few weeks. The past few months, come to think of it. Once, they had been close. Their Friday get-togethers would take place in a restaurant or each other's homes. The talk would veer from pricing, to mutual friends, to politics and religion. They had been partners since the beginning, since the Atco trailer parked on-site.

Now Bruce was married, his wife expecting their second child. He couldn't always spend the time Paul wanted him to on job sites and often cut their Friday meetings short.

Paul spun back and forth in his chair as he searched for the right questions, tired of trying to feel his old partner out. Bruce's answers had been noncommittal, so Paul decided to go for broke.

"How would you feel if I declined to buy out, if we put the whole business up for sale?"

Silence hung between them as the question settled into each of their minds. Bruce pursed his lips as he studied the tip of his burning cigarette. He sighed then looked up at Paul. "To tell you the truth, right about now I'm ready for anything," he said slowly. "I'm getting tired of all this stuff, this paperwork.'' Bruce waved his cigarette over the papers scattered on the desk. ''I surely never expected to be spending half of my day cooped up in an office chasing down a paper trail.'' He took another deep pull on his cigarette. ''Never thought I'd take up smoking again.''

Paul laughed mirthlessly. ''I'm tempted to myself.''

Bruce looked up at Paul thoughtfully. ''How about you, buddy? All those years we were carting concrete in wheelbarrows, drawing up our own plans, putting in bids, did you imagine yourself sitting up here, running around carrying a briefcase, of all things, instead of a shovel?''

''I did, actually.'' Paul shrugged. ''I got exactly what I wanted...once.''

Bruce shook his head and stubbed out his sixth cigarette, half-smoked. ''Well, I didn't.''

Paul glanced back over his shoulder, catching a glimpse of the mountains behind him. Rhonda's words came back to him. Did he want to fight for this, he thought as he looked back at the office, the desk completely covered with papers, blueprints hanging on the walls? It was seven o'clock. His parents would be finished supper, sitting with a cup of coffee, chatting after a day of work outside.

He'd been fighting traffic all the way back from the job site at the Upper Narrows. He had a two-page list of phone calls to make yet, verifying subcontracts on the new malls Henderson Contractors were to build. He wouldn't be done until ten o'clock tonight. Then tomorrow morning he could get up and do it all over again.

Was this really what he wanted?

''I hate to rush this momentous occasion, Paul, but Lois wanted me home on time tonight....''

Paul nodded, acknowledging Bruce's comment.

Home. Bruce had a wife and a child waiting for him. Paul had nobody. And the girl he wanted would soon be married to someone else.

''We'll talk about it more on Monday,'' Paul said quietly. ''You may as well go home.''

* * *

"So that's the best you can do for me?" Paul leaned his elbows on the cold glass table between him and his banker, Les Visser. He frowned at the pages in front of him.

"You're a good customer, Paul, but the rates have risen since your last loan." Les shrugged. "I can't do better than that."

Paul rubbed his finger along his jaw, calculating. Debts for the next fifteen years. Sky-high payments. Higher service charges. "Maybe I should try for a second opinion?"

"I hope you're kidding," Les said, his tapping finger betraying his agitation with Paul's casual comment. "I had to twist O'Brien's arm to get you as much as I did." He leaned forward, his expression earnest. "Paul, I've helped you right from your first loan for that forklift and I've been with you all the way until now. This really is the best I can do. You won't get better in any bank in Vancouver, or the lower mainland for that matter."

Paul gathered the papers and fussed with them, making the pile neat. "I wonder if another accounts manager would have more pull." He grinned up at Les, unable to resist one more dig.

"If you wait a couple of months, we're getting some hotshot young guy coming into the branch pretty soon. You could try your luck with him. His old man's in big with O'Brien."

"Pass," Paul replied, his voice dry as he slipped the sheaf of papers in his briefcase. "If he's cozy with O'Brien, I don't know if I'd want to do business with him." He smiled at Les. "Don't worry. I know what you've done for me. If it wasn't for you, I'd still be pushing cement in a wheelbarrow." Paul snapped his briefcase shut and stood up. "Where's this young 'hotshot' from?"

"Your old home town, maybe you even know him."

Paul hesitated, frowning at Les.

"Tim Enders. He asked for the transfer a couple of weeks ago, and it came through this morning."

"He asked for the transfer himself?" Paul raised his eyebrows, his voice hard.

"Well, he's had a lot of help from Momma and Daddy Enders." Les frowned. "You sound ticked. You know the guy?"

Paul heaved his briefcase off the table, his movements quick, decisive. "Yes. I think I know him better than some people do."

"Careful, Amy." Fred Henderson caught Amy's arms, preventing a collision in the hospital corridor.

Amy took a step back to catch her balance and grinned up at Fred. "Well, hi, there. What are you doing here?"

"Visiting your dad."

Amy felt like she should take another step back. She tilted her head to the side, her eyebrows lifted in surprise. "Visiting my dad?" she repeated stupidly. "And you're still in one piece?"

"It's not that bad," Fred said with a smile.

"Maybe not. But I haven't heard my dad say anything complimentary about you since I could talk. I'm surprised he let you in the room."

"He did come to our place for your engagement party."

Amy pursed her lips, considering. "That's true."

"I've actually come a couple of times to see him since he's been here."

Amy shook her head, still trying to absorb the idea of Fred Henderson chatting with her father. "He's never mentioned it." Amy grinned up at Fred. "I still have a hard time imagining it, but—" She stopped a moment, suddenly overcome by a wave of emotion. "I'm so glad." She reached out for him, dropping the package of flowers she had brought for Judd, her heart welling with happiness. It had been too long since she had something to truly celebrate. She squeezed hard. She had loved Elizabeth and Fred all her life. To have her father, now, after all those years of resentment and dislike, allow Fred to visit him was more than she could have hoped for.

"It's okay, Amy." Fred held her close, patting her on the back. He straightened and smiled down at her. "I have had my own difficulties with your father. He's had a lot of bitterness and anger. I've had to learn to forgive him and have prayed for an opportunity to talk to him. He seemed quite happy at your engagement party, so I took a chance. We spoke for a while, and I sensed that he was ready to have me come and see him." He stroked Amy's cheek. "Besides, you've had so much on your mind, I thought if there was some way I could make things easier for you then I should do it."

Amy shook her head slowly, as if trying to absorb this very welcome piece of information. She felt a surge of happiness lift her heart. "I've always loved you and Elizabeth so much, it was so hard for me at times. I'm so glad."

"Me, too. Especially if we're going to keep living close to each other." Fred bent over and handed Amy the package she dropped. "I better get going. I promised I'd meet Elizabeth in a couple of minutes at the grocery store."

"I probably could have kept on working there, Dad's been in the hospital so much."

"It will all even out, Amy. We're praying for you." He winked at her, turned and left.

Amy watched him go, her heart overflowing with happiness. "Thank you, Lord," she said softly. "I really needed something wonderful."

She turned, her step light as she walked down the hallway and into Judd's room. His roommate had gone home the day before, and now her father was by himself. He sat on the edge of his bed, his back to her, playing cards on his food tray.

Probably cheating, Amy thought, walking into the room and bending over to give him a kiss.

He jumped, then smiled up at her. "Hey, girl. How are you?"

"I'm feeling great, what about you?" Amy set the flowers on his bedside table and pulled up a chair.

Judd shrugged. "Not bad. Not good. My eyes are kinda blurry. Nurse says it's 'cause of the diabetes."

"Will it go away?"

"Hope so. Hard to cheat with poor eyes."

"At your age, you should start to play fair."

"At my age, I don't need to play fair." Judd rubbed his eyes, blinked a moment and gathered up his cards. "So, how are all the critters?"

"One of the new heifers was a little lame. Gave it a shot of long-acting penicillin and now it's okay. I think we'll get some really nice calves from them. I wish we had more pasture, then we could put their calves on grass over the summer and make even more from them in the fall.''

"You might want to sell them in the spring. Even out your cash flow. That way you've got money coming in spring and fall.'' Judd pushed the table away and pulled his IV pole closer. "Looks like nice weather outside.''

"It is. Sunny, warm. Slight breeze. Really good haying weather. I'm hoping to get the baler fixed next week and it will be ready to go. Rick is working on our tractor. Things are finally pulling together.'' Amy leaned back in the chair, her arms crossed. "I just met Fred Henderson in the hallway. He said he's been seeing you.''

Judd shrugged. "Yah. He's been coming.'' He looked up at Amy. "He's okay.''

"I've known that a long time, Dad.'' Amy struggled to keep the note of censure out of her voice, thankful that her father was finally able to see Fred for who he was.

Judd merely nodded and sat back on the bed, pulling his bathrobe around him. He lay back fiddling with the IV tube. "Anything exciting happen since last I saw you?''

Amy thought of Noreen's phone call and rubbed her fingers against arms that were suddenly cold. "I...I got a phone call yesterday.'' She bit her lip then hurried on. "It was...Nor...I mean, Mom.''

Judd frowned, leaned forward as if to hear better. "Who?''

Amy cleared her throat and tried again. "Mom. Your wife. Noreen Danyluk. She phoned yesterday. She saw our wedding announcement in a Vancouver newspaper and took a chance and called.''

"Noreen?'' Judd lay back against the stacked pillows of the raised bed, staring off into the distance. "Noreen called?''

"She phoned to congratulate me on the wedding.'' Amy couldn't keep the bitter note out of her voice. "She's known our number for a long time. Why didn't she call sooner?''

Judd closed his eyes, his lips pressed together.

Amy sat up, alarmed at the look of anguish on his face. "Dad, what's wrong?"

Judd said nothing, only shook his head slightly. Amy eased back into her chair, ready to jump up and call the nurse. "Are you sure you're okay?"

"Stop fussing, Amy," he grumbled. He opened his eyes but still wouldn't look at her. He seemed to be in another time, another place. "Did she say anything else?" he asked finally.

"I told her you were in the hospital. She didn't say anything about coming to see you."

Judd nodded slowly, his eyes now on his daughter. "You don't sound happy about her calling."

Amy bit her lip, trying to compose her thoughts, her emotions, surprised at her father's calm. "I just want to know what took her so long. Why didn't she ever call. Not once. Not even for birthdays or Christmas..." Amy stopped talking as her anger rose. "And why doesn't she want to visit you?"

"Guilt. Guilt is a soul-destroying emotion."

Amy wondered who he spoke of. He looked grief stricken.

"I made a mistake..." Judd hesitated. He sighed and straightened. "If she doesn't want to come for a visit, I understand. Tell her I said that."

"She might not phone again." Amy thought of her response to her mother and wondered if Noreen would even want to try.

Judd crossed his arms and looked away. "How does Rick like his job?" her father asked, abruptly changing the subject.

"Loves it." Amy retorted, glad to move to a less-emotional topic. "Comes home late, tired, dirty and happy." Amy wrinkled her nose, unable to imagine that he would prefer working with cold hard metal instead of warm animals and soft grass.

"So what are you going to do about Rick working out?"

"Not much I can do. Keep plugging. Prices look good for the fall, so I'm hoping we can buy a round baler this year. Then I can feed the cows myself."

"That would make things handy." Judd looked at her, his face suddenly concerned. "It's not too much for you, is it, with Rick gone?"

"Now that I quit my job, I can manage. It's going to be a

bit tight financially until we sell the calves, but after that it will be okay.'' Amy shrugged. ''It will be less hectic once you're home and Tim and I are married.''

Judd nodded slowly.

''What?'' Amy frowned at her father. ''You don't look like you believe me.''

''No, that's not it.'' He tapped his fingers together. ''I just don't know if it would be such a good idea for me to live with you and Tim when he moves onto the ranch. I don't want to see you doing all of this just because you think you have to look after me.''

''Don't be silly, Dad. Of course you'll stay with us. Especially now. Where else would you go? What would you do?''

''I don't need much, Amy.'' Judd grinned at Amy. ''Just a television and a remote control. I've got my disability pension, I could live on my own.'' He paused a moment, looking down. ''The ranch is a lot of work for you.''

''It's not a burden to me.'' Amy laughed. ''I love the work. I can't imagine living anywhere else.''

''And Tim won't mind driving to work every day?''

Amy looked at her hands, twisting her ring around her finger as she remembered the conversation she'd had with his mother over his work and his prospects. ''He has never complained about it.''

''That doesn't mean he wouldn't mind.''

Amy shrugged. ''He's not henpecked yet. I'm sure he would have said it fairly clearly if he minded.'' Amy reached over and patted her father's arm. ''Don't worry, Dad. It will all work out just fine.''

Chapter Eleven

A my stepped into Tim's car. As she leaned over to give him a kiss, she caught the unfamiliar whiff of a different scent. "New aftershave for Sunday?" she teased, sniffing his cheek.

"Gift from my mom."

Amy fell back, puzzled, as she mentally ticked off any possible reasons for the present. His birthday wasn't for another four months. They'd already received engagement gifts...

"Relax, Amy," he said with a smile as he drove out of their yard. "It was one of those 'just because' things my mom likes to indulge in at times."

"Thank goodness." Amy laughed. "I'm down to my last few dollars. I'd have to knit up some socks if I wanted to get you something." She wrinkled her nose. "I don't miss cashing at the grocery store, but I sure miss the paycheck."

"Speaking of paychecks, when do you figure on shipping your calves?"

"I'll have to do it earlier than I figured—October instead of November. I won't have to buy as much hay then."

Tim only nodded, his forehead creased in thought.

"What?" Amy asked. "Do you think I should wait?"

He lifted one shoulder, as if unsure. "Do you think the income from the spring calves will give you enough money for the winter? You've got the heifers and you'll have to buy hay. Your expenses are going to be higher over the winter. Things could get tight.''

"I know," Amy sighed, disturbed by the serious tone of his voice. "But as I've said before, the price looks good. And if we can weather this winter, by spring, I'll have another crop of calves to sell and things will really roll.''

Tim pursed his lips as he stared at the road ahead. Amy didn't like that look, either. It usually meant "Time to talk about your financial statement.'' All those people who teased her about the advantages of having a banker for a fiancé, didn't understand her frustration with discussing financial planning on dates—or planning honeymoons around banker conventions.

"It's Sunday, Tim," she added. She needed time to let the worries of the week lay at rest, to remind herself to trust in God.

"You're right.'' He glanced sidelong at her. "I'm sorry.''

Amy winked back at him with a smile of forgiveness. But she couldn't seem to shake the sense of unease his words brought up. The discussion wasn't finished, just postponed, and she wondered what he really wanted to talk about. They drove in silence, the thrum of the car the only sound.

Amy let herself relax against the seat, disturbed at the tension that dogged their relationship the past week. Neither she nor Tim brought it up, but for herself it dated back to the trip to Vancouver and her future mother-in-law's comments.

She had tried to broach the subject of his career on the way home from Vancouver but he had been evasive.

And it hadn't helped that Rick had talked about Paul on their arrival. Tim had been extra touchy where Paul Henderson was concerned. Amy wanted to get Tim's jealousy out in the open so she could reassure him, but Tim disliked talking about Paul even more than he disliked talking about Noreen.

And that was another thing she wanted to tell him but didn't dare. She was hoping to bring up Noreen's phone call this morning, but he looked a little tense as it was.

Amy reached out to smooth his hair, her fingers lingering on his shoulder, wanting to reassure him, to show him. He smiled then, tilting his head toward her.

"Are you still heading off to Vancouver this afternoon?" she asked, seeking for a touchstone, something that would draw them together. The wedding plans always managed to be common ground.

"Stanley managed to get some time off work, as well, so I thought we could pick out our tuxedos tomorrow." He smiled at Amy. "You really should have had your dress picked out long ago. It's getting closer. Have you had a chance to look through those books my mom bought?"

Amy felt a prick of guilt as she thought of the heavy, glossy magazines lying on the couch in the living room. Shannon had glanced through one while Amy was making supper, oohing and aahing over some of the styles. Amy managed a quick glance over her shoulder, but couldn't seem to work up enthusiasm for the lace and sequined confections that Mrs. Enders had earmarked for Amy's consideration. They looked expensive and totally out of her reach. "The dresses in there are lovely..."

"But..."

"Out of my price range, I think."

"How many times do I have to tell you, my parents will gladly help out."

"I had thought I could sew my own dress..."

"You won't have time for that." Tim reached over and folded his hand over hers. "You barely have time to buy one. So don't get all proud on me. For once in your life take what someone is offering and don't think you have to either earn it or deserve it. After all, the future wife of an M.C.S. has an image to keep up."

"M.C.S.?"

"Manager of Commercial Services. It's a promotion."

"Tim, are you serious?" Amy whirled on him, grabbing at his shoulder. "You got a promotion? When? Why didn't you tell me sooner?"

Tim grinned at her exuberance. "I only got the phone call a couple of days ago."

Amy sat back, pleased and very proud of her future husband.

"I can't believe you got promoted over Bob Delaney. He has more seniority than you."

Tim's expression became serious and Amy felt a small tingling of dread. "I think you should know..." He wrapped his fingers around the steering wheel, rotating his wrists. "The promotion isn't for the branch in Williams Lake."

Amy swallowed, her heart beginning a long, slow thump. "Where is it?" she asked quietly.

Tim bit his lip, took a deep breath and glanced sidelong at her. "Vancouver."

"What?" Amy's mouth fell open as the single word registered. She sat back, staring at Tim, as her whole world rearranged. "Vancouver? Why there?" she asked stupidly even as his mother's comments came back to her with aching clarity.

"I know for a fact I'm not going to get anywhere at the branch in town, Amy," Tim said hurriedly. "I'm the least experienced accounts manager, and talent isn't recognized as quickly in a small place. Seniority is what counts. This chance came up in Vancouver, and I know I'll be able to go a lot further than if I stayed here." He looked at Amy, his gaze pleading. "I can't turn it down, Amy. It's a great opportunity."

Amy slumped against the seat as his words washed over her, clear, sensible and so very destructive. How could he do this without asking her? How could he just assume she would go along with this? First Rick gets a job and leaves the ranch, now Tim gets a promotion and wants to leave town. Was God trying to tell her something? Or was his mother, she thought unkindly.

Over and over it seemed doors closed on her, limiting her options, pushing her into corners. Was she being selfish to ask him to take her needs into consideration? She hadn't known he was unhappy in Williams Lake, he'd never said anything before, had he? She didn't think she was that blind. "And what about my father and the ranch?" she asked when her thoughts finally settled down.

Tim bit his lip as his hands continued massaging the steering wheel. "I've been thinking about that one long and hard." He threw her a pleading glance. "Don't think it has been easy for me to set aside what I know you want." He looked straight ahead again, hesitating. "I think you should sell it, Amy. Your father doesn't seem interested, Rick's got a job..."

"And you don't want to live there," Amy finished for him. She looked away. She truly hadn't known. What his mother had said was the first inkling she had of where he wanted to go. "Do you have any other surprises you want to spring on me before we get married?"

"I'm sorry, Amy. I thought I would be happy here. But every time I go back to Vancouver, I realize what I'm missing. In the bank here, there's only so far to go. We would have been moving sooner or later, anyhow. This is just sooner."

Amy nodded slowly, his words slowly sinking in, heavy and ominous.

"I know you'll be able to sell it. Your dad had often said he wanted to live in town, and now with his diabetes..."

"Please," Amy put up her hand, then let it drop idly into her lap. "Can we please not talk about this right now?" For a moment anger surged through her, but she pushed it aside, drawing in a deep breath. She sent out a quick prayer for trust and that God would turn this into good.

They drove in a heavy silence, and this time Amy didn't seek to dispel it. She wanted to get to church where more people would dilute the atmosphere that was so heavy between her and Tim.

How could he do this to her? Why didn't he tell her? She was sure his parents had talked him into it. And if that was so, why didn't he consult her? She hadn't known he would have preferred to live in Vancouver.

Did she have the devotion she would need to follow him to Vancouver?

She wanted to. She wanted to be a faithful wife and do what was best for him. But could she give up her dreams to help him follow his?

Okay, Lord. You put me in this. I really need You to help me out right now. I need to be at peace with this. Even though I can't, she added to herself as she stared sightlessly out of the window.

Tim pulled into the parking lot of the church and without a

backward glance, Amy stepped out and almost ran up the church steps.

"It is with great joy that we announce the return of Mark and Sheryl Andrews's twin girls from Kamloops Hospital to home." Pastor DeJonge smiled at the congregation. "We thank God that all is well with the babies and that they could finally go home to Sweet Creek. Mark and Sheryl wish to thank the congregation for your prayers." He paused a moment to adjust his glasses as he looked down. "Of course we'd like to continue to remember the Danyluk family as Judd is still in hospital." Pastor DeJonge looked around the congregation. "Are there any other prayer requests?"

Amy swallowed, wishing she could slow her beating heart, wondering if she should ask for what truly lay on her heart. What would Tim say if she asked the congregation to make him change his mind? And was that what she really wanted?

She stole a sideways glance at Tim who looked down at his folded hands. What would he say if she stood up? What would he think about her request?

It shouldn't matter.

She bit her lip, and unbidden, her glance turned sideways to the Hendersons' pew and found herself looking directly into Paul's eyes. For a moment their gaze held, and Amy felt a well-known tingle. When she first stepped into church the sight of his blond head both frightened and thrilled her. He had said he was going to come up this Sunday, and she didn't think he was serious. Until she saw him sitting in the pew. She bit her lip, remembering his phone call.

You know exactly why he's here, Amy. The thought pushed its way through all the other difficulties of her life, all the other sorrows and burdens, and for a brief moment she clung to it.

Then Paul winked at her, and the moment evaporated. What was she thinking about? Amy suddenly stood up.

"My mother..." She faltered and cleared her throat. In her peripheral vision she saw Tim frown. "My mother phoned me a few days ago," she continued, her voice sounding so small, almost lost in the full church. She clung to the pew in front of her and drew another breath. "I'm struggling with forgiveness, and I ask for your prayers." Amy hurriedly sat down, looking neither to the right at Tim nor to the left at Paul. She closed her eyes, folding her icy hands tightly under her chin.

There was a general silence, and then Pastor DeJonge invited them to join him in prayer.

Amy felt a wave of peace softly soothe her ragged thoughts and as she slowly released the tension in her body, she gave her problems to the Lord. His strength washed over her, renewing and strengthening. Thoughts of Noreen, Tim, Judd and especially Paul, and all the emotions that came with them, slowly slipped away.

Thank you Lord, she silently added after the minister said Amen. *Thank you for your peace.*

Slowly she looked up, taking a cleansing breath. They stood for the last song, and when its notes faded away, she felt Tim clutch her elbow.

"Amy." His voice was quiet, his tone admonishing. "Why didn't you tell me your mother phoned?"

Amy turned to look over her shoulder at him, hurt at his intrusion. She found it ironic that he should demand disclosure from her so soon after his own surprising news. "I'm sorry, Tim. You always seem embarrassed when I talk about her." She clutched her handbag tighter, drawing on the peace she had just felt. "I didn't want to bring it up." Given what he had sprung on her in the car on the way up here, she was surprised that he would be chiding her over withholding a much-smaller piece of information than he had.

"But I should know these things before you get up in church and ask for prayer requests." Tim bent over to pick up his Bible and put the song book back into the rack, his words considerate, but his tone chastizing.

Impatience coursed through her. Impatience and a residue of anger at his quick dismissal of her needs. She knew they should talk, but they could hardly have it out here in church. Silently she turned and stepped into the flow of people, head down, unwilling to see if Tim followed.

"Careful, Amy," a deep voice behind her cautioned. She

looked up just in time to prevent herself from bumping into Mrs. Masterson, shuffling along behind her walker.

Amy slowed her pace and risked a backward glance. She saw the broad expanse of Paul's white shirt, slashed vertically by a black tie. Paul shoved his hands in the pockets of his charcoal dress slacks, looking down at her with concern in his deep blue eyes.

"How are you doing?" he asked quietly.

She turned away. Her emotions were still in a turmoil. It didn't help that Paul had come as he'd said he would in his phone call. What if he came up every weekend? What would she do?

It doesn't matter, she reminded herself bitterly. The way things are going you'll be gone in November, anyways.

She bit her lip, wishing she could find a way to graciously slip by Mrs. Masterson, needing to find a quiet place to gather her wits. But the dear, elderly lady chatted amiably to her neighbor who had slowed her pace to match. Short of rudely pushing past, she couldn't get away from Paul as easily as she eluded Tim.

"I saw your dad yesterday. He seemed pretty good." Paul spoke quietly.

Amy nodded, unwilling to get drawn into conversation with Paul. It was all too easy to end up confiding in him, something she should be doing with her fiancé. Always, in the back of her mind, Paul's declaration hovered, preventing any confidences.

"Are you and Tim visiting him today?"

She shook her head, watching Mrs. Masterson's feet drag slowly along the carpet. Amy wished she could escape, but short of pushing past the dear old lady, was stuck answering Paul's quiet questions. "I am, but Tim has to run into Vancouver to make arrangements for the wedding."

"Oh, yes. I almost forgot that's still in the works," he replied, though his gaze communicated just the opposite.

Amy chanced another glance behind her, wishing Tim had come after her. But he had obviously taken her reprimand to heart, and as she looked past Paul, she caught a glimpse of

Tim's brown suit coat just as the doors at the front of the church swung behind him. She looked ahead again, concentrating fiercely on Mrs. Masterson's soft gray hair as it bobbed and weaved in time to her awkward gait, trying to ignore the person directly behind. If she hadn't spoken so sharply to Tim, he might be beside her now.

As if that would have been better, she thought. She didn't know which was worse—Tim and his probing questions or Paul and his probing eyes, which even now, felt as if they burned the back of her head.

She jumped as warm fingers brushed over her neck.

"Take it easy," Paul murmured, "You've a strand of hair caught in your collar. It's been driving me nuts."

"Stop doing that," she whispered fiercely over her shoulder, trying to ignore the tingle that quivered down her back as his fingers lingered. "We're still in church for goodness sakes."

Paul leaned slightly over to catch her eye. "Stop doing what?"

"Oh, don't give me that innocent wide-eyed look, Paul Henderson. You know exactly what I'm talking about." Amy glared straight ahead, her heart pounding just a little too fast, her fingers trembling as she clutched her purse.

"Okay. I'm sorry." His finger slid between her dress and her neck tucking the hair back in again. "There you go. Right as rain."

Amy pressed her lips together. Why wouldn't he just leave her alone?

"Hey, Amy, just teasing." Paul touched her shoulder and she jerked away, her back rigid.

They moved a few painfully slow steps forward, then Paul leaned over and whispered, "I am sorry, Amy. Really."

She only nodded.

"I want you to know I'll be praying for you and your mom," he continued, his voice still soft, intimate.

Amy couldn't keep her anger up. Other than Pastor De-Jonge's sermon, his was the first encouraging voice she had heard today. Her shoulders dropped and her fingers loosened their death grip on her purse as she thought of her mother. How many more questions hadn't that unexpected phone call raised.

"How do you feel about her contacting you?"

Amy hesitated between needing to share her own confusion with Paul, who had known her mother, and feeling that doing so would be disloyal to Tim. Need won out over loyalty. "I don't know, Paul," she admitted. "I have so many things I want to ask her and yet..."

"It must be hard to know what to think."

Amy only nodded, thankful for his understanding.

"If she comes for a visit and needs a place to stay," he continued, "I'm sure Dad and Mom will put her up."

Amy glanced over her shoulder at him, a tremulous smile hovering at the corner of her mouth. "Thanks."

Paul shrugged. "It's not a big deal, Amy."

Maybe not to him. She didn't know how she felt about her mother, but was thankful for Paul's easy acceptance of her mother's contact. He truly was a good friend.

But as she looked ahead, trying to ignore the reality of his presence behind her, she knew that *friend* was a feeble description of what had grown between them. Because each time she saw him, his words sang through her head.

I love you, Amy... I love you, Amy...

The encouragement Paul felt from Amy's confidences waned as soon as he saw Tim waiting directly below him at the bottom of the church steps, one hand resting on the metal handrail, the other shoved in his pocket. He ignored Paul and smiled up at Amy, a faint lift to his eyebrows as if asking for forgiveness. Paul glanced sidelong at Amy. She drew in a deep breath and with her returning smile, seemed to grant it.

Paul tried to ignore the quick lance of jealousy as Amy tripped down the church stairs, reaching out for her fiancé. He tried not to see how the sun danced in her hair, tried not to watch as Tim pulled her closer.

He leaned against the rail, his eyes scanning the chattering group of people gathered below him. Rick stood with Shannon, laughing with a bunch of other young people. Fred and Elizabeth chatted with another couple.

Everywhere he looked, people had gathered in groups. It's what happened on Sunday mornings and any other time the community got together.

Paul looked beyond the crowd, feeling suddenly alone. It shouldn't surprise him that it would take a while before he found his place. The very bonds that formed a community also precluded an immediate belonging.

However, he wasn't the only solitary one. On the edge of the parking lot, staring fixedly at someone in the crowd, stood a woman, isolated and alone. Paul frowned as he tried to place her. He hadn't seen her around, yet she looked familiar. She stepped to one side, as if trying to get a better look, and as Paul followed the direction of her gaze, it came to him with stunning clarity who she was.

Noreen.

She looked straight at Amy.

Amy hadn't seen her yet. She stood with her back to the lot, talking earnestly to Tim, as always, and Tim was frowning, as always.

Paul didn't think Amy would mind a little interruption.

He stepped down and touched her shoulder lightly. Amy turned, then stopped when she saw him.

"What can we do for you, Paul?" Tim didn't try to hide his peevish tone.

Paul ignored him and leaned closer to Amy. "I think your mother is here," he whispered.

Amy straightened, glancing first at Tim, fear in her eyes, then up at Paul. "Really? Here? Tell me where?"

"On the edge of the parking lot."

"Who is? What are you two talking about?" Tim demanded.

"My mother," Amy whispered, pressing her fingers against her mouth, the other hand blindly reaching out towards Tim.

Tim turned around, trying to find Noreen Danyluk, missing the appeal in Amy's eyes and her outstretched hand.

But Paul didn't.

He caught her icy hand in his own, squeezing it in encouragement. "You don't have to talk to her if you don't want to, Amy."

Tim turned around, his eyes narrowing at the sight of Amy clinging to Paul. He caught Amy's elbow, pulling her close to him. "And I'll thank you to keep your hands to yourself," he warned Paul.

Paul relinquished his hold on Amy, frustrated with Tim's obtuseness and jealousy. Amy needed support and help. After ten silent years, her mother stood forty feet away from Amy, and all Tim could think of were his so-called rights.

Amy seemed unaware of Tim and his little games, her hands twisting around each other, her face mirroring her anxiety. She took a step toward Noreen, then hesitated.

"It's okay Amy," Paul said quietly, ignoring Tim. "All you have to do is go to her and say hello."

"I don't know if I can. It's been so long."

"Amy, I think we'd better go." Still unaware of what was happening, Tim tugged on Amy's arm, and with an uncharacteristic display of independence, Amy jerked her arm back.

"Don't pressure me, Tim."

Paul felt like dragging Amy away from her fearful fiancé, toward Noreen. But if he did that, he realized, he would be no better than Tim. Amy had to decide for herself.

Paul laid a gentle hand on her shoulder "It's been ten years. Maybe 'hello' is the best place to start," he said, his voice quiet, encouraging.

Almost unconsciously Amy's free hand slipped up to cover his, and for a moment their fingers intertwined. Paul gently squeezed and then let go. "No matter what has happened, she's still your mother."

Amy pushed her hands into the pocket of her coat and clenched them. Drawing in a deep breath as if making a decision, she started walking.

"Amy, wait," Tim called out, following her. She ignored him, and Paul began to pray in earnest.

Chapter Twelve

A gust of wind tossed Amy's hair across her face, and as she reached up to brush it away, she caught her mother's gaze. That sudden contact made Amy feel as if someone had pulled all the air out of her.

She stared at the elegantly dressed woman who had left her, her brother and her father all those years ago. The face was familiar and yet not. The hair was grayer, fashionably cut, wrinkles fanned out from eyes as brown as ever. Her mouth had acquired a hardness, her cheeks a hollowness. Her eyes seemed to devour Amy's, to draw Amy to herself.

They both stood unmoving, waiting, looking, until finally Noreen allowed the ghost of a smile to creep across her mouth. She drew her long raincoat about her and slowly turned away.

Amy blinked as if coming out of a trance. Her mother. The figure on the parking lot was her mother, and she was leaving.

Memories drifted out of a place she had kept locked and silent, like light intruding through the cracks beneath a door. Pictures, sounds, words, feelings, all mingling and overloading until she had to see her close-up, to touch Noreen to make sure she was real.

"Mother," Amy called out. "Wait. Please wait."

Noreen continued walking past the cars. The wind that caught Amy's hair must have blown away her words, as well.

Should she follow, Amy wondered? Should she try to connect with a person who hadn't been a part of their life for so long?

She's my mother.

Amy took a step, then another. Finally she was running, each step precarious in ankles unaccustomed to high heels.

Noreen was already in her car, reaching out for the door handle to shut the door. Amy shoved her hand against the door, holding it open.

Breathless from more than just the chase, her heart pounding in her chest, Amy stared at the person she had dreamed would someday return.

Her face was familiar and not. It was as if someone had taken the picture Amy kept in her bedside table and smudged it, loosening the features in some places and pulling them in others. Noreen half turned, swung her legs out and put her feet on the ground, as if to get out of the car again.

"Hello, Amy." Noreen looked up as she spoke those two words, and in them Amy heard entreaty and fear.

Amy hung on to the door, a sob gathering in the back of her throat. This was her mother. No matter what Noreen had done, for this brief and shining moment the woman Amy had cried out for in the night, had prayed would come back, was here. In person. Not a dream, not a figment of her imagination.

Amy slowly knelt, slipped her arms around her mother's waist, laid her head on her mother's lap.

She remembered the loneliness of ten years with no female voice to greet her at the end of the day. She remembered the frustrations of growing up without a mother to guide her.

Noreen stroked her hair. "Oh, honey. Oh, Amy, I just wanted a look... I didn't think you would want to...talk to me," she murmured, her fingers tangling themselves in Amy's hair, her voice breaking.

Amy closed her eyes, inhaling the scent of unfamiliar perfume, feeling hands holding her that were known and yet unknown.

My mother, she thought, taking a deep breath.

Amy wished the world could stop, wished this pure moment could last. But as she pulled away, looking once again at Noreen, she knew that couldn't happen. The past years would drift in as sure as would the reality of kneeling on the hard pavement.

Amy straightened, rubbing her knees, staring in dismay at yet another pair of ruined panty hose. "Still a tomboy, Mom," she said with a shaky laugh.

Noreen bent her head as she wiped her eyes. Clutching the tissue, she glanced at Amy's knees then up into her daughter's face. She shook her head and reached out to stroke Amy's arm.

"My dear girl." She faltered.

"Can I have one of those?" Amy asked, indicating the tissue packet.

Noreen looked up. Rick stood beside the car, hands shoved in his pockets, his expression uncertain. Amy stepped aside, gesturing toward Noreen with a discreet movement of her head.

Rick came forward and Noreen got out of the car. Her mouth trembled as she was faced with her other child. Rick, however, only nodded toward her. "Hi," was all he said.

"Hello, Rick." Noreen had lifted a hand, but as Rick kept his distance, she lowered it again.

"So...?" Rick's hands jingled the change in his pocket. A slight trembling of his lips betrayed his own inner turmoil. "Why did you come back?"

"I just wanted to see you."

"After ten years?"

"I know." Noreen looked down at the tissue she twisted around in her delicate fingers.

With that admission Rick seemed to sag against the car. His belligerence left as his expression became that of a young confused boy.

"Why did you leave, Mom? What did we do?"

Noreen took a shaky breath as if to speak, then firmly closed her mouth.

In spite of her own conflicting memories, Amy felt a sudden burst of pity for her mother. She could see pain and anguish clearly etched on her face. But Amy didn't know where to go from here, either.

"Noreen, how are you?" Elizabeth Henderson interrupted the tableaux, offering reprieve from the tension that enveloped the trio. Amy moved aside. Elizabeth smiled down at her old neighbor. "Glad you came."

Amy wiped her nose, listening to Elizabeth ask a few questions, chatting to Noreen as if she'd been gone only a few days instead of ten years. As she watched them, Amy let her breath out in a careful sigh.

She looked past Elizabeth and Noreen to where Rick stood. He still leaned against the car. Shannon had come up beside him. She threaded her arm through his, talking to him in quiet, reassuring tones.

She felt a quick stab of jealousy at Shannon's support. Tim still stood at the bottom of the church stairs, watching them. She couldn't read his expression from this far away. She didn't know if she wanted to and turned away.

"Why don't you all come over for dinner?" Elizabeth asked suddenly, her invitation encompassing the small group gathered around the car. "Rick, Shannon, you'll come, too?"

"Sure we will. Thanks Mrs. Henderson," Shannon offered. Rick shot her a thunderous glance, but she held his gaze, smiling sweetly back.

"Noreen?"

"I couldn't..."

"Please?" Elizabeth laid her hand on Noreen's shoulder. "It won't be anything special. But we'd like to have you. We've a lot of catching up to do."

"Hello, Noreen."

The deep voice over her shoulder caught Amy's heart in a tight fist. She didn't need to look behind her to know how close Paul stood to her. Too close. Yet for a moment she felt a yearning for his comfort. She almost leaned back against him, almost reached out for him, knowing he would give her what she needed.

As he reached past her to shake Noreen's hand, Amy stepped aside. Paul winked at Amy and stepped around her. He dropped one hip against the car, his head bent as he talked to Amy's mother. Amy could not help but envy the ease with which he renewed an old acquaintance. He asked questions and laughed. All Amy could do was watch, unsure of how she should feel.

Out of the corner of her eye she saw Tim walk toward the group, and she tensed.

When he stopped beside her, Amy looked at him, then her mother. "Mother, I'd like you to meet Tim Enders. My fiancé. Tim, this is my mother, Noreen."

Noreen smiled at him and reached out to shake his hand. Tim hesitated, but then took it. "Hello, Noreen," he said, his smile stiff.

"Elizabeth has invited us for lunch, Tim." She fingered the strap of her purse as she spoke, a light quaver in her voice. "I'd like to go."

Tim looked at Noreen, up at Paul then back at Amy, his expression unreadable. He gave a curt nod and reached out for Amy's hand.

Amy put her hand in his, then glanced back at Noreen. "Will we see you at Hendersons', Mother?"

Noreen looked around, then with a slow nod of her head, assented.

Amy gave her soup another stir, listening to the hesitantly spoken conversation around the Hendersons' dinner table. Elizabeth and Fred brought up old stories as they reminisced with Noreen. They seemed careful with Judd's name and anything associated with him as they sought exactly the right words to bridge a space of ten years.

Shannon asked questions about Noreen's job, expressing interest in the travel magazine she worked for. Paul brought up names of restaurants they had both frequented—Bishop's, The Cannery, with its excellent wine and seafood selection. Slowly they drew Noreen out, asking questions about her work and her life. Amy contributed an occasional comment, content to listen to her mother's familiar voice, awash in memories.

Tim and Rick were both quiet.

"How are the wedding plans coming?" Elizabeth turned to Tim to gently draw him into the conversation.

"I still have to get my future wife to decide on a dress." Tim took a sip of water and glanced at Amy.

"You'll have to do that soon. If you don't, Amy will be just as glad to get married in jeans and cowboy boots," Fred said with a grin.

"I wouldn't put it past her," Tim replied above the polite laughter.

"And are you planning any work on the house?" Elizabeth asked. "I know Amy wanted to do some renovating before you move in."

Amy's heart gave a mighty thump, and she shot Tim a warning glance, but he only shrugged.

"We haven't decided on where we're going to live yet."

A strained silence descended, and Amy swallowed down a lump that had gathered in her throat.

"Actually my parents have given me a down payment on a house," Tim continued.

"How does that affect the ranch?" Fred asked.

"It will be up to Judd, but I'm going to advise him to put it up for sale."

Amy bit her lip at his bald statement, developing a sudden interest in the noodle her spoon had been chasing around her bowl. She felt manipulated, as if Tim deliberately provoked her to make a decision. And mentioning his parents' contribution put another load of guilt on her shoulders.

"Have you talked to your father about this?" Fred turned to Amy.

"We've discussed it briefly." Amy caught the noodle, but couldn't put it in her mouth. She knew she wouldn't be able to swallow it.

"Where will you live if not at the ranch?" Elizabeth put in.

Amy shot Tim another warning glance, but he didn't, or wouldn't, catch her eye. "My parents have been looking around for us," he said. "In Vancouver."

"Well—" Fred nodded, a note of uncertainty in his voice "—I'm sure you'll be very happy—wherever."

Amy swallowed, and Tim finally met her gaze. His smile was diffident, but Amy would not be assured. She looked away, directly into Paul's questioning eyes.

She held his gaze a moment as if to say, What's your problem? then returned her attention to her soup.

The rest of the lunch conversation stumbled along, desultory, strained. Amy said a silent prayer of thanks when Paul got up for the Bible and said the closing devotions after dessert.

After the Amen, Amy jumped up to clear the dishes and food from the table. She knew Elizabeth and Fred always sat around the table for a while after devotions. This was their time to chat, to share and enjoy being together.

But today Amy was weary of trying to smile and pretend. She wanted the meal to end. Shannon and Noreen helped. After a few moments Elizabeth joined them. Fred asked Rick a question about his work. Tim got up to get his coat. Paul lounged in his chair, staring at Amy.

His steady gaze unsettled her, so she ignored him, gathering up the plates with the leftover cold cuts, cheese and buns.

"That was a great lunch Elizabeth," Tim said as he pushed his chair under the table. "Amy, if you want to visit your dad yet, we should go."

Amy didn't reply and took the plates into the kitchen. Elizabeth caught her arm as she marched back toward the dining room for another load.

"Just go on ahead, Amy," she said kindly. Her blue eyes looked up with understanding. "You go and visit your dad. We'll clean up here."

Amy stopped and suddenly reached over and gave Elizabeth a hug. "Thanks so much," she murmured into her ear. "For having Mom here, and us."

She straightened, drawing in a quick breath. As she walked through the dining room, she bent down and gave Fred a quick kiss on his cheek. She waved goodbye to Rick and Shannon and couldn't resist a quick glance at Paul. He still sat at the table, chair pushed back, tie loosened, cuffs rolled up, his unwavering gaze on her.

As she looked, an expression of unspeakable longing came

over his features. She paused, their gazes locked. Slowly, hesitantly, something deep within her unfolded at the entreaty in his eyes. An answering urge deep within her responded, pulling her near. When he got up, she realized she had unconsciously taken a step toward him.

She took a steadying breath, her heart pounding.

The pain and desire on Paul's face told her more than any words he could have spoken. This was not the face of a man intent only on a conquest. This was the look of a man in love.

But it couldn't be returned.

Amy avoided looking at Tim, who waited by the door. She couldn't face him right now.

Instead, she turned to her mother. There were many things she wanted to tell this familiar stranger, many questions she wanted to ask. But Tim hovered, and every moment she spent with her mother made her feel as if she had chosen against her father.

"Will I see you again, Mom?" she asked. It was a difficult question to ask. But she had to ask, had to go through some semblance of the normal give-and-take of rebuilding relationships. For in spite of the past, her mother's reappearance filled a void in her life.

Noreen tilted her head to one side as she reached out to gently stroke Amy's arm. "I'd like that."

Amy bit her lip and forged on. "Are you going to see Dad?"

Noreen shook her head gently. "I can't. Not yet. I didn't even think I'd have this much time with you and Rick. I'll see him sometime."

Amy nodded. "How long are you staying here?"

"I have to get back to Vancouver tonight." Noreen smiled, then touched her daughter's cheek. "Thank you," she said softly. "You don't know how it felt to be able to hold you once again."

Tears pricked Amy's eyes. A few quick blinks and they were gone. "I guess I should say goodbye," Amy returned, regret tingeing her voice.

"We'll leave you two alone." Fred regarded the other occupants of the room as he stood. Rick took the hint and left without a backward glance. Shannon threw a wink over her shoulder at Amy as she followed.

Tim hesitated, and Amy looked at him, a silent plea in her glance. He turned and left.

Paul stayed sitting until Tim closed the door, then got up. He stopped in front of Amy's mother. "Glad to see you here, Noreen." He turned to Amy. "And I'll be seeing you around, Punky." Without any warning he leaned down. His warm lips grazed her cheek. His hand stroked her shoulder. When he left, the sound of the door closing behind him pierced Amy's heart.

Elizabeth clucked in dismay. "Don't you mind him. Paul can't seem to make up his mind lately."

"That's not new." Amy took a shaky breath, trying to re-assure herself as much as agree with Elizabeth. She rubbed her arms, then turned to Elizabeth. "Thanks again for lunch, Mom."

"You're welcome," Elizabeth said with a slight frown, tilt-ing her head discreetly in Noreen's direction. As Elizabeth turned to leave, Amy realized what she had done.

Addressing Elizabeth as Mom came so naturally to Amy she often didn't realize it until someone else pointed it out. But now, with her own mother in front of her, Amy heard it through Noreen's ears and felt a sadness engulf her.

Noreen bit her lip, looking away. "I really had no right to come back, did I?" she asked, pain obvious in her soft voice.

Amy was unsure of what to say.

"Well..." Noreen lifted her hands, and for a moment they hovered. She repressed a light sob, Amy stepped forward and was enclosed by her mother's arms. "Oh, honey. None of this was supposed to happen. After I talked to you on the phone, I wanted so badly to get a look at you and Rick. Just a look, and I was going to leave." Noreen murmured against Amy's hair.

Amy closed her eyes, trying not to think of ten lost years and her own sorrow. Instead, she thought of the pain so clearly etched on Noreen's face, the loss she had suffered.

A verse from II Corinthians came to mind. "You ought to forgive and comfort him so he will not be overcome by exces-sive sorrow." Except in this case *him* became *her*. God's forgiveness blanketed so many of her own sins, how could she withhold one iota of forgiveness from her mother, who carried her own burdens?

Amy drew back, taking in her mother's features, changed by time, yet so familiar. "I'm glad you came back, Mom."

A quiet descended as each took in the changes in the other, regret and questions hovering.

"Are you sure you don't want to see Dad?" Amy asked, wondering again how her father would react to the sight of his wayward wife.

"I would like to...but I'm afraid."

"He's been asking the congregation to pray for you the past few months," Amy blurted out.

Noreen shook her head, her look wistful. "That's good."

The comment puzzled Amy and she wanted to ask more.

"So Tim's the one?" her mother said briskly, changing the subject. "He seems like a decent fellow."

Amy nodded. Listening to her mother sing his praises was difficult after what he had told her this morning.

"He must be quite something if you're willing to leave the ranch and live in a city." Noreen smiled taking in Amy's clothes. "He must have quite an influence on you. I never thought I'd see you give up your blue jeans for a dress. Nor your oath of undying love for Paul."

Noreen's casual mention of Amy's childhood promise brought a flush to her cheeks that seemed to deny her next words. "I'm a big girl now."

"He still calls you Punky."

"Paul's been gone for a while himself. He's forgotten that things change."

"I suppose," Noreen replied, her voice wistful. "I know this is awkward, Amy. So much has happened. I've missed so much..." Noreen's hand waved in the direction of Amy's, clenched together, the engagement ring winking brightly. "But I really want to thank you for coming to the car earlier." Her voice caught. "It meant so much to me."

Amy looked at her, trying to sort out her own feelings—

sympathy, anger, fear, distrust. Her own memories—kisses, hugs...love.

"I've got to go," Amy said, aware that Tim waited outside. She hesitated, then reached out and hugged her mother once more. "When will I see you again?"

Noreen stroked her cheek, her expression pensive. "Whenever you want."

Amy smiled, took a step back, then left the house. Her step faltered, however, when she saw Paul leaning against Tim's car, his arms crossed over his chest. Paul looked up as she approached and stepped away from the car.

Amy took a breath, willing her heart to stop its renegade beating at the sight of him. His light kiss still lay warm on her cheek. Would she have to go through this each time she saw him? If so, it was better that she and Tim move away.

Paul frowned, and Tim stared straight ahead. Amy could tell from Tim's strained expression that he and Paul had had a weighty discussion.

"I'm sure we'll talk again," Paul said to Tim. Paul's expression was enigmatic as he gave Amy a curt nod, totally at odds with his behavior only moments ago.

Amy ignored him and got into the car.

Tim reversed, put the gearshift in Drive and left. They drove in silence, the hum of the car's engine and the pinging of rocks against the undercarriage the only noise in the car. His anger was palpable. His knuckles were white. His jaw clenched.

"What's the matter, Tim?"

"Nothing." His curt reply tempted Amy to just let things be and not delve deeper. But they were to be married in a couple of months and she didn't want to start that lifelong, difficult trip with anything between them. They needed to talk, and not just about Noreen.

"Something is wrong, Tim." She reached over, touching his hand with its white-knuckled grip on the steering wheel.

Tim clenched his jaw, then finally blurted out. "I wish you'd tell your old boyfriend to stay out of our business."

"He's not my old boyfriend."

"That doesn't seem to stop him from giving me advice."

Amy looked at him, puzzled. "Advice?"

"Told me that Noreen is my future mother-in-law, then he told me I was rude to her."

"Well, you could have said something if only 'pass the bread.'"

"Don't *you* start, Amy. I don't know her from Adam. Then she shows up and suddenly she's 'Mom' and we're having a warm family meal with her."

Amy paused, choosing her words carefully. "As I recall, Jesus did the same thing—sinners and tax collectors and all that."

"That's different." Tim shook his head. "I've heard what she put you, your father and Rick through." Tim glanced at her, his expression pained. "Your father's health is poor. He's in the hospital..."

"That's not her fault."

"You weren't talking that way a few months ago. At that time you didn't want to talk about your mother. Now she shows up and all is forgiven. She's not even going to visit him."

She looked back at Tim, realizing there was more to her mother's return that upset him. She heard his words but wanted to understand the unspoken meaning beneath them.

"Why does my mother make you afraid, Tim?"

He glanced at her, then hit the brakes, a cloud of dust and gravel roiling in their wake. He put the gearshift in Park and turned to her.

"I'm afraid that if you can change your mind that quickly about your mother, you can change your mind just as quickly about me." He caught her hands in his own, squeezing them. "I love you, Amy. I don't want to lose you."

His clean-shaven cheeks were warm against her cool fingers, his dark eyes fixed on hers.

"I love you, too, Tim." She let him hold her hands awhile longer before pulling them back. She had hoped to talk about moving to Vancouver and instead ended up getting sidetracked into a conversation about her mother. But now, as she watched him, she felt taken aback at the intensity of his expression and his open insecurity. He's unsure of himself, she thought, surprised. "I love you a lot."

"Really?" Tim laughed, a harsh sound. "Then why were you so entranced with Paul back there?"

He saw, thought Amy, pierced with guilt. She could say nothing in her defense.

"You say you love me, Amy, but I'm wondering how constant that love is. Your mother shows up, and all is forgiven. Paul comes back, and you can't keep your eyes off him."

His words frightened as they burrowed and took root. Was he right? She wore his ring on her finger, yet a glance from Paul had the power to make her heart beat faster. She was on her way to visit her father, yet she'd just had dinner with the mother who had been unfaithful, a mother who hadn't contacted any of them in ten years. Was she that fickle, that unfaithful?

This is so hard, Lord, she prayed, looking away from Tim's angry eyes. *I love Tim, I do. I love my father. Is it wrong to want to see my mother again?*

"I can't say anything else except to assure you that I love you." And she did. She knew that. She tried to tamp down the confusion that coursed through her as she tried to explain her feelings toward her mother. It seemed that somehow the same accusations she had thrown at herself were also interwoven through Tim's mind. "I've struggled most of my life with what my mother's done to us. But I've also missed having her around." She paused for the right words, knowing that Tim needed to understand if they were going to build a relationship of trust. "I want to have my own mother to share things with. I missed her."

Tim said nothing as he seemed to ponder her words. "I'm sorry, Amy," he smiled apologetically. "You're right. I haven't been fair to you or your mother. Mark it down to pre-wedding jitters, I guess," he said with a short laugh, putting the car into gear and pressing on the accelerator.

Amy blew out a sigh as the tension that held them in its tight grip loosened.

She glanced at Tim, trying to analyze her love. Just a moment ago she saw a side of him she hadn't seen yet. Only this morning he had sprung the move to Vancouver on her. They needed to talk about the move, something she thought of as being far more important to clear up than her relationship with her mother.

But now that peace reigned, she didn't want to bring it up.

As they drove, Tim relaxed, becoming the man she was going to marry, not the unforgiving, unsure stranger she had glimpsed a few moments ago. But she knew she wouldn't forget the part of him he had just shown her.

At the hospital they woke Judd from his nap. He was in good spirits and chatted about inconsequential things—the weather, the hay crop, their wedding plans.

"One more day, the doctor figures, then I'll be out of here," he said, displaying more enthusiasm than he had in a while.

"That's great, Dad. The house is so empty without you." Amy plumped his pillow and pulled a chair closer.

"Just turn on the television," Judd replied. "It will seem like I'm still there. How has your day been?" Judd asked.

"Good." The meaningless word couldn't begin to cover what had happened, as Amy's mind tripped over the events of the past few hours. Her awareness of Paul's presence, Noreen's sudden appearance, Tim's anger. She knew she had to tell Judd about his wife, however. She looked at him and caught his hand, as if to help him. "Remember I told you the other day that Mom phoned? She came today."

Judd sank back against his pillows as a soft smile slipped across his wan features. "When?"

"She showed up after church this morning. We had lunch at Hendersons'."

Judd nodded, his eyes shut. "That's good."

His words were spoken softly, fervently, and Amy felt taken aback at his casual acceptance of something that a few years earlier would have almost given him a stroke. He caught her hand, squeezing it as he turned his head to look at her. "Will you pray for me, Amy?" he added.

"I always do." She frowned, puzzled at his reactions. "Anything specific?"

He nodded. "That Noreen will forgive me."

Chapter Thirteen

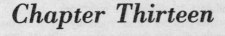

Amy dropped her father's hand and sat back, trying to assimilate her father's words with her own emotions toward her mother. "What do you mean, forgive you?" What was there to forgive? she wondered. It was her mother who had left, not the other way around.

Judd looked away, folding his hands over his stomach, tapping his fingers in agitation against each other. "I don't want to talk about it now," he said, his voice taking on his usual gruff tone. He looked at Tim. "So how's the banking business been?"

"Busy," Tim replied, leaning forward, relief tingeing his voice. Amy guessed he didn't want to talk about Noreen, either. "There's been a number of land deals lately that needed financing..." Tim shrugged. "The usual boring, banker-type stuff."

"How many you turn down?" Judd asked.

Amy rolled her eyes as Tim neatly deflected his question. Her father was always trying to find out who was buying, who was selling and for how much. But Tim never got intimidated by her father's bluntness and always managed to turn away Judd's curiosity with a few carefully chosen words.

"Land prices going up?" Judd continued, trying to find another angle.

"Actually they are. It's a seller's market right now."

Judd directed a triumphant look towards Amy. "There you go, Amy. That's how you can make some money off that ranch."

Amy frowned.

"What do you mean, Judd?" Tim asked.

"I've been wondering if we shouldn't get rid of the ranch," Judd continued. "I think it's a good idea."

Amy stared past her father, suddenly angry. So that's where he was leading the last time she came to visit. His careful questions about living on the ranch and how much work it was for her.

Tim shot a surprised look first at Amy, then at Judd. "Are you serious?"

"It's up to Amy, of course," said Judd. "She does most of the work, but now with me sick and Rick gone, I don't think it's fair of me to expect her to keep working it."

"I think selling it would be the best solution," Tim said reasonably.

Amy stood and ignored them both. This was all she needed. Both her father and Tim aligned in the same camp. She looked sightlessly out of the window. You're moving to Vancouver, what difference does it make. The thought settled deep within her, disquieting and fearful.

She leaned her forehead against the cool window and wished she could stop thinking, planning and trying to make things fit that just wouldn't. All she wanted was...

Amy's heart thumped in fear. All she wanted was...

She couldn't complete the thought.

Things that had seemed relatively tidy a month ago were now all mixed-up. It reminded her of a wagon of blocks she had received as a child. When the blocks were taken out, they could only be put back in a certain pattern, otherwise they wouldn't all fit.

Her life had been dumped out, and she didn't know how to put it together again.

"Amy?" Her father's voice pulled her back to the present and the persistent problem of what to do. "Are you okay?"

She gave herself a shake. "Yes," she said softly. "I'm fine."

"I really think you should sell the ranch, Amy," Tim continued, his voice calm and reasonable. "I'm not only talking as your fiancé here, I'm also talking as your banker."

Tim tried to catch Amy's eye, but she couldn't look at him right now. She didn't want to hear his logical arguments, didn't want to hear sensible solutions. It was all too quick and easy for him.

"I know it's not what you want, Amy," Tim continued, reaching out for her hand. "I know you love living out there. I've always known that, even though you seem to think that I haven't understood that. But I have." He stroked her fingers, looking down at the ring that sparkled back at them both. "I didn't always give you the encouragement you wanted, but don't you see?" He looked up at her then, touching her cheek lightly with one finger. "I couldn't. And as your banker I still can't. We have other plans now, other dreams."

Amy let Tim's soft, reasonable voice wash over her, and she gained some measure of comfort from his words. He *did* understand her. Amy only nodded, her eyes on the polished floor, on the toes of her cream-colored shoes. She let him convince her that he cared, that he had her best interests at heart.

But we're still moving to Vancouver, she couldn't help but think. And you had that all planned. "So what's the best thing for me to do?" she asked, looking directly at him. She wasn't going to say it and put an end to her own hopes. She didn't want to speak the words aloud.

"As things stand right now, the ranch could keep operating if you were to rent it out. However, with the loans you've got against it and the money you still have to put out, it's going to be too close to the bone, and renting it out won't give you enough money to cover everything and realize any kind of income for yourself." Tim dropped her hand and sat back. "The only way it can keep going is if you stay there." He shrugged, avoiding her eyes. "Rick isn't there anymore, Judd just recommended that you sell it and—" he hesitated, then looked her straight in the eye "—you and I won't be living there. I would suggest that the sooner you put it up for sale, the better."

Amy released her breath, praying for peace, patience, anything to stop the chill his words laid on her heart.

She had fought against it and twisted and turned, but her life was headed in this direction. There was no way around it.

If she wanted to be married to Tim.

Amy rolled slowly over and blinked at the clock beside her bed. It read 5:00 a.m. She smiled as she gathered the blankets around her, relishing one more hour of sleep.

She needed it. Monday had been busy. At Tim's urging she had gone into town to list the ranch. She had paused in front of the real estate office, frowned, then had written up her own advertisement. She'd pinned it alongside all the other "Real Estate for Sale" postings on the huge bulletin board in the grocery store. A real estate agent would just take an eight-percent cut anyhow, she reasoned, looking over the mobile homes, houses and parcels of land posted by people who felt the same way she did.

Tim had been only too willing to give her a figure that he said was nonnegotiable, and Amy put a few more thousand on top of it as insurance. She knew even better than he did what the value of their land was, anyhow. She had worked it most of her life, had fenced it, had hayed and fertilized it. If anyone knew how much money had gone into it, she did.

She had stopped in to see her father. He asked her if she had put the ranch up for sale. Thankfully she could tell him, yes.

She could give the same answer to Tim when she met him in town.

Once home, she spent the rest of the afternoon getting the baler ready. It made a paltry two rounds around the field, then quit. She dragged it to the yard and called Rick. He said he would take home the parts she needed, and work on it tonight. Then he phoned later to say that he had an emergency up in Likely that he had to work on.

Amy took a stab at fixing it, literally. She ended up with grazed knuckles and parts scattered all over the garage as a result. At 11:00 p.m. she gave up, showered and had fallen into bed only to end up tossing and turning, thoughts of her father and mother and Tim and the ranch chasing themselves in circles as she tried to neatly categorize feelings and emotions.

She couldn't do it.

From a shadowy figure whose features had been dim for most of her life, Noreen had become real and solid and had raised in Amy feelings of love and caring—emotions she didn't think she would ever have toward her mother.

Emotions that, pure as they may be, made her feel as if she betrayed her father.

Betrayal seemed like a constant companion now, thought Amy, turning over once again, frowning up at the ceiling now lit by the early-morning sun. Betrayal hovered around her every time she saw Paul, every time she was with Tim.

She questioned Tim's advice to her and when she had put that notice up on the bulletin board, she'd felt as if she betrayed the ranch. Her brother didn't want it. Her father didn't. Tim didn't. Even her mother hadn't.

Which brought her back to Noreen and her father's cryptic request that she would forgive him. What did she have to forgive him for? What had happened?

With a disgusted sigh, Amy threw back the covers and sat up, pushing her tangled hair back from her face. She needed to keep her body busy so her mind would have something else to think about.

A quick shower chased the remainders of sleep from her body and mind. On her way through the living room, she paused at her father's recliner.

She missed him. He had never been much help since she'd started doing more of the work. She had always thought her labors and encouragement would inspire him to keep going. But it wasn't enough. She always knew, deep down, that she had wanted the ranch for herself, but she had also hoped her love for the land and the work would be absorbed by those around her. It hadn't worked that way.

She dropped in the chair, pulling her father's Bible off the table and letting it fall open. Her devotions of late had been

quick and hurried. Too often she rattled through them, hoping
for some kind of instant inspiration. She filtered what she read,
taking what she needed and ignoring what she didn't think
applied.

Now she stopped at Psalm 20. ''May the Lord answer you
when you are in distress...'' Well that certainly applied. ''May
he send you help from the sanctuary...'' She could use all kinds
of help right now. ''May he give you the desire of your heart
and make all your plans succeed.'' Amy placed a finger on that
verse, rereading the words, trying to let them become a part of
her.

Trouble was, she no longer knew what the desires of her
heart were.

She wanted the ranch. She was attracted to Paul.

The ranch was for sale, she and Tim were planning their
wedding and further than that, she didn't want to think or plan.

She dropped her head against the back of the recliner, closing
her eyes as the words of the Psalm filtered through her mind.

Trust in the Lord.

Let go.

She closed her eyes as her mind drifted over her needs, lifting each one of them to the Lord.

Trust, trust, trust. She knew she failed each day. She loved
Tim, but the thought of moving to concrete and stone and leaving the soft hills and trees and open spaces of her home was
too painful to contemplate.

A shrill ring shattered her thoughts and propelled her out of
the chair. The phone.

A quick glance at the clock on the wall made her frown in
puzzlement. It was too early for someone to call.

That must mean...

The hospital.

Amy leaped off her chair and ran into the kitchen, grabbing
the phone off the hook. She fumbled in her haste, almost
dropped it, recovered and caught it with both hands.

''Hello.'' Her tone was abrupt, her voice breathless.

''Amy Danyluk?''

''Yes.'' Please don't be a doctor. Please let my father be all right. She clutched the phone with one hand, her chest with the other.

"Chester Drozd. Sorry to call you so early in the morning, but I was scared to waste any time. I saw your ad on the bulletin board. The one putting your place up for sale. Is it sold yet?"

Amy leaned back against the kitchen cupboard, her hands suddenly clammy both with reaction and a new fear. "No, it isn't." Her mind struggled with the name, familiar to her.

"I don't know if you know me. We have a place up by Lac La Hache."

Amy finally placed him. "Yes, I remember you." She sucked in a deep breath as her mind realigned itself. She didn't know what was worse. The hospital phoning or this.

"Well, then, I guess you know why I'm calling." He paused a moment to let the reality of it all sink in. "I'm interested in having a look at your ranch. I think it could be a perfect place for one of my boys."

Amy listened, each word falling like a piece of lead into her heart, weighing it down with a heavy sadness. So soon, she thought.

When she had composed the ad, she tried to be fair, but deep in her heart she hoped no one would want to purchase the ranch. She had tried to look at it dispassionately. She knew its faults. The house needed some work. The corrals needed some more. As a matter of fact everything needed some work. She had consoled herself with the notion that no one would want to buy it.

But the voice on the other end of the phone quickly dispelled the one hope she clung to.

"I'd like to come and have a look at it," Chester continued. "It will take me about three quarters of an hour to get there. I can be there around two."

"Today?" Amy asked, almost breathless with the speed with which things were moving.

"If that's okay."

"Sure." It was why she had put the ad up on the bulletin board.

"I'm glad you decided to list it on your own. No sense

dealing with a real estate agent if you don't have to," Chester continued. "Well, I guess I'll talk to you more in a while. See you then." He hung up the phone with a decisive click.

Amy stood, motionless, pressing the receiver of the phone against her chest, as if trying to absorb the reality of what had just happened. For a moment she wished she *had* gone through a real estate agent. It would have taken at least a week before it was even listed. Now, this afternoon, a potential buyer was coming to look at the place.

He might not like it, she thought. He might decide that there's not enough here for his son, that it will all be too much work.

But when Chester arrived with his two sons, Amy could see from the eagerness on his face that here was a man who looked like he had made his decision even before he had seen the place.

He stepped out of the truck and looked around, a grin stretched across his wide face. "Been looking around for a place up in this area for a while," he said as he shook her hand. He put his hands on his hips and looked around with a satisfied smile. His denim shirt strained across his barrel chest. "Buying this place is like getting a toehold in the valley," he continued. "Don't you think that'd be a good idea boys?"

He tilted his chin toward his sons, one a carbon copy of his own short girth, the other taller, but also heavy set. They nodded, grinning at Amy, but said nothing. They didn't have to. Chester said it all.

"The way I figure, boys, some of the ranches around here will be coming up in a few years—Kincaids', Hendersons'." Chester looked back at Amy and grinned. "This place is going to do us just fine."

Sold even before he's seen it, thought Amy ruefully.

"So, can I have a look around?"

"Sure," Amy took a deep breath, readying herself.

"Fine." Chester nodded to his sons. "Let's go."

And go they did, thought Amy as she hurried to keep up with him. In the space of twenty minutes they marched around the corrals, zipped through the barn and checked out the hay sheds. Despite Chester's short legs, Amy almost ran to keep up with him and his sons. While they made the whirlwind tour, he snapped off a few questions about the pasture, the hay crop and, of course, the price.

His easy acceptance of her answers made it easy to be dispassionate about the ranch's flaws. Not that Amy could have hidden much from him. Chester noticed every broken board, every missing piece of fence. He even made a quick diagnosis on the baler still scattered in pieces in the garage.

"The barn is solid, but it needs some repairs," she said trying to keep the note of apology out of her voice as she heaved open the heavy door. It needs more than some work, she thought ruefully, seeing it through a buyer's eyes. It needs to be knocked down and replaced with a new structure. "There's a few calving pens in the lean-to. I just put those in a while ago," she gestured to the pens that stood ready. "I've got some heifers that we bought that will be calving in a couple of weeks. The stock isn't included in the price, however, neither is the machinery. The price is just for the land, buildings and the house."

"Fine by me. I've never particularly cared for fall calvers. Use a lot of feed over the winter with them," mused Chester as he noted the pens. He tilted his head to the boys, and in unison they turned and strode outside. "Just out of curiosity, though, what breed are they?"

"Purebred Fleckvieh Simmental..."

"Lousy exotics," he grumbled. " Give me Hereford or Angus any time."

Amy felt her back stiffen at his easy disclaimer of her stock. But she didn't want to get into a discussion over the economics of raising animals that raised a high price at the auction or animals that were the traditional stock for this country.

Chester grabbed a corral post and shook it. "How long these posts been in the ground?"

"Some for about ten years. I've replaced others."

Chester nodded in acknowledgment, then turned to the shorter of the two. Amy guessed he was the oldest. "What do you think, Jason? How would you like to start up here?"

"I think we'll take it," Jason said, smiling.

"Done." Chester turned to Amy. "We'll take it," he repeated.

Amy heard the words twice, but they still took time to register. She felt as if someone had pulled the earth out from beneath her and if she looked down, she would see emptiness below her.

"We'll take it," Chester repeated, obviously noting the dumbfounded look on Amy's face.

"I'm not moving on the price."

Chester waved a hand dismissively. "The price is right, the location is good. Needs work, but a Drozd has never been shy of that."

"Sure," she said, exhaling then inhaling, trying to find her breath. "Okay."

"You're not going to change your mind on me, are you?" Chester leaned forward, his cap pushed back on his head.

"No." Amy thought of Rick working in Williams Lake and the conversation she had with her father yesterday. She was the only Danyluk who wanted it, and once she and Tim were married, they would be living elsewhere.

"No, it's still for sale," she replied softly.

"So. I'll make an appointment with the lawyer in town and we can get the papers drawn up." Chester rubbed his hands as if in anticipation. "Who are you going to get to auction off the stuff?"

Amy frowned, her mind still trying to absorb the implications of his whirlwind visit. "Auction?"

"You said the stock and machinery aren't included in the price. I presumed you were going to have a farm auction. It's the best way to get rid of this stuff."

Amy looked from Chester's bobbing face to Jason's grinning one, trying not to resent them and their easy dismantling of a place where all her childhood memories were stored. It was just a ranch, and they wanted to buy it. His suggestion was a valid one. This was a good lesson in letting go of the things of the world. The way things were headed, she knew it was what God wanted of her.

It had to be. It was the only way things made sense to her.

"I'll probably call Vanderwell's Auction," Amy was pleasantly surprised to hear how casual and even her voice was. "They can take care of everything."

"They're good." Chester nodded in approval.

As they walked back to the truck, Amy remembered.

"Did you want to see the inside of the house? We re-sided it a couple of years ago and hoped to do more work inside." She forced a smile, thankful she could act as if none of it mattered. As if she was merely getting rid of the calves, like she did every year.

Chester pursed his lips, giving the house a cursory glance. "No. Jason will probably want to build. He can move a trailer on the yard until then."

Amy blinked again. Just like that. A few words and her home, the place she had lived in all her life, was casually dismissed. It was hard not to resent his casual attitude.

"I'll phone our lawyer this afternoon and tell him we'll be coming in to sign an Agreement for Sale and he can get the searches going," Amy said as they walked back to the pickup truck.

"I'll call my own lawyer, as well. May as well get this thing going as soon as possible." Before Chester climbed into the pickup, he reached out and shook Amy's hand. "I think it will be a pleasure doing business with you. You look at the world with a steady eye."

Steady? Amy felt like she could be knocked over by a day-old calf. But she smiled her thanks at the compliment and stood back, her arms crossed over her chest, her fingers digging into her skin.

Chester climbed into the truck and rolled down the window. "I need to make a few phone calls. Who do you deal through in town?"

"All our stuff is at McKnight and Grieg's," Amy said.

He nodded, tugging on his cap. "Good. We deal with them, too. That should make things easier. We can talk later about possession date and all the other dirt." He turned the key in the truck, took another satisfied look over the yard, tossed a quick wave at her and roared down the driveway.

Okay, Lord, Amy thought, crossing her arms across her chest against the sudden chill she felt. *Things have gone way beyond me. This isn't the desire of my heart, but this is what You gave me. Help me to see that. Help me to let go.*

She sucked in a full breath, all the way to the bottom of her lungs, and let it slowly out. *And we're going to need something for my dad to do.*

She walked back to the house. She had some phone calls to make and appointments to set up.

As she walked up the steps to the house, she looked once more over her shoulder. Would she be able to let this go when the time came? It would mean choosing between Tim and the ranch.

And what about Paul?

Amy turned her back on the yard and walked resolutely into the house. Paul was not an option.

Chapter Fourteen

❧

"Awright, folks, lets see what we got here...." The auctioneer bent over and with an audible grunt pulled another cardboard box toward him over the grass. He had set up his podium and table between the barn and the corrals, which was the highest point on the yard, creating a natural amphitheater. The late-morning sun shone brightly. The birds sang cheerfully. The flies behaved, keeping a low, lazy profile.

It was a glorious Saturday. Perfect for an auction sale. Most of the people in the area thought so, as well. Amy had never seen so many people at an auction sale.

The auctioneer hoisted up the box onto the table beside him and riffled through it. "Box number twelve contains some old toys," he peered inside again and pushed some items aside. "A few books, and," he straightened, holding up a dusty ceramic bowl, "this antique." He turned it over, read the markings on the bottom and glanced back up at the crowd. "Mint condition, worth a small fortune." He put it back in the box and turned to the crowd. "Okay. What am I bid? We'll start with seventy, here now whaddya say..." He grabbed the microphone with one hand and held the other out, encouraging people to bid.

"Is he kidding? Seventy dollars for that stuff?" Tim's voice was incredulous. "He'll never get that," he said to Amy as they hung back at the edges of the crowd, watching and listening.

"Of course not. It's psychological. He's trying to give people the idea he thinks it's worth that much." Amy leaned back against the barn, her hands in the pockets of her denim jacket as she listened to the auctioneer drop the opener ten dollars, then another ten. "That way if someone pays twenty dollars for it, they think they got a deal."

"If someone pays twenty dollars for it, they got a very expensive bowl." Tim frowned as the auctioneer dropped once more. Someone jumped in, another two people upped the ante and they were away. One man worked the front of the crowd, spotting the bids, catching the eyes of the people bidding, encouraging, badgering people he knew, calling out each time the price increased.

"Doesn't seem to matter once you get caught up in the bidding." Amy felt surprised at the amounts of money people were willing to pay for boxes of, basically, junk. She was going to throw most of it away, but the auctioneer told her to pack it all up in boxes and put one or two items of value in each one.

And he was right. Some of the boxes had gone for a ridiculously high price, and all because someone had wanted the old Mason jars stuffed in a box with old books or the cream can that held an assortment of kitchen utensils.

"Looks like I'll get enough to retire on," Judd grunted as he lowered himself to the straw bales Amy and Tim had placed against the barn for anyone who wanted to sit. But no one did. Everyone wandered around poking and prodding. The auction had started fifteen minutes ago, and people still arrived. Most people stopped to chat a minute, then went on to look at what was available. Having it on a Saturday had brought quite a few people out.

"It's going a lot better than I thought," Amy commented. She scanned the crowd, her heart stopping each time she saw a blond head, then chastised herself.

Figures milled about, and one detached itself from the group.

"Hello, everybody." Elizabeth Henderson breezed up. She smiled at Tim and hugged Amy and nodded at Judd. "There's a lot of people here today." She looked over her shoulder at the crowd and then back at Amy. Elizabeth caught her gaze and looked her directly in the eyes. "How are you doing?" she asked quietly.

Amy lifted one shoulder in a negligent shrug. "Okay." She didn't want to talk about how she felt. This morning she had prayed for strength to get through the day, and so far she had managed to keep a delicate hold on her emotions. It was harder than she thought to see her life auctioned away to people who wouldn't hold the things as dear as she did.

Elizabeth sensed her reticence, pausing a moment to stroke her shoulder. "I'd stick around, but I promised Fred I wouldn't buy anything, and if I stay, I will. I was on my way to town and thought I'd stop in and see you a minute. You're welcome to come over for supper," she swung her gaze to Judd and Tim, both of whom only nodded. She looked back at Amy. "I hear you're finally shopping for your wedding dress? That's cutting it close, my girl. When are you leaving for Vancouver?"

"Tonight," Amy replied.

"How long are you staying?"

"Not long. I have to be back—" Amy caught herself. She didn't have to be back for anything. The Drozd boys were going to bale the hay, and Rick was going to oversee the shipping out of the cows and heifers. She drew a breath and tried again. "I'm hoping we can find a dress quickly, though. Just in case it needs to be altered."

"I'm sure we'll find something." Tim wrapped his arm around her waist and squeezed. "My mother has had a number of dresses picked out for weeks now." He laughed lightly and Amy forced a smile.

"I'm sure you'll find something you like," said Elizabeth with a reassuring pat on Amy's shoulder. "And what about you, Judd. Do you have your suit?"

"Tim got me a tux," he replied. "Ordered special. Got a deal on the pants because I didn't need a full pair."

Amy frowned at him.

Judd caught her look and winked. "Look, honey. I'm trying. Cut me a little slack here."

Amy relaxed. It had been a long time since she heard her father crack a joke. The doctor had told her his previous mood swings were the result of fluctuating blood sugars and that once balanced, Judd would become easier to get along with.

And he was surprisingly correct. Amy still could not get used to her father's bantering. She often had to look at him twice to make sure his remarks were said in jest and not his usual cutting comments. His blood sugar levels had finally come under control, but Amy also noticed a lightness pervade his attitude after the sale of the ranch. Ever since the deed was signed over to Jason Drozd, it was as if a burden had been lifted from her father's shoulders. This, of course, made her feel doubly guilty and selfish for hanging on to the place as long as she had.

"Why did you want to get rid of that?" Judd sat up, then pulled himself onto his crutches. "That's a box of your old toys."

"Why would I want to keep them?" Amy frowned as the auctioneer displayed an old doll with one eye missing and a ratty teddy bear, both pulled out from another box.

"I'm going to need something for the grandchildren to play with."

"Dad, that's a long way away. And where are you going to store them? I'm sure Rick wouldn't thank you if you came to his place with a whole truckload of old toys and junk."

Judd looked away, as if finally realizing what he had set in motion when he agreed to sell the ranch. "Your mother bought you kids some of those."

Amy refused to think about that. The change in her father had been happening for a while, but since her mother's visit he was more willing to talk about her, to recognize the relationship they once had.

Amy only shrugged and looked away.

"Ten I have ten, do I have ten fifty, ten fifty…" The auctioneer held up his hand ready to drop it to end the transaction when a voice called out, "Fifteen."

Mr. Vanderwell's head whipped around. "I've got fifteen,"

he called out. "Thank you. Do I hear seventeen?" He cajoled some more, but no one came in. Mr. Vanderwell pointed to a person in the middle of the crowd as Amy wondered who would be willing to pay fifteen dollars for something they could pick up for five. "Sold, to Paul Henderson, for an even fifteen."

Amy's heart skipped a beat.

Elizabeth spun around and sighed audibly. "That boy," she muttered. She turned back to Amy. "Don't pay him any mind. He's just..." But she paused, glanced at Tim who now stood, staring out over the people.

Amy could almost feel his antagonism.

The next item up was a set of wooden patio chairs. Amy had put them in the sale reluctantly. They were a project from high school shop class. Judd had designed them, and together they had labored over them endless hours. She ended up getting a mark of ninety-seven percent. It was the closest anyone had ever come to perfection in that teacher's class, and once done, they had sat outside. Judd had thought it a shame to leave them out in the rain, so he'd stored them in a shed.

This time the first bidder came in sooner and the prices escalated quickly. Amy relaxed as the price went higher and higher, thankful Paul wasn't bidding. Things slowed down and the auctioneer threw out another sales pitch. "These are genuine homemade chairs, folks. You won't find anything like this in your regular stores. And—" he paused, glancing around the crowd "—these were handcrafted by Amy Danyluk herself."

A voice called out, "Three hundred."

A few gasps went up. Elizabeth glanced back at Amy then, shaking her head, pushed her way through the crowd to her son's side. He bent his head to hear her, shook it and straightened as the auctioneer waited to see if anyone else wanted to tangle with Paul.

"Three hundred and fifty."

Tim.

Amy's heart sank, then began pounding in earnest as Paul added another fifty to that. She looked over at Tim, wondering if she could talk him out of this skirmish. His jaw was set, his hands planted firmly on his hips.

She couldn't.

The price jumped by fifty each time, going higher and higher. Amy felt a flush warm her neck as people turned around to watch Tim do public battle with Paul, squirming under knowing looks.

The price had gone up to seven hundred dollars with neither contestant showing any sign of backing down.

Eight hundred and Tim stood his ground, matching Paul's bid almost as soon as Paul spoke. Paul occasionally hesitated, tilting his head as if contemplating, completely ignoring his mother who now glared at him. But then, just at the last moment, upped the ante another ten.

Back and forth they went, people laughing outright, the auctioneer encouraging, calling out, "Does the winner get the girl, too?"

Amy blushed, wishing she could leave. She turned her head neither to the right to look at Paul nor to the left to look at Tim. Instead she concentrated on the hills just over the auctioneer's shoulder, watching the trees swaying in the wind, wishing she was anywhere else but here. She didn't want to know why Paul was buying things she knew he didn't need. She didn't want to think of the unspoken message she knew he was sending her. In six weeks she and Tim were getting married.

"It's a beautiful wedding dress, Amy." Elizabeth fluffed the top of the leg-of-mutton sleeves, the lustrous satin material shimmering in the rays of early-morning sun slanting through the living room window. "I wish your mother could see this."

"She did. We met at the store." Amy forced a covered button through the satin loop on her sleeve. The material dug into the curve of her elbow, almost cutting off her circulation.

"Was Mrs. Enders there?"

"She was the one who decided on this dress."

Elizabeth thankfully said nothing, only nodded in acknowledgment. "It looks lovely on you."

Amy wondered. When she had looked at herself in the mirror in the bridal salon, a beautiful stranger looked back at her with curious eyes. It didn't seem like her.

She ran her hands down the front of the full skirt, then snatched them back. She was constantly aware of its cost. She had almost left it at the store in Vancouver, but Tim wanted her to bring it here.

"I'm surprised you picked this style," Elizabeth said.

"I had my eye on another dress." Amy's voice became wistful as she worked on the button. "It was linen with open-work embroidery around the hem and neckline and the bottom of the sleeves. My mother had picked it out."

"But..." prompted Elizabeth.

"Mrs. Enders didn't think it was the kind of gown the future wife of a bank manager should get married in." Amy pushed down the feelings of resentment she felt at Mrs. Enders's casual dismissal of what she had chosen. What could Amy say? The Enders were paying for it. Noreen's offer to pay was suavely brushed off by Delia, effectively giving her control.

Elizabeth stood back, tilted her head to one side, her expression thoughtful. "You sound unhappy. Is it your mother?"

Amy shook her head as her fingers fluttered over the sequin-and pearl-encrusted bodice. The hesitant steps she and her mother took toward reconciliation, difficult though it may be, were less taxing than Amy trying to impose her will over Mrs. Enders. "I'm going to stay with her this week. I can't say I'm really excited about going back to Vancouver. But she offered to help me with some of the wedding preparations." And help pay for them. This had eased some of the guilt about all the things she'd already had to accept from the Enders family and had given her some measure of choice. It was frustrating to her to watch what was supposed to be a joyous occasion break down into a battle of wills.

"When are you leaving?"

"Tomorrow. She's coming here to pick me up."

"So soon?" Elizabeth's face fell. "Will you be back?"

"I have to be back for the closing date to sign the final papers for the ranch. I'm only going to be there a few days."

Amy tilted her head toward Elizabeth, still doubting her own decision. "Do you think it's the right thing to do?"

Elizabeth smiled and shook her head. "She's your mother, you can't change that and you need to get to know her. What better time than just before your wedding?"

Amy nodded in assent. "I know you're right, but there are times that all the lonely years get in the way. When I came home and saw Dad sitting on the kitchen chair, his leg stuck out in front of him, his crutches leaning against the table, I went through another whole range of emotions again—like it was her fault he's the way he is."

"I've never wanted to say too much, but I have different emotions when I see your mother," Elizabeth replied. "I think she's had to carry more than she should have."

Amy frowned. "What do you mean?"

Elizabeth sighed, then unfolded a small sequin that had become tucked against Amy's neck. She rested her hand on Amy's shoulder a moment, then drew back. "I think your father has a few more explanations to make to you and your brother. I sense that he's ready to make them now, where he wouldn't have been a few years ago. If you're going to stay with her for a while, you need to have those things explained to you. Ask your father when you go home. Ask him to tell you more about your mother." Elizabeth fussed and straightened, her fingers warm, caring.

"What are you talking about?" Amy felt a headache brewing behind her eyes. The same headache she had fought during the three days she'd spent at the Enders's home. They kept talking about the wedding, finalizing plans, and she kept trying to work up enthusiasm for something she felt had gone way beyond her.

And now Elizabeth was hinting that there was unfinished business between her father and mother. She had too many things to think about.

"I'm sorry, Amy," Elizabeth replied. "I stepped out of line."

"No. You said exactly the same thing my mom said when I met her for coffee. She told me to ask Dad about her, to ask him to tell me what happened. What's going on? What don't I know?'' Amy felt as if she was balancing very carefully on the edge of something, and she didn't know where to step next.

Elizabeth pursed her lips, as if thinking. ''I never knew before, so don't think I've kept anything from you all this time. When Noreen came, I asked her a few point-blank questions.'' Elizabeth quirked a half smile at Amy. ''You know me. She answered them. But for now I'm only going to say that your father was right. Your mother did leave, but there's more to the story than just that.'' She stepped back, her voice holding a note of finality. ''And now we're going to change the subject and talk about your future instead of your past.'' She knelt down and fluffed out the full skirt. ''Did you find a place in Vancouver?''

''Yes.'' Amy rubbed her temple with one finger, knowing Elizabeth was right. But somehow she couldn't shake the idea that the future and the past were inextricably interwoven. ''We looked at a number of different places.'' They had finally agreed on a condominium tucked in among others, overlooking a small patch of green Tim called a park. When she stood inside, looking out at all the concrete and glass, panic had gripped her and she had to get out.

Elizabeth glanced upward, her hands still holding the skirt. ''And living in Vancouver is a certainty?''

The question hung in the quiet air of the sunlit room. Amy took a deep breath, feeling her body strain against the taut material of the dress. ''Yes. That's one of the biggest reasons we sold the ranch.''

''You'll find all kinds of things to keep you busy there, no doubt. Paul was always going on about all the things there are to do,'' she continued, leaning back on her heels, looking up at Amy with thoughtful eyes. ''It will be a change for you, though.''

Amy lifted one shoulder, thinking of the small apartment and the even smaller balcony. Suddenly she could hold it in no longer. ''I don't know, Mom,'' she blurted out. ''I just don't know if I can move there.''

Elizabeth got to her feet, and handed Amy her veil. ''This

is a hard time for you to have doubts. Have you talked to Tim about this?''

Amy bit her lip. ''We did before. And he'd always given me the impression that he was going to live at the ranch. Then he throws this Vancouver thing at me, and suddenly we don't have time to talk about it.''

''I think you had better find the time.''

I know, thought Amy, but when? Each day brought the wedding closer, each thing they bought with Tim's credit card laid one more burden of obligation on her shoulders, one more thing she felt she couldn't go back on.

She wished she could just postpone the whole thing, wait and see.

But wait for what?

The question hovered unanswered. Fear kept it in the back of her mind where it couldn't be examined too closely. She turned the veil over in her hand, watching the sun spangling on the sequins of the headpiece.

''I guess, I'll have to.''

''And in the meantime, things keep moving on.'' Elizabeth walked once more around her, examining, checking for loose buttons, threads. ''Do you want some help taking the dress off? If not, I have to leave. Fred and I are going into town.'' Elizabeth winked at Amy. ''Got to decide on a wedding present.''

Amy felt the entire room close in on her. She felt like a rudderless boat on a river, hurtling toward an unknown destination, powerless to stop anything. What had she started with a simple yes?

''So that's your wedding dress.''

Amy whirled around, clutching the gauze netting of the veil to her stomach, her heart in her throat at the sound of the deep voice.

Paul! What was he doing here in the middle of the week?

He leaned against the door frame, arms crossed, eyebrows raised. Pushing himself off, he sauntered into the living room. He shoved his hands in his rear pockets, pursed his mouth in a soundless whistle and walked once around her.

''You picked this out?'' he asked, his deep blue eyes meeting hers. He stepped away as if to get a better look, his hand rubbing his chin. "Doesn't look like the Amy Danyluk I know and love."

"Doesn't matter." Amy almost snapped at him, more angry at her own reaction to him than at his steady perusal. She didn't want Paul to see her in her wedding dress; it seemed so final.

Especially when the sight of him shot a thrill through her....

"I better get ready to go," Elizabeth said. "Amy you're welcome to stay for supper." She got up, adjusting her hip-length sweater.

Amy shook her head. "Sorry, I have to meet Tim in town to do some arranging for the wedding, and then we have premarital classes. Dad is staying over at Rick's tonight. But I was wondering if I could leave the dress here."

"Okay." Elizabeth smiled at Amy, patting her icy hand. "I hope you have a nice evening." As she left, Elizabeth shot a warning glance at her son. He ignored it.

Paul stood in front of Amy, trying to act nonchalant. Hard to do when the sight of her in that wedding dress terrified him like nothing ever had before. She was going through with this!

"He still determined to pull you out of here and drag you to Vancouver?" Paul didn't even try to keep the bitter tone out of his voice.

"We do plan on living in Vancouver, yes."

Goodness she sounded prim. But Paul was encouraged by the sudden glint of fear in her soft gray eyes.

"Think you can do it?"

She said nothing, just bit her lip and stared down at the veil she slowly crushed with her fingers.

"Amy..." He shoved a hand through his hair, trying to find the words, trying to figure out what he could say to make her wait. He had told her he loved her; he wasn't arrogant enough to think those words alone would make her change her mind. "Amy, he can't make you live there. It's not your place."

The soft rustling of the netting was the only sound in the heavy silence.

"Amy, you have nothing in common with him. You two are so different from each other. You like things simple, he likes them fancy. I know you want a casual wedding, he certainly doesn't. Not from the things Shannon tells me. I mean, look at this dress. I know you didn't pick it out."

She kept her head down, her fingers working at a loose sequin.

"And now you're moving to Vancouver?"

Amy clutched the veil harder, her fingers white. Tension clenched her jaw tight, and her words were forced. "The ranch is sold. Tim's job is there, where else would I live?"

He stepped closer, peeling her fingers away from the ruined veil, all his pent-up frustration trying to find a release, trying to find a crack in the wall she had built around herself since he came back. "Amy trust me. You can't live in Vancouver. I know what I'm talking about. It will kill you."

"I don't know why you're getting caught up in this, Paul." She lifted her chin, her pose belligerent. "You come in and out of this place as often as the grader shows up on our road, and every time you come you've got a different girlfriend. You throw a few words at me and expect me to drop a man who has promised to share his whole life with me...."

"Amy, the words I gave you were the only ones I had a right to. I can give you a whole lot more, but I have some sense of honor, believe it or not." He swallowed down his anger and hurt at her accusations. "As long as you've decided you're going to marry Tim Enders, I can't say more than I love you."

"Like you've said to Stacy and Alicia and Juanita and...and—?" Amy sounded almost desperate "—a dozen other girls."

Paul swallowed, hurt at her accusations, seeing himself through her eyes. "You may not believe this, Amy, but I've only told one girl that I love her." Paul caught her by the arms, forcing her gray eyes to look directly into his. "And that girl is you."

She looked up at him, shaking her head in disbelief. "I don't believe you," she said, her voice hard. "I know you too well, Paul. You've had so many girlfriends, lived away so long..."

"You may think you know everything about me, Amy, but

believe it or not, somewhere between ten years ago and now, I've changed."

"That's convenient." Amy narrowed her eyes as if challenging him. "You know what your problem is? You're jealous and you don't like it that maybe, for once in her life, Amy Danyluk likes someone other than Paul Henderson."

"*Like?*" he asked, incredulous. "You are getting married to someone you *like?*"

She pulled back, her voice bitter, ignoring his comment. "I wish you'd just decide what it is you want."

"I've made that very clear. I want you. I've always wanted you. I've just never deserved you."

Amy's shoulders sagged, her eyes drifted closed, then she shook her head, once.

"I'm not a possession you can pick up and put down whenever the mood strikes you," she whispered. "I made a promise to Tim, not you."

"I have never seen you as a possession, Amy. I've always respected you for your beliefs, your strong faith. And it was that faith that kept me away from you. I've had to make some decisions myself in my own faith life. I've told you about them." Paul watched her face, praying for some sign that she was listening, that she wasn't shutting him out. "But I've had to make other decisions as well these past few weeks. I've sold everything I had in Vancouver."

Amy lifted her head, her eyes wide with disbelief.

Paul laughed shortly. "It's all gone. Henderson Contractors has been officially sold, and I've moved back home. And do you know *why,* Amy?" He held her eyes, his gaze steady. "I did it for you. For us. I did it because I love you, and I'll keep telling you until you believe it."

"No," she said, shaking her head as if to push away all that he had just said. She held out the skirt of her dress, her eyes pleading, her voice strained. "See this, Paul? This is the dress I'm going to wear when I marry Tim. It's him that I love."

"Are you trying to convince me or yourself?"

Amy clenched her hands tighter around the soft material of the dress. "How can you say that? Since you've come back

I've never, with any word or action or—'' she faltered ''—*anything,* encouraged you.''

''And what about before that?''

''That's unfair.''

Paul took a steadying breath, trying to still the urgency that coursed through him. Forcing himself to relax, he kept his eyes on hers, a wry smile curving his lips. ''You may think you haven't encouraged me, but you did, Amy. Every time we look at each other, it happens. Every time we touch each other, every time we're together.'' He took a step closer, unable to keep his hands away from her. He traced the delicate line of her lips, touched her eyebrows, cupped her chin.

She resisted his touch, stood her ground, her back stiff in that virginal white dress, that dress in which she was bound and determined to marry Tim Enders. ''That isn't love, Paul,'' she said. ''That's what's left of some foolish old crush that I should have gotten over years ago.''

''But it started out that way...''

''Why do you throw that in my face?'' Amy cried out. ''I've tried so hard to get you out of my life.''

''Why?'' Paul lowered his voice, forced himself to keep quiet. They hovered on the brink of a discovery that, once unearthed, would change their futures. His prayers and yearning became one as his hand slipped around her neck, his fingers tangling in her hair at the nape of her neck.

''Do you know how much Tim's spent on this wedding—on the invitations, the decorations...this dress? I can't just call it off.'' She hugged herself, her hands cupped tightly around her elbows, as if holding herself steady. ''If I do, how am I supposed to live with the knowledge that I'm just as bad as my mother, just as easily swayed, just as unfaithful?''

And finally Paul understood.

Oh, Lord, he prayed, *put the right words in my mouth, give me right motives. Help me say what I say out of love for Amy. Help me to show her that what she is doing, she's doing for the wrong reasons.*

''Amy—'' his voice was quiet, pleading ''—if you go ahead and marry Tim...'' He hesitated, and Amy pressed her chin against her chest. He couldn't stop himself from touching the red-gold of her hair, her delicate shoulder. His fingers feathered up and down the silk covering her arm, as if urging her to look up at him. "If you marry Tim now, knowing how I feel about you, having to convince yourself that you love him..." He dropped his hand and Amy almost sagged with relief.

"Amy if you do that, you will end up exactly like your mother."

Chapter Fifteen

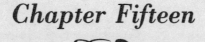

Once home, Amy walked around the empty yard, trying to still a pounding heart. She couldn't dwell on what Paul said. It cut too deep, the promise in his eyes hurt too much. He was a few years too late with his avowal of love.

She had made a promise to Tim. He was a good man. He was a Christian.

So is Paul.

I can't break my promise. I can't do that.

Her thoughts chased each other around. Her mind was too busy and she had no work to alleviate it with. The cows had been shipped a couple of days ago. The Drozd boys had baled a few rounds then quit. Amy itched to get out there and do something, anything, but both the tractor and baler had been sold at the auction.

Tomorrow she would leave for Vancouver. In a couple of weeks everything she owned would be moved to the condo in Vancouver where she and Tim would live after the honeymoon.

She leaned on a rough board fence as the cool wind of fall swept down the hills, a harbinger of the cold weather to come.

She shivered a moment, wondering what winter was like in a city. There would be no snow to shovel, no animals to feed. No tractors to start in twenty-below weather.

It could be okay. It would have to be okay.

So why did Paul's words echo through her mind each time she thought about moving? His declarations of love promised her something she had been waiting for since she was a young girl.

But she had gone past that, had grown out of it. She'd made a promise to someone who loved her and had made a commitment to her. Sure they had their differences. Didn't any married couple? She wasn't about to turn her back on that on the basis of a few words from someone who was probably just jealous.

But a man wouldn't sell everything he owned to come back just because he was jealous. He did that for stronger reasons.

Amy leaned her elbows on the fence, rested her chin on her stacked hands wishing she could just get married and be done with all this second-guessing. It would all go away then.

Once again she looked to the mountains, the line from the psalm coming back to her "I lift up mine eyes to the hills, from where comes my help?"

"My help comes from the Lord," she breathed out loud, the words drifting with the soft wind that teased the grass beyond the fence. She closed her eyes, letting God's peace flow over her as she prayed for patience, wisdom and strength and whatever else the Lord thought she might need.

She pushed herself away from the fence and walked back to the house.

Her father sat at the kitchen table, papers scattered around. He looked up when she came in and smiled at her.

Amy dropped into a chair across from him, turning a piece of paper toward her. On it was a drawing of a chair portrayed from different angles. "What are you working on?"

Judd made a few more notes, then looked up. "I got the idea during our auction sale." He frowned, added a few numbers and sat back. "You know those deck chairs we made?"

Amy held his gaze, her own face impassive. As if she'd forget. Paul Henderson bought them for one thousand, five hundred dollars. Tim had finally backed down when he knew that Paul wasn't going to quit. Tim was angry all the way to Vancouver.

"Well—" Judd cleared his throat, as if he knew he had trod on shaky ground "—I had a bunch of people ask me where they came from. One guy that came up for the auction has a furniture place in Surrey. He's been looking for unique and well-made deck furniture. He wants me to make him a couple more, maybe a table to go with it. If they sell, I got me a new job."

"Where would you make them?" Amy asked hesitantly, hardly daring to think that her prayers for her father had been answered so quickly.

"Rick said Jack has a place in town with a shop that he never uses. Does all of his work at the garage. He said I could set some stuff up in there. From what we made at the auction, I can buy a couple of really nice power tools, add them to what I already have, and I'm in business." Judd grinned at Amy. "Can even sit down on the job most of the time."

The peace she felt when she came into the house seemed to swell, and she sent up a silent prayer of thanks. "This sounds pretty promising, Dad."

"I think it'll fly. Rick's picking me up later, and we're going to check out the shop. I'll be staying at his place tonight."

Amy nodded. "What material would you use?"

"I've been phoning around. There's a little mill on Vancouver Island that has a deal on some cedar and will custom cut some of the squares. He knows a guy that will kiln dry them as well. All I have to do is plane them down." Judd leaned forward, pulling the plans out of Amy's hands. "I figure I'll stick with the pattern we came up with for the chairs Paul bought. Give it a European look. Maybe stain the frame a darker color than the back slats." With an eagerness Amy had never seen before, Judd laid out his plans explaining how he would join them, how long it might possibly take.

"Will you be able to compete with the assembly-line furniture makers?"

Judd waved his hand in a dismissive gesture. "No one makes really good lawn furniture. The guy seemed really excited. Said he'd never seen chairs like that." Judd rubbed his chin. "It might not go anywhere, but it's a start." He leaned over the paper and jotted down a few more numbers and glanced up at the clock. "I thought Tim was coming for you in fifteen minutes. Shouldn't you be getting ready?"

"Yes," Amy looked at the paper with her father's handwriting scrawling across it willy-nilly, wishing she could go along with her father and Rick instead, making plans for her father's future instead of hers.

"You don't sound really excited about it."

"Well, Tim has enough excitement for the two of us. I'm lucky he's so organized. If it was up to me, we'd probably end up having to elope."

Judd nodded, rubbing his whiskered chin once again. "Tim still ticked at Paul?"

Amy shrugged, pressing her fingers on the paper in front of her and turning it. She watched the picture of the chair go around and around and around. "He hasn't said anything, but I suspect he's gotten over it. Tim doesn't hold grudges."

"No." Judd grinned again. "It still makes me laugh to see those two go at each other over a pair of chairs that you or I could have made them for one-twentieth of the price." He shook his head, remembering. "I don't know why Tim didn't buy them. I would have given him the money back."

Amy said nothing, only spun the paper faster.

"Why do you suppose Paul bought that stuff?" Judd leaned forward, suddenly serious. "I got the idea he was trying to tell you something."

Amy still gave no answer, her breath catching as she remembered the entreaty in his eyes, the feel of his hands on her arms only moments ago.

"I heard he sold his business in Vancouver," Judd continued. "I heard he and his dad are looking to buy the Kincaid place."

"Yes. He told me that he's moved here for good."

"When did he tell you that?"

Amy rubbed her eyes with her fingertips, hoping to erase the memory of his words and what they meant. "Just this afternoon, at his parents' place."

"That will make things interesting."

Amy dropped her hands. Judd's arms were crossed over his chest as he stared past her, out of the window. "A couple of months ago, I would have challenged you on that statement, asked what you meant by that. You used to dislike Paul and his father. But now, after knowing Fred has been visiting you and you've been enjoying his visits, I know you mean different, don't you?"

Judd shrugged, not meeting her eyes. "I used to be jealous of the Hendersons, that much is true. Rick has never liked Paul and made no secret of it, although I suspect that's over now, as well. I made some mistakes about their family, and I've jumped to wrong conclusions about Fred and Noreen."

Amy took a steadying breath. "Elizabeth hinted that you had something to tell me about Mom. If that's so, I need to know before I spend a few days with her."

Judd nodded. "Elizabeth is right." He looked up at his daughter, his expression sorrowful. "I should have told you long ago, but the longer I waited, the harder it got." He tapped his fingers against his arm as if thinking. "It's still not easy."

Amy sat back, sensing she was on the verge of something important. She refused to look at the clock, refused to think that Tim might be coming at any moment. Noreen's visit and Elizabeth's comments had raised too many questions. Amy felt, deep within her, that she needed to know the answers, soon. "Maybe not, Dad. But I need to know if there's anything you've held back from me."

Judd cleared his throat, as if getting rid of years of holding back. "I'm a hard man to live with. You know that." He paused a moment, shrugging. "This is real hard for me, Amy. I'm not the blabbing type." He fiddled with the papers in front of him, frowning.

Amy nodded. "I know that much, Dad." She waited a moment, sensing that she might have to help him along. "Why did Mom dislike living here?"

Judd shook his head. "It wasn't the romantic ranch she thought it would be. Animals stink and are ornery and machinery won't work. Husbands get dirty and cranky. It's lonely out here. And that was hard for her."

"Didn't she have any friends?"

"A few. But to visit them you need a vehicle, and we only had one truck at the time. I used it mostly. And when you and Rick came it was that much harder. I needed her help on the ranch. I had just started and was trying to work for extra wages at other ranches at the same time. She had never worked with animals before, or equipment. I wasn't very patient with her. She stopped helping. When you were old enough I got you out there driving the tractor and mowing hay. Noreen hated it, but couldn't say anything because she wouldn't do it."

"And your marriage..." Amy prompted.

"Was getting worse. We fought and bickered. She would go out and wouldn't come home. I imagined the worst and then I found out I was right. She had been fooling around with some guy. I stayed up one night and confronted her. She told me, yes, she had been unfaithful but she wouldn't say who with." Judd laughed bitterly. "In my anger I thought, for many years, it was Fred Henderson. I was wrong about that, too."

Judd paused, lost in the past, his face set in the same hard lines Amy remembered so well and hadn't seen in a while.

"And then," she prompted.

Judd sighed, crossing his arms across his chest, avoiding Amy's eyes. "Then I told her to leave and not come back. She did. Then, a week later, I caught my foot in an auger at the place I worked and lost half of it. When I came out of the hospital, Noreen called. She wanted to come back. Said she was sorry and wouldn't do it again. She wanted us to take marriage counseling and everything. I told her it was a bunch of bunk. Then I told her to leave us alone and not bother me or you kids again. Told her she didn't deserve to see us."

"Mom wanted to come back?" Amy sat back, stunned. This was the information Elizabeth had alluded to.

Judd nodded, then turned to Amy, anguish etched on his face. "I didn't want her to come back because I was scared. If she couldn't be faithful to a man with two good legs, how could she be faithful to a man with only one? I couldn't take the chance."

Amy didn't reply. She held down her own hurt and let her father continue.

"The past year I've been praying for Noreen, you know that. I hope she can forgive me." Judd stopped. Amy was shocked to see a tear slowly drift down his wrinkled cheek, her own emotions in conflict.

She could have had a mother, she thought, could have had a family if her father had been more forgiving.

"I'm an old tired man," Judd continued. "I've made big mistakes." He covered Amy's hand with his own. "I'm sorry, Amy. I've wanted to tell you. The longer I waited the harder it became. I tried to fool myself that it didn't matter, but I know it did." He looked up at Amy. "Can you forgive me?"

Amy took her father's hand, suddenly tired and worn-out. "Why didn't you tell me sooner, Daddy?" she asked. All the struggling she had done, all the recriminations she had thrown against her absent mother now became as dust in the wind. Noreen had wanted to return, to make a family, to try again. "Why did you wait so long?"

"Pride." He spoke the word softly, his tone showing her even more how far he had come. "I blamed God, Noreen and everyone else. I felt sorry for myself, and I lost interest in everything."

"What made the difference?"

"Fred Henderson."

Amy dropped her father's hand, surprised at this piece of news.

"He'd phone once in a while," Judd continued. "I'd hang up and he'd keep trying. He'd tell me that I had to let go of anger and bitterness. He didn't even know I thought he was the one fooling around with Noreen. Told me I had a wonderful daughter and son and not to miss out on their life. He showed me that a relationship with God can change things." He laughed lightly, reaching out to touch her once again. "It was more than my blood sugar that got balanced in the hospital."

Amy looked into her father's gray eyes, lined with wrinkles. His face had more color now, he spent more time outside in the sunshine.

Fred Henderson had helped bring about this change. She felt a burst of thankfulness followed by a feeling of bittersweet envy as she thought of what Paul offered her. It didn't matter. Fred and Elizabeth would always be her other parents. That wouldn't change once she was married.

But you won't see them as much. Amy closed her eyes a moment. She shut that thought away and with it all the dreams of bringing her children over to the Hendersons' on horseback, the plans she had made when she and Tim were going to live on the ranch. It hurt to think about that.

"Do you regret selling the ranch?" she asked, moving to other problems that needed discussing.

He bit his lip, looking sorrowfully at his daughter.

"No. I'm sorry for you that Tim didn't want to live out here. Things might have turned around, had I been a better manager. I knew Rick would never be interested and I never imagined you would. I wanted to tell you already back then not to bother, but I was so glad to still have my family around me that I didn't want to discourage you."

"And all along I thought you wanted to keep the ranch, wanted to stay here."

Judd brushed his hand over her hair again. "I guess we should have talked more to each other."

Amy nodded, thinking back to her mother, wondering what might have changed had she known that Noreen wanted to come back.

But it didn't happen, and she still had a wedding to plan.

As she stood up, she saw the clock. While she felt as if time had stilled, in reality the minutes ticked relentlessly on and Tim would be here shortly. She bent over and kissed her father. "Thanks for telling me the truth, Dad. I have to go. Tim will be here in five minutes."

She hesitated a moment, then turned and ran up the stairs, wishing for the second time that she could stay home instead of running around town finalizing wedding plans.

Tim came just as she finished running a brush through her hair.

She kissed her father goodbye. "I probably won't see you

until I get back from visiting Mom in Vancouver.'' She straightened. ''Watch your blood sugar, okay?''

''Yes, I will.'' Judd caught her hand. ''I'm sorry, Amy,'' he whispered.

She only nodded, bent over to give him another quick kiss and left.

As she settled into Tim's car, Judd's words joined all the other thoughts that roiled around in her head. Her father's revelation suddenly changed her own perception of her mother and therefore, herself. Her mother had made a mistake and had paid dearly for it because of her father's self-righteousness. Her father's idea of faithfulness had been true, but too ardently applied. There had been no room for mistakes.

Was her own notion of faithfulness also extreme?

She glanced over at Tim, remembering Elizabeth's words and even more important, Paul's. She'd spoken to her father as Elizabeth had encouraged her to do; now she needed to talk to Tim, to voice the questions that had been fed by Paul's comments.

Tim however, was excited and full of plans and didn't notice Amy's reticence.

They stopped at the florist and double-checked the order of flowers for the church and the reception hall. Amy's bouquet had been ordered the week before, as had Shannon's. Red roses interspersed with pink lilies.

''I'd like to change that order,'' Amy said quietly as the florist laid out the pictures.

Tim frowned at her, then shrugged. ''Sure, honey. What do you want?''

''I prefer yellow roses and tiger lilies.'' She turned to him, her voice matter-of-fact.

''But the wedding colors are red and white.''

''I don't like red.''

''But my mother picked out the colors.''

Amy held her ground. Tim looked taken aback, tried once more, then took out his charge card and paid for the order. From there they checked on the hall and the decorations that

Mrs. Enders ordered the week before, also in red. Amy changed them to peach and white.

The caterer needed a final count on how many people were coming. She laid a binder on the table. Across the top of the pages were written "Enders/Danyluk Wedding" and the date. Below that a brief menu.

"I thought the chicken cordon bleu would be a good entrée," Mrs. Menzies flashed a conspiratorial grin at Amy. "Mrs. Enders recommended it."

"Veal would be more reasonable," Amy put in, emboldened by her success in the florist shop. "All those ranchers, you know."

Tim and Mrs. Menzies exchanged surprised glances. Tim only nodded. They discussed entrées and desserts as Amy tried to imagine Mrs. Masterson trying to work her mouth around the names of the food, let alone her false teeth. And what would that dessert do to her father's sugar levels?

"Do you have any preferences, Amy?"

"Well my first preference is ice cream in a cone," she said succinctly, "but I'll go with cheesecake and pie."

"And the final tally on the guest list?" Mrs. Menzies asked.

"I don't have a final count, yet," Amy said, thinking of the returned envelopes piled up under the livestock manifest book. They had shipped the livestock just as the price came up. Rick had worked off the bill at Dilton's. The payment from the Drozd boys was due to come. For the first time since she could remember, the bank account had a healthy balance.

"And have you decided on a cake? The bakery in town usually gives us a discount." Mrs. Menzies looked up at them, handing Tim a photo album. "This will give you some idea of what's available."

"Do you want to have a look, Amy?"

Amy's moment of rebelliousness ebbed. It seemed pointless. There were countless decisions that had already been made, and changing them all served no purpose. If she had wanted things done a certain way, she should have been more forceful from the start.

Except the Enderses were paying for everything, and that

made it difficult to exercise control. She glanced disinterestedly at the pictures and let Tim choose.

"You must be excited." Mrs. Menzies smiled at Amy. "Can I see your ring?"

Tim caught her hand and stretched it out for the caterer to see. Somehow it irritated her. Like she was a prize to be shown off.

I've never seen you as a possession, Amy. Paul's words drifted down, catching up to her thoughts, making her grit her teeth in despair.

Why are you going through with this? Paul's question wouldn't leave her and spun its insidious web as they drove to the restaurant.

Once inside, Amy slipped off her coat and draped it over the back of her chair. They sat down, opened the menus, and Amy tried to concentrate.

"What do you want?" Tim asked, scanning the menu in front of him.

"I'll have the baked chicken," Amy said. As Tim ordered, she excused herself, got up and left for the washroom. Thankfully it was empty.

She fixed her lipstick with trembling fingers, examining herself in the mirror.

Okay, Danyluk, what were you doing today? She dropped the lipstick in her purse as she remembered Tim's shocked look as she changed plans willy-nilly. She knew she should tell him why. But how to explain to him the sudden need to establish a foothold when she began to see his mother's influence behind most every decision they had to make?

Closing her eyes she dropped her hot forehead against the cool mirror. Things were moving too fast. She wished she could have a few days on her own so she could absorb what had happened—what she had learned from her father, what Paul had told her. She wanted to sort out her own feelings. Her brief moment of rebelliousness was too little, too late. The very magnitude of the wedding would overwhelm her if she let it.

She didn't want to think about weddings. She didn't want to sit through yet another premarital class and talk about the importance of communication in a relationship when Tim had kept something as vital as his decision to accept a job in Vancouver from her.

She felt as if she was constantly twisting around trying to grasp the threads of her life and pull them into some kind of coherent mass. But she couldn't see them all. She needed someone who understood her confusion, her fears, her needs. Someone who would just listen.

He's here, Amy, he's just waiting for you to finally, once and for all, finish struggling.

Amy left her head where it was, knowing what she had to do. In the fret and bother of life, yet again she had tried to fix it herself, to be strong on her own.

She closed her eyes and slowly, one by one laid all her burdens on the Lord.

To articulate her problems, to say them out loud, to pour out her heart to the One who knew and understood and cared more than anyone else fully relieved the weight she had been struggling under.

"Sorry, Lord," she breathed raising her face to heaven. "Sorry for trying to figure all this out myself. Someday I'll learn, and once again, I'll let go. You love me more than anyone, Your love is ever faithful."

As she prayed, as she let go of each problem, she felt God's peace flow through her. She felt as if gentle hands tugged on the strings of her life, untangling them for her, lifting burdens. Her heart slowly filled with praise, her clenched hands loosened and opened up to Him. She was allowed to take.

And she knew that she had to make one more decision.

She left the washroom feeling lighter, peace pervading her mind and lightening her step. She hesitated a moment when she saw Tim looking out the window.

A quick prayer encouraged her, and she slipped into the chair across from him.

He looked up at her, reached across the table and caught her hand.

"Okay, Amy. What's wrong? You've been acting peculiar lately and I'm worried about you." His dark brown eyes soft-

ened with love as he stroked her cool fingers. His hair was
neatly brushed away from his face. He looked as handsome as
when she had first fallen in love with him.

But it wasn't enough anymore.

"I need to tell you—" She faltered, knowing that what she
was going to say would hurt him, for she knew that Tim loved
her. She took a steadying breath, trying to keep her eyes on
his. "I can't do this, Tim. I can't marry you."

His hold on her hands tightened, squeezing her ring. "What
are you saying, Amy? What are you talking about?"

His stricken look cut her deeply. "I can't marry you," she
repeated, looking away. "It would be a mistake."

"Amy." His voice broke, hurting her even more. "You can't
mean it. You've been under a lot of stress, I know that. I know
it wasn't easy giving up the ranch, but you know it's the best
thing." He cupped her face, turning it toward him. "If you
need time, we can wait. I'll be willing to postpone the wedding."

"It wouldn't make any difference," she said softly, pulling
her hands out of his. "I've struggled with this, prayed about
it. I'm sorry."

"It's Henderson, isn't it?" Tim sat back, his voice suddenly
harsh. "Ever since he's been back, you've been withdrawn.
And I've seen the way he looks at you."

Amy didn't know what to say to that. He was correct, par-
tially. "It's more than just Paul. It's living in Vancouver. I can't
live there...."

"Paul's only attracted to you because he can't have you,"
Tim interrupted, ignoring her last comment. "I'm positive that
as soon as he knows you're free, he'll leave and find someone
else."

"I don't think so." She had known Paul all of her life. And
she knew that what he had done, what he had told her, was
true and real. "But that doesn't have any bearing on our relationship."

"Of course it does, Amy. We have a lifetime ahead of us.
We have a good relationship, don't throw it away. I know
you're upset about selling the ranch, but you couldn't hang on

to it much longer." Tim leaned forward again, his voice pleading as he tried another tack. "Amy, we love each other. I know God meant for us to be together."

Amy blinked, slowly, looking down at her hand. She turned her ring around, watching the rainbows of light shoot out from it. She stretched out her fingers and with deliberate movements, slipped the ring off.

"You can't be serious." Tim didn't take the ring. "We've got everything planned, the condo, the caterer, the invitations, the decorations. My mother is counting on this. I don't mind postponing it, but at least let's try another date. A month, maybe two. Whatever you need."

"Will we still be living in Vancouver?" Amy asked.

Tim hesitated. "That's where my work is. I love my work, Amy."

"I know, Tim. And I don't expect you to give up everything for me." She paused, still holding on to his ring. "But I'm afraid that if we were to marry, I would resent what I had to give up for you." She looked up at him, pleading. "I can't live in the city, Tim. I just can't, not even for you. And if I can't, then I don't think my love for you is strong enough."

Tim's expression hardened. "So as long as Paul wasn't available I was good enough for you, and now that he's come back, it's over." He narrowed his eyes. "Maybe you're like your mother after all."

Amy blinked, cold pressure tightening her temples at his words. She couldn't dredge up anger, couldn't manufacture any feeling other than the dull ache that clutched her heart.

Her mind however, processed his words, words she had once intoned to herself in rebuke, words that had lost their power since she'd spoken with her father.

But coming from him they were words of betrayal.

She reached out and dropped the ring with a hollow thunk onto the table.

"Amy," he whispered, looking from the ring to her, shaken. "I'm sorry. I didn't mean what I said. I was upset."

Amy pushed herself carefully back from the table. Tears threatened but she suppressed them. She had loved Tim but she felt she had no right to mourn a relationship whose loss gave her more relief than pain. "I'm sorry, Tim. I loved you, too, but I don't think I loved you enough." She slipped on her coat and, turning, left the restaurant. She walked a few steps down the street, faltered, then resolutely walked on. After a few minutes, reality intruded. Tim had brought her here and she could hardly walk home. She glanced down at the dainty high-heeled sandals she wore. Especially not in these shoes.

She opened her purse, found a quarter and walked back down the street to the pay phone she remembered seeing by the restaurant.

She dialed Rick's, but there was no answer. Ditto for her own home. She pulled the quarter out of the machine and stared at it. Did she dare? She had just broken up with her fiancé, how would it look?

She ignored her doubts. With shaking fingers she deposited the coin in the phone and punched in Hendersons' number. Elizabeth answered.

"I'm stuck in town, Mom. I need a ride. Can someone come?" She wrapped her fingers around the cord.

"Paul and Fred are riding the lease, but I can come."

Amy swallowed her disappointment. "That would be nice." She shivered as another gust of wind blew down the street. "I'm at the pay phone across from the tire store."

"I'm leaving right away. See you later." Elizabeth hung up, and Amy held the receiver a moment, thankful that Elizabeth hadn't asked any questions.

She pulled her coat closer around her as she leaned against the wall of the phone booth. The restaurant door opened and Tim walked out. He hesitated, turned and walked toward her.

"C'mon, Amy. I'll drive you home."

She shook her head. "I just called Elizabeth, she's going to pick me up." She couldn't spend the long drive back home with Tim. Not after what she had just done, what he had just said.

"I'm sorry, Amy. I shouldn't have talked that way." He plowed his hands through his thick hair. "You have to understand. I didn't expect this. I can't believe you want to end this.

We had a good relationship. Things were going well before—"
He stopped and Amy knew what he was going to say.

Before Paul came back.

"It doesn't matter how or why," she said, choosing her
words carefully. "I've been having doubts for too long now,
doubts I didn't have the courage to face. And yes, like you
said, I was afraid I was like my mother. That fear kept me
engaged to you and kept me from facing my own doubts. However, I just found out that my mother wanted to be faithful. She
wanted to try again." Amy drew her coat closer, shivering,
thinking about how close she had come to going through with
a wedding to a man to whom she felt more loyalty than love.

For a moment the thought of all the arrangements weighed
on her mind, but she couldn't take that burden on. Had it been
up to her the wedding and its subsequent celebration would
have been simpler, smaller.

"You didn't even give it a chance."

"No, Tim. Don't you understand? I couldn't *take* the chance.
In spite of how hurtful it was, I was afraid that you were right.
That I was just like my mother. If I had married you, 'given it
a chance' I'm afraid of what might have happened to both of
us."

"So this is it? On the streets of Williams Lake, two years
are swept aside?"

Amy looked around, remembering the mountainside where
he had proposed to her. "I'm sorry I couldn't oblige with a
more romantic locale, but I didn't think of it as a particularly
romantic thing to do."

"No, I suppose not." He shifted his weight, glanced once
more at her and then took a step backward. "Well, I'll be away
from here in two weeks. I imagine that can't be soon enough
for you."

Amy saw the hurt in his eyes and regretted once again putting it there. She resisted the urge to reach out for him, to
comfort him. "Please don't talk that way. I don't hate you. I
did love you..."

"Not enough to move."

She shook her head. "I would have ended up hating you."

"Not you, Amy. You don't know how to hate. I could learn something from you about forgiveness and loving." He touched her cheek lightly, turned and left.

Amy dropped her chin on her chest and bit back tears. She had hurt him, she knew that and took no pleasure in it.

She felt a lone tear trickle down her cheek and she wiped it carefully away, wishing Elizabeth would come so she could talk to her.

Half an hour later a Henderson farm truck pulled into the street. Amy felt an apprehensive lift of her heart. But as it drew near she saw Elizabeth was driving. When it stopped in front of her, she tried not to feel disappointed. She got in and shivered in the warmth of the cab.

"It seems like you're always rescuing me," she said to Elizabeth as she buckled up her seat belt.

"Not a problem, dear," Elizabeth replied, pulling away from the curb. "I wasn't busy." Thankfully she said nothing more until they left town behind them and were driving on the highway.

"So, now you have to tell me how you ended up in town at 7:00 p.m. all on your own when you were supposed to be with Tim." Elizabeth smiled at Amy as she settled back in the driver's seat.

Amy bit her lip, wondering how she was going to explain to the mother of the man she thought she loved, that she had just broken an engagement with the man she was supposed to love. She decided on a pure Danyluk approach. "I broke up with Tim."

Out of the corner of her eye Amy watched for Elizabeth's reaction. Elizabeth only looked ahead, nodding slightly.

"I'm not too surprised, dear." She kept her eyes on the road. "Fred and I could see it coming. I wondered if your love for Tim was strong enough to move from here to Vancouver."

"I did love him," Amy added, feeling she needed to justify her actions.

"Yes, dear, I know you did. Everyone knew you did." Finally she turned to Amy and smiled. "Don't load too much guilt on yourself over it, but I think you loved someone else more.''

"Was it that obvious? I tried so hard," she said sadly. "I was always so afraid that I was just like..." Amy stopped, feeling like a scratch in a record, always returning to the same place.

"Just like your mother." Elizabeth finished the sentence for her. "My dear girl. You've been carrying that around ever since you were little, and it's been even worse since Paul came back. But you know who you are." Elizabeth reached across the truck and squeezed Amy's hand in reassurance. She straightened, taking the wheel again, looking ahead. "In some ways you're very much like your mother," she continued, "but in other ways, so different. You have your mother's sensitivity and your father's stubbornness. Your mother's selflessness and your father's self-righteousness. And mixed in with that you have a very caring, loving nature that is pure Amy."

At Elizabeth's kind words Amy felt a deep sadness well within her. She didn't know where it came from, only that she needed to let it go. She dropped her face in her hands and began to cry.

Elizabeth pulled the truck over and drew Amy into her arms. "It's okay, dear, you just cry. It's been a hard few months for you." She stroked Amy's face and let her pour out her sorrow. Each sob, each tear seemed to cleanse and draw out all the confusion of the events of the past month. Her sorrow mingled with prayers for guidance as she lay in the secure comfort of both her surrogate mother and her God.

When the heartache was drained from her soul, Amy straightened and sniffed. Elizabeth reached past Amy to the glove box, pulled out a box of tissues and handed it to her. "Blow your nose and stop thinking. Trust that God will take care of you and let Him do the fussing."

Amy nodded and, drawing in a deep breath, sat back as Elizabeth pulled onto the highway. She closed her eyes, as peace washed over her once again. She didn't know what she was going to do, didn't want to think past this moment, but for the first time in months, the future wasn't something to avoid.

Elizabeth pulled up in front of Amy's house and left the truck idling. "Why don't you run in and get a few clothes together. You should stay at our place tonight."

Amy turned her head toward Elizabeth and smiled her thanks.

Upstairs in her old bedroom, she quickly gathered up a spare change of clothes and her overnight things and dropped them into her suitcase—the one she had just unpacked a few days ago when she came back from Vancouver. But this time a sub-dued excitement hurried her motions, quickened her heart.

She was going to Hendersons' and Paul would be there.

Chapter Sixteen

Paul drew his horse to a halt and arched his shoulders forward. His back was stiff, his knees hurt, and he was aware of muscles and bones he didn't even know he possessed.

He had forgotten how tiring eight hours in the saddle could be. All the way down the hills he had been calculating how much longer before he could get out of the saddle and whether he would ever be able to walk upright again.

Sasha shook her head, reminding Paul that she had been carrying him eight hours. With a groan he dismounted and, pressing a hand on his back, arched backward easing the stiffness out of it.

His father drew up beside him and easily stepped out of the saddle. He grinned at Paul, tossed the reins over Trooper's head and without missing a beat led him to the hitching rail.

"Show-off," mumbled Paul as he stretched his stiff legs and slowly started walking.

"Long day isn't it," said Fred amiably as Paul tied Sasha up.

Paul said nothing, only gave his father a level look and began tugging loose the latigo holding the cinch strap. By the time Paul had the saddle back in the tack shed and the blanket laid out to dry, his father was already done and leading Trooper out to pasture.

It took Paul a little longer to brush Sasha down and take the bridle off. He let her go to join her friend who was already rolling on the ground, and Paul joined his father leaning on the top rail of the fence.

"So, son. Day like today didn't make you change your mind about staying?"

Paul yawned so hard his jaw almost cracked, but as he did so he slowly shook his head. "No," he said finally, his hands dangling down as he watched Sasha and Trooper lift their tails and tear off to the other end of the pasture. "Not at all." He smiled almost dreamily, rotating his shoulders. He was exhausted, but it was a good tired.

Fred crossed his arms and leaned his chin on his hands. "And what about Amy?"

Paul stiffened at the mention of her name. He couldn't help it. "What about her?" he asked, affecting a nonchalant air.

"She's going to be married and moving away. Does that make a difference?" Fred turned his head slightly and, with his thumb, pushed the brim of his cowboy hat up a little.

Paul sighed lightly and shrugged. "It does. But I still want to be out here." He looked up at the darkening sky. The cooling air held the bite of fall, a reminder of winter approaching. He smiled a slow smile. "I can't go back to the city. I feel sorry for Amy if she thinks she can. I tried to tell her, and I'm resisting the urge, sore as I am, to get back on Sasha and ride over there and try again." He took a deep breath, stilling the panic that started within him whenever he thought of Amy's approaching marriage. He struggled again to let go, sending yet another quick prayer heavenward. "I feel closer to God here, Dad, and I know that shouldn't change with my surroundings, but it does."

Fred straightened and squeezed Paul's shoulder, hard and quick. A man's hug. His father wasn't given to overt displays of affection, but his boys knew clearly that they were loved and cared for.

"I'm going in. I'm sure supper's overdone by now." Fred turned and walked away, a soft whistle trailing him.

Paul waited a moment, relishing the emptiness of his stomach. It didn't matter if supper was dry or overcooked, it would taste delicious. He drew in a deep breath of cool air, rolled his head, prayed again that Amy would be happy and turned to the house.

He pulled his boots off in the porch and almost dropped them on top of a pair of dainty high heels. Looked like his mom had company. Saleslady, Paul thought, nudging the shoes aside to make room for his boots. He hung his coat up, finger combed his hair, pushed open the door to the kitchen and stopped.

Amy half turned, her hair slipping across her shoulders, her gray eyes softening as she saw him. She wore a pale bronze dress that brought out the highlights in her hair and emphasized the delicate tones of her skin.

Paul swallowed, curbing the desire to drag her out of her chair and wrap his arms around her, hard. Instead he nodded at her curtly, mumbled a quick hello to his mother, then turned and headed for the bathroom to wash up.

The soft murmur of voices reached him as he ran the water over his hands, concentrating on getting all the grime out from under his fingernails, stalling.

What was Amy doing here? She was supposed to be in town making plans for her wedding.

Maybe she had finally changed her mind? Maybe she had come to tell him she had made a mistake and she was now ready to live with him, happily ever after?

Paul rinsed the sink out and looked up into the mirror. He needed a haircut, he needed a shave and he needed to have his head examined. Amy was as stubborn as Judd, and she carried around the burden of her mother's unfaithfulness. He couldn't fight that.

He wiped his hands on the towel, dragged his hands over his face and steeled himself to hear more of her wedding plans. *I just wish I could be truly happy for her, Lord,* he prayed. *But I can't. And I can't because I don't think she will be happy if she goes through with this.*

He entered the kitchen.

Amy stood by the table as if waiting for him.

"Where's my mom and dad?" Paul frowned as he glanced around the kitchen. A place was set for him at the table, a covered plate on a place mat, flanked by silverware.

"Your mom and dad thought maybe we should talk," Amy said softly. "Alone."

Once again Paul swallowed, his heart speeding up, his breathing shallow. "What..." He stopped and cleared his throat, feeling as uncertain as a teenager. "What are we supposed to talk about?" He pulled the chair out from the table and sat down, concentrating on uncovering his food, arranging his silverware just so.

Amy sat down diagonally from him, her hands folded on the table in front of her. He heard her draw a breath, and just before he closed his eyes to thank God for the food, he saw it.

She no longer wore her engagement ring.

Paul reached over and caught her hand, separating the intertwined fingers, running his own over the spot her engagement ring had once been. "Where's your ring?" he asked, hardly daring to hope.

"I gave it back to Tim."

Paul continued rubbing her finger as her words slowly sank in. "Why?"

"Because you were right. Because I didn't love him enough. Because I was staying faithful to him for the wrong reasons."

Amy let her fingers slowly twine through his as she spoke— hers now soft, his callused. She squeezed his hand, as if encouraging. Paul slowly lifted them to his mouth, resting his lips against them. He drew a deep breath and slowly let it out again.

"Amy," he whispered against her hand. He lifted his gaze to meet hers. Slowly, so slowly, he reached out to touch her face, his fingertips barely touching her cheek, as if he was afraid she would disappear if he pressed too hard. "When did this happen?"

Amy laughed her voice shaky. "About two hours ago."

Paul gave in to the impulses he'd stifled for the past month, stood up, and with a gentle tug, drew her to her feet. Relishing his right to finally do so, he pulled her close, wrapped his arms all the way around her tightly, holding her against him, rocking slightly, hardly daring to believe she was in his arms. He buried his face in her silky hair. Her arms slipped around his waist, slender but strong. He rubbed his rough cheek against her, nudging her face around until their lips met.

"I love you, Amy Danyluk," he said against her mouth, his words caressing her lips. And then finally, oh finally, they kissed, long and tenderly, as if each had to catch up to the place their hearts were at this moment. They clung, laughed and kissed again, caught up in the moment, catching up on missed opportunities.

Paul finally drew back, still holding her, his eyes traveling over her face, taking in each beloved feature, touching each with his lips. "I love you," he repeated, his shoulders lifting in a relieved sigh. "I want to marry you."

Amy blinked quickly. Then she laughed. "Just like that," she said, her voice tremulous.

Paul grinned, dropped another kiss on her mouth. "Just like that," he repeated. "I don't want to give you too much time as a single girl, you might enjoy your freedom too much."

"I may as well start bossing you around, then." Amy pulled away, giving him a gentle push. "You'd better eat. I'm sure you're hungry."

Paul bent over and gave her another quick kiss. "I'll live." But he did as he was told and sat down. He reached across the table to take her hand before he bowed his head in prayer. His heart was full, overflowing and his prayer became an outpouring of thankfulness.

When he was finished he looked up, squeezed her hand. Her head was bent and Paul could see a glint of tears on her cheeks, but a smile on her mouth. He reached into his pocket and pulled out a dusty handkerchief.

"It's seen cleaner days, but it's fairly absorbent," he said, sensing a need to ease the mood. "And your mascara won't stain it."

Amy laughed a shaky laugh and took it from him.

A polite cough from the doorway heralded his mother's arrival. She entered the kitchen and leaned against the kitchen counter, her arms crossed over an old well-loved sweater, a benevolent smile on her face.

Fred paused a moment in the doorway, surveying the scene with a grin. "So, declarations of undying love all done and over with?"

Paul just smiled back at his father. "We were just getting warmed up."

Elizabeth emitted a sound that sounded suspiciously like a choked sigh.

"Say something, my dear?" asked Fred.

"Nothing worth repeating."

Paul looked up at his parents, his heart overflowing with love and peace. Life was good. God was good.

And just because he could, he reached over and stroked Amy's hair, his hand lingering on her cheek. She smiled back at him, and he thought of all the things he needed to know about her and the plans he wanted to share. It would take weeks to catch up, to reconnect, to establish a new and better relationship.

And the best part was, they had all the time in the world.

The next morning Amy picked up her suitcase and looked around the room to make sure she hadn't forgotten anything. She blinked back her tears, frustrated with the fragility of her own emotions. It took so little these days to make her cry.

She sniffed, swallowed, took a breath and turned to leave the room. Paul waited in the hallway and took her suitcase without a word. He preceded her down the stairs, his hair sticking out well below his baseball cap. He needs a haircut, she thought, following him, clutching her cosmetic bag. Paul walked through the living room and shouldered open the front door, allowing Amy to pass him. She paused a moment looking up at him, meeting his blue, blue eyes. He smiled back, and she had to resist the urge to stop and lean against him.

She didn't want to go.

But there, standing on the step, stood her mother, her strawberry blond hair glinting in the morning sun, her pale gray silk suit hanging elegantly from her slim frame. Elizabeth stood beside her looking like a before picture in her worn sweatshirt and faded blue jeans, her feet hastily shoved into a pair of moccasins.

One had given her life, the other, faith. One had taken care of her as a child, the other as a young girl growing up with too many questions and no one to answer them.

Until now.

Amy had forgotten about her mother's visit until the shrill ring of the phone had interrupted the Hendersons' breakfast. Fred had grumbled, said a contracted 'hello' then handed it to Amy. Noreen was on the other end calling from Williams Lake, trying to track her down to take her to Vancouver for their planned visit. No one had answered at the home place, and she hadn't known where else to call. She had come up the night before and stayed at a motel in town. Amy felt she could hardly tell her mother that she didn't want to go with her, after she had traveled all that way.

It didn't seem fair, she thought. She and Paul had only been able to spend one night together free from the guilt of other relationships. One night to try to catch up on the past, to discover when and where and how they had first fallen in love with each other.

"There you are, Amy," Noreen turned to her with a smile. She saw the single suitcase Paul carried. "Is that all your clothes?"

"It's all I'm packing," said Amy. Paul and she had made a quick trip to her place after breakfast to get a few more clothes, steal a few more kisses and get back in time for Noreen's arrival.

She felt the warmth of Paul's hand on her neck, giving her a proprietary squeeze, and she resisted the urge to turn into his arms, lay her head on his chest. In just the few stolen moments they'd had together, she had discovered one of the things that had been missing from her and Tim's relationship. The need to connect, to touch and the awareness of the other's presence. Now she knew exactly how close he stood behind her, how much he wanted to hold her.

"Well, then, I guess we had better get on our way." Noreen smiled at the group, slipping on her sunglasses. "I'm hoping to make Vancouver before rush hour starts."

Amy bit her lip remembering too well the snarls of traffic in Vancouver and the cars and trucks whizzing by. She gave Paul a pained look over her shoulder. She wanted to do more, but was restrained by her mother's presence and the fact that Noreen knew nothing about her and Tim's broken engagement.

"Have a good time, Amy." Elizabeth gave her a hug and squeezed her shoulders. "We'll be thinking of you." Elizabeth's blue eyes, so much like her son's, held Amy's, as if letting her know that she both understood and approved of the sacrifice Amy made by going with her mother now. She took a step back as Amy walked down the verandah stairs and followed her mother to the car.

"Wait, Amy," Elizabeth called out, holding up her hand as she turned toward the house. "Just hold on a minute."

She disappeared and a few moments later stepped out of the door holding the shiny plastic garment bag that held Amy's wedding dress. "You may as well do something about this."

Amy turned back to get it, but Paul stopped her, handing her the suitcase. "Here, you put this in the car, I'll get that thing." His tone indicated exactly what he thought of the silk and lace confection.

Amy couldn't help but smile at the sight of Paul tossing the bag over his shoulder as if it were a sack of feed. Noreen frowned as Paul headed toward the open trunk, about to flip the garment bag in.

"Don't put it in there. It's far too expensive to ride in the trunk of the car. Put that in the back seat," Noreen directed, opening the door. "We don't want Amy walking down the aisle in a dusty dress."

"We don't want Amy walking down the aisle wearing that dress, period," Paul said firmly.

Amy frowned at him. Noreen didn't know what was going on, and Amy didn't want to discuss her breakup, standing around her car.

Paul held her gaze a moment, then winked. "You take care, Punky."

Amy wished again she could stay but knew for her mother's sake she should go.

Noreen's questioning gaze moved from Paul to Amy, and Elizabeth broke the moment, hugging Amy once again. "Have a good time, girl. We'll see you in a few days." She turned to Noreen. "Thanks for coming up here to pick her up. But next time you're more than welcome to stay here, you certainly don't need to stay in a motel in town."

Noreen smiled her thanks, waiting for Amy to make a move.

Amy looked once more at Paul trying to show him in one look how it hurt to leave. She stepped into Noreen's car. As they drove away, she turned in her seat, watching his figure as it grew smaller and smaller, then she turned around, facing ahead.

"Why do I get the feeling that I didn't exactly come at a very good time?"

Her mother's softly spoken question broke the quiet in the car. Amy glanced sidelong at her mother, feeling suddenly guilty for not showing more enthusiasm for her visit.

Amy shook her head. "I'm looking forward to spending time with you, Mom. Besides, I think we need to do this."

And as she thought back to her broken engagement, she realized she was right. All her life the shadow of her mother's defection had hung over her and had colored so much of her relationship with Tim.

Now, as she was on the threshold of a relationship with Paul, she knew she needed to dispel any and all doubts and fears from her past. She needed to reestablish her relationship with her mother in order to make her relationship with Paul secure.

"I almost hate to ask, but is there a story behind the wedding dress?" Noreen glanced sidelong at Amy, then ahead, as if questioning her right to pry.

Amy laughed, remembering the sight of Paul carrying it. "I guess I should tell you." Amy unconsciously reached for her absent engagement ring. "I gave Tim his ring back."

Noreen threw Amy a surprised glance, then looked back at

the road. "I see," she said inanely, as if unable to find the right words. "That would mean the wedding is off."

Amy nodded.

"And the dress is to be returned?" Noreen continued.

Amy nodded again.

"When did this happen?"

"Yesterday."

More silence.

"So that's why Paul was staring at you like he wished he could be alone with you."

"I guess so." Amy swallowed a sudden pain at the thought of leaving Paul, but it wasn't the pain of uncertainty, merely the hurt of parting. She would see him again, and she prayed that God would keep him safe until she returned.

"I guess I should have known. His feelings for you were quite obvious the time we had lunch at Fred and Elizabeth's place."

Amy remembered that particular afternoon and for a moment wondered what her mother really thought about the situation. Did she think less of Amy for breaking up with Tim who had so much going for him?

Noreen glanced sidelong at Amy again, smiling. "You know something?"

Amy shook her head.

"I never really liked that dress, either."

Amy laughed and, for the first time since her mother had picked her up, began to look forward to their being together.

"This is where you'll be sleeping." Noreen flicked the switch on beside the door, flooding the bedroom with subdued light.

Amy stepped carefully through the doorway, her stockinged feet sinking into the soft, green carpet. The room was done up in shades of sea foam and gray, coordinated from the bedspread to the prints that hung on the wall.

"This is lovely." Amy dropped her suitcase with a muffled thump. She luxuriated in the soft pile of the carpet, her footsteps silent as she walked to the large window. Her mother's economic situation was evident from the luxury of the four-teenth-floor condominium.

Rain tapped against the window, turning the lights of the apartment building across the road into hazy patches of light. A shroud of gray hung over the harbor, hiding the mountains beyond the strait.

"On a clear day you can see Vancouver Island," her mother said.

Amy touched the cool window, craning her neck to look down at the tiny lights that scurried along the street, cars with people on their way home or out for an evening of entertainment.

"Well, I'm impressed."

"I know you don't have the view that you do from your bedroom at home, but this place has its own appeal."

Amy turned away from the window. Noreen sat on the bed as her hands twisted nervously around each other.

"I'm glad I came." Amy smiled in reassurance.

"Then I'm glad, too." Noreen tilted her head to one side as if studying her daughter anew. When she spoke, her voice was quiet, tight with emotion. "I didn't tell you, but I stopped in to see Judd last night when I was in town. We had a lot to talk about and only got a little bit covered. It's just a beginning, but I know it's only fair to you and Rick to start."

Feelings vibrated between them, each afraid to make a move, forgiveness toward her mother an unfamiliar emotion for Amy, guilt a far too familiar one for Noreen.

Amy took a step forward, was met by her mother and they embraced.

Noreen was the first one to pull away. She smiled a shaky smile, wiped a tear from her eye, smudging her mascara. "Sorry. I'm not usually this emotional."

Amy smiled as her mother found a tissue, wiped her eyes then became brisk and efficient. "I had a number of things planned for this week, but I guess shopping for a wedding gift is out of the question." Noreen blinked, then returned Amy's smile. "We could do clothes. I'm sure we can find something that isn't silk with sequins that would suit you."

Amy laughed. "We could. I haven't gone clothes shopping for years, and I guess the money I had set aside for a new fridge could cover that."

"Are you still using that old thing that always froze my lettuce?"

"And the milk if you didn't put it exactly on the right shelf."

"I always scolded you for putting it in the wrong spot...." Noreen stopped then laughed self-deprecatingly. "Well didn't that sound exactly like a mother." She looked down at her watch. "Goodness. It's late and you must be famished. I'll get supper going, you just unpack and relax."

Amy watched the door close behind her mother. There were still a lot of emotions that entangled themselves in encounters with her, but somehow each visit became easier.

Her comment about the fridge gave Amy a glimpse of what she could expect from the next few days. Different memories. New insights into her own childhood seen from eyes that beheld things with different emotions and from a different place than her father.

Amy opened her suitcase and immediately thought about Paul. She sent up a quick prayer for patience for herself and Paul. And, in spite of herself, a prayer that he would still be waiting when she got back.

She couldn't discard all those years of unrequited love in just one day, and her own insecurities hovered, always reminding her that Paul had had many girlfriends, many of them far more glamorous than she could ever hope to be.

Please, Lord, help me to trust. And to be satisfied that You are ever faithful.

Paul shoved the pitchfork back into the bale with a quick jab. Sasha stood on the other side of the corral, head down, munching on dry hay, making it look more appetizing than it was.

A chill wind knifed down the mountains, and Paul pulled his coat closer around himself. He would have to haul out his winter clothes pretty soon, he thought, as he rubbed his hands together to keep warm.

The sun drifted down toward the mountains, the sky opposite already darkening. The days were getting shorter, and he figured it would freeze hard tonight.

Paul sighed as his eyes followed the hills to the road that lead to the Danyluks' place. Amy had been gone two days. He'd missed her from the first minute she'd driven away in Noreen's car.

The small spark of fear that ignited when she left, glowed again. Each hour she stayed away it seemed to burn hotter. Would she come back? Had he misunderstood?

He spun around and vaulted over the fence separating the frozen pasture from the yard and strode to the house. His mom probably had supper ready, and he was cold and hungry.

He stepped into the house just as the phone rang. His heart skipped a beat. Maybe it was Amy.

"Is that you Paul?" His mother poked her head into the porch and handed him the cordless phone. "Phone for you."

He grinned and clutched the receiver, turning his back to his mother as he pulled his boots off. "Hello," he said, his voice breathless.

"Paul Henderson?"

Paul's heart plunged. Not Amy. Some man. "Yes," he replied, unable to keep the disappointed tone out of his voice.

"I'm sorry to bother you. I realize that you might not want to talk to me, but I have some news that might interest you."

Paul frowned as he recognized the voice. "What can I do for you, Tim?" He clutched the receiver, his mind racing as he wondered what Tim could be calling about, other than Amy.

"What I'm about to tell you is confidential but..." Tim stopped a moment while Paul silently urged the words out of him. "The Drozd boys couldn't get the financing together to buy the Danyluk place. I...I know I'm stepping out of my bounds here, but I thought you might be interested in knowing that it's still up for sale."

Paul's breath left him in a rush. *Thank you, Lord,* he prayed. He had thought the worst, had thought Tim was going to tell him that he still wanted Amy, still loved her. "Why did you tell me?'' Paul couldn't stop the question, wondering about Tim's motives.

A moment of silence fell, then, ''I know how much that place means to Amy. I also know that she has feelings for you—'' Tim was quiet a moment ''—as I do for her.''

Paul felt a moment of regret for all the times he had wondered if Tim really cared for Amy. What he had just done showed Paul that he did, and in spite of previous antagonism, he felt sorry for him. ''I don't know what to say, Tim, but I'm really glad you called. Is it Rick or Judd I should deal with on this?''

''Judd signed power of attorney over to Amy a number of years ago. You'll have to talk to her.''

Paul felt his heart lift. He and his father had been considering the Kincaid place and couldn't come to an agreement. Danyluks' wasn't as large, but it would work better into their operation. ''I'll do that. Thank you.'' He said goodbye, hit the Talk button on the handset to hang up and clenched his fists. ''Yes,'' he shouted, punching the air. ''Thank you, Lord.''

Chapter Seventeen

"I feel terrible, leaving you alone tonight." Noreen buttoned up her coat and then yanked her briefcase off the table. "Are you sure you don't mind? I'll try to cut the meeting as short as possible."

Amy shook her head and pushed the sleeves of her peach-colored corduroy shirt up her arms. She got up and walked to the door. "No. I don't mind one bit. It's been a long time since I spent an evening alone. I think I might like it."

"Well, I've spent far too many of them, and I really begrudge the time." Noreen smiled regretfully at Amy. "But I am consoled in knowing that you'll be here when I get back." She reached over and stroked her daughter's cheek.

Amy smiled back and caught her mother in a hug. "I'm so glad I came, Mom."

Noreen straightened and nodded. "I wish I could tell you what a blessing you have been to me. I thank God for bringing Tim into your life."

Amy frowned. "Sorry, Mom. I missed that. You mean Paul don't you?"

"No. Tim. If you hadn't gotten engaged to him, the notice would never have been in the Vancouver papers. And I wouldn't have had the nerve to call you otherwise." Noreen smiled at Amy. "I guess any mother can't resist getting in on their daughter's wedding."

Amy sighed, thinking how close it had been. She would have missed this time and any future times. For the past few days she had wondered if being engaged to Tim had been wrong. Even if it was, God had used it for good. "Then I'm glad I got engaged to him, too."

Noreen smiled and glanced at her watch. "I've got to go." She opened the door and paused. "Are you sure you're going to be okay? I could just cancel the interview."

"And sit here feeling guilty the rest of the evening." Amy laughed. "I don't mind, Mom. Just go. I'll have tea ready when you get back."

Noreen nodded, turned and closed the door behind her.

Amy waited a moment, relishing the quiet sounds of her mother's condo. No noise from outside intruded, and inside, the only sound was the quiet hum of the refrigerator in the kitchen and the bubbling of a large fish aquarium dividing the living room from the formal dining room.

The space and luxury of the condo was still unfamiliar, even after three days. But what had been the best surprise was the enjoyment she had, being with her mother. They browsed through the designer boutiques on Robson Street, visited the Granville Market, saw a play at the Queen Elizabeth Theater and on the one clear day they had, walked around Stanley Park.

The days went by far too quickly as she caught a glimpse of her mother's life, the loneliness she had lived with and how she had filled it. It was almost sad to see how much Noreen enjoyed each minute they spent together.

And each evening Paul phoned. He never asked, and Amy didn't volunteer, but in the back of each conversation hovered the question, When are we going to be together? She felt so torn. Each smile her mother directed at her, each hug that occurred with increasing spontaneity, anchored another tiny barb of regret for all that her mother had missed out on because of Judd.

But now, alone for the first time in a few days, Amy felt her love for Paul overwhelm her. She ached to be with him, yet a new emotion had reared its head.

She was afraid to make herself vulnerable to him. As she and her mother talked, she was reminded again of herself as a young girl, hanging on Paul's every word, stealing pictures that she placed under her pillow at night. Again she felt the way it had been to be treated as a younger sister, and she wondered if that would ever go away.

She dropped onto the couch, the cordless phone beside her, and picked up the book she had been trying to finish.

After about an hour she put it down and glanced at the clock. Eight-thirty. Paul still hadn't called. Amy picked up the TV remote control and flipped through the various channels, turning up her nose at what was offered.

When the phone rang beside her, she jumped. "Noreen Danyluk's residence, Amy speaking."

"You always answer the phone so primly, are you sure you didn't take secretarial training?" Paul's deep voice reverberated through the lines, sending shivers down Amy's back.

"Hi." She leaned back, curled her feet under her, relaxed and smiled.

"So what are you and Noreen doing?"

"Mom's gone to an important interview, and I'm trying to find something equally exciting to watch on television." Amy fiddled with the remote and finally shut the television off.

"So you're all alone."

"Yah. What about you. What are you up to?" Amy lay back and closed her eyes, letting his deep voice wash over her and soothe all her apprehensions.

"I've been traveling."

Amy listened, positive she could hear the sound of a police siren on the phone. "Where are you? Williams Lake?"

"No. Not Williams Lake." He was quiet a moment, and the siren died down. "Why don't you get up and look out your window?"

Amy jumped to her feet and ran to the patio doors. She pulled the vertical blinds aside and squinted into the darkness. All she could see was her pale reflection, her face framed by her hair hanging loose. She cupped one hand and held it between her face and the window.

And then she saw him, standing by the pay phone across the street, looking up at her, waving.

"Can I come up?" his voice asked in her ear.

Amy nodded, then realized he couldn't see her. "Yes, please," she said breathlessly.

"I'm going to hang up now. I'll buzz you."

"Sure," was all she could manage.

The click in her ear galvanized her into action. Paul was here. He was coming.

She whirled around the apartment, trying to clean up an already immaculate room. She clapped her hands to her head. Her hair! She had just pulled it up into a ponytail and left it. She would look a fright.

She spun around and headed down the short hall toward the bathroom when the phone rang. Skidding to a halt, she looked left then right. Paul was waiting, but she looked terrible. What to do?

She ran to the phone and picked it up. "Yes?"

"It's me."

Amy hit the buzzer to let him in, hung up the phone and headed back down the hallway.

She stood in front of the bathroom mirror, her pale reflection staring back at her. Were her eyes really that big? She looked like she hadn't slept. And her hair was a mess. At least the shirt was clean. Its pale peach color was a perfect complement to the earth-toned jeans she wore.

Amy yanked on her ponytail, jerked open the drawer and pulled out a hairbrush. But her hair wouldn't cooperate. She grimaced at it, still holding the brush when the doorbell rang.

He was here already!

Amy dropped the brush, rammed her fingers through her hair, wincing as she hit a tangle.

The doorbell rang again and again.

"Oh, brother," she sped out of the bathroom, ran down the hallway, her heart hurrying her along, her insecurities holding her back. She stopped in front of the door, took a deep breath, smoothed her hands over her hair and opened the door. Paul stood in the hallway, his hands shoved in the pockets of faded blue jeans, tiny droplets of water shining in his hair and misting the shoulders of a cream-colored cotton sweater, the tension around his mouth relaxing as he saw her.

He stepped inside, closed the door behind her and without speaking a word gathered her into his arms. He buried his face in her tangled hair, pressed her close and whispered her name over and over.

She clung to him, her eyes closed, one hand clutching his back, the other his neck as they rocked slightly, clinging to each other, filling the emptiness of the past few days, no, months.

Paul straightened, only enough to cup his hand behind her head, then lowered his head and finally kissed her. And Amy's heart leaped against her chest, her own fingers tangled in his hair, holding him close.

Paul pulled away slightly, ignoring her small sound of protest as he dropped featherlight kisses on her cheek, her eyelids, her temple, his fingers traveling over her face as if remembering each feature.

"Paul," she whispered, enjoying the sound of his name. "I missed you."

"I know," he said confidently, pulling away.

Amy frowned, then saw his grin. "You are terrible."

He looked down at her, his blue eyes suddenly serious as they traveled over her face. He sighed once and shook his head lightly. "I can't believe you are actually here."

"In Vancouver? In my mother's condo?" she asked, letting him know that two could play his game.

"No." He gave her a little shake. "In my arms." He touched her hair, running his fingertips over her hairline, traced her eyebrow, down her nose and then touched her lips. "I love you, Amy," he said softly. "I have loved you longer than I even knew I did."

Amy looked up at him, at the face that had been in so many of her dreams, the face that she had thought of in so many of her waking moments. "I'm not dreaming, am I? I'm not going to wake up and find you gone, back to a place I can't reach you.''

He shook his head and kissed her again. "Let's go sit where we can talk.''

Amy laughed, caught his hand and pulled him toward the couch. "Will this do?''

Paul tilted his head to one side, glanced at the television, then back at the couch. "Who gets the remote?''

"I hid it.''

He laughed, dropped on the couch and pulled her beside him, cradling her shoulders with his arm, pressing a kiss against her temple. He drew her against him and sighed.

"You drove all the way up from the ranch?'' she asked, pulling back to better see his beloved features.

He leaned back on the couch and rolled his head to look at her. "Yes. I have a question to ask you.'' He straightened and reached into his back pocket.

Amy felt her heart lift. He had already asked her to marry him at his parents' place, and she hadn't quite believed it. This time it was going to be official and real, she mused.

She frowned when he pulled out a long white envelope. She had expected a small velvet box. "What's that?''

Paul waggled his eyebrows at her. "You don't know?'' He tapped her on the nose with the envelope and then opened it up. "This is a very important document pertaining to our future.''

"A marriage license?'' Amy asked carefully.

"Almost as good.'' Paul spread the paper on his knee and handed her a pen. "This is an offer from Paul Henderson to purchase the Danyluk property from one Amy Danyluk, who holds the power of attorney granted her by her father...blah, blah, blah.''

Amy snatched the paper from his hands and held it close, scanning the contents. She lowered the paper, shaking her head. "What...'' She couldn't figure this out. "I thought the Drozd boys were going to buy it. They just had to sign the papers.''

"They had trouble coming up with the money.'' Paul leaned

back, grinning. "I got the information from a very trustworthy source."

"Who?"

Paul's face became serious and he took her hand in his, rubbing her fingers. "Tim phoned me to tell me. He thought I would be interested. He knew how important it was to you, and he knew how important you are to me. He told me he did this because he loved you."

Amy smiled a bittersweet smile. "I thought he would hate me for what I did—" she looked up at Paul "—just weeks before the wedding."

Paul touched her lips with a finger. "Like my mother told me when I broke up with Stacy, 'Better before the wedding than after.'" He smiled down at her and reached into another pocket, this time to pull out a small velvet box.

He carefully opened it and pulled out a golden ring with a blue sapphire bracketed by delicate swirls of gold. He turned it in his hands a moment as it caught the light. Then he carefully slipped it on her finger replacing the diamond that had been there only a week before. "Will you marry me, Amy Danyluk?"

Amy watched as he slid the ring over her knuckle, then she curved her fingers over his. She felt her heart lift, her breath shorten and her throat tighten. "Yes," she whispered, reaching out for him. "Yes, I will."

They embraced again, kissed again and laughed again.

"And will you sell me your ranch?" Paul asked, cupping her face in his hands.

"I'll have to talk to my dad about that," she said, her mouth almost sore from smiling. She laughed, pulled Paul close and planted a kiss on his mouth. "I thank God for you, Paul Henderson."

Paul grew serious at her words. "Not as much as I do, Amy. Not as much as I do." The moment stretched out like a prayer.

Then Paul pulled Amy closer. "When can you come back?"

Amy rubbed her cheek against the soft wool of his sweater. "As soon as possible."

"Tonight?"

Amy hesitated, suddenly thinking of her mother and her loneliness. But as she looked up at Paul she also realized where she wanted to be with all her heart. She opened her mouth to say something, but at that moment the door opened and Noreen came in.

She stopped, looking first at Amy, then Paul. "So you did come."

Amy frowned at Paul, then looked back at her mother. "Did you know?"

"Oh, yes," Noreen said, dropping her briefcase on the floor and shaking the droplets of water from her coat. "I phoned him and told him to come."

Amy bit her lip and shook her head.

"Hey," Paul said quietly, touching her trembling lip. "Don't cry."

She smiled at him, and in front of her mother leaned over and kissed him full on the mouth. Then she sat back, shaking her head at the two of them. "Thanks, Mom," she said softly. A gentle quiet was shared by the three of them.

"I figured you had spent more than enough time with me, and I thought it was time Paul came and got you," Noreen explained, reaching out to touch her daughter's face. "I knew it was time for you to start the part of your life you've been waiting for since you were a little girl." She stood up. "I took the liberty of packing your bags, hoping you wouldn't notice. They're ready to go."

Amy looked at Paul, then at her mother. She got up and caught Noreen in a fierce hug. "Thank you. I can't thank you enough." Amy stepped back and shook her head. "I do love you, Mom."

Noreen's eyes grew suspiciously shiny, and with a shaky laugh she turned away. "I'll get your things and walk you down to Paul's truck," she said over her shoulder as she disappeared into Amy's room.

She reappeared a moment later with two suitcases. Amy had come with one, but her mother had insisted on buying her new clothes, and the increase in her wardrobe necessitated another.

"So, let's go." Noreen smiled at Paul, then at Amy.

"Okay." Paul reached up and pulled his keys out of his pocket. "My truck is across the street." They left the apartment. The ride down was silent, each lost in their own thoughts. When they came to the bottom, Noreen sniffed, but stepped out of the elevator and walked across the foyer and out the double doors without a glance backward to see if Amy followed.

"Woman with a mission," said Paul with a sad smile, hefting Amy's suitcases and following.

It was still drizzling outside. Paul put Amy's suitcases in the cab of the truck, next to the window. "You're sitting beside me," he said with a grin.

Amy winked back, her heart overflowing with thanks and love. She turned to her mother and for a moment regretted leaving her.

"You'll come and visit?" Amy said, clutching her mother's shoulders as if to force the concession from her.

"Of course. As much as I'm allowed." Noreen caught Amy close to her in a fierce hug. She kissed her on the cheek and then stepped away. Paul bent over and kissed Noreen soundly on the cheek, wrapping one arm around her in a casual hug.

"So we'll see ya later," he said, "Mom."

Noreen smiled, then flapped her hands at them. "Get going. You've got a long ride ahead of you."

Amy stepped into the truck, Paul right behind her, and as they drew away, she turned to look out of the back window, much as she had only a few days ago, only this time she was beside Paul, heading home and it was her mother that stood on the pavement. She felt a measure of sadness and at the same time she thanked God for having had the time with her. There would be other times. She turned around, catching sight of Paul watching her.

"You'll see her again, you know."

Amy nodded, for the second time that night close to tears.

Paul drew her against him and negotiated the busy streets, one-handed. They said nothing until he turned onto the Trans-Canada Highway, his windshield wipers creating a hypnotic rhythm.

Amy straightened and reached up to touch Paul's cheek. "I

love you, Paul Henderson, and I'm glad you let me have the space I needed to be with my mother.''

Paul turned his head slightly, his eyes still on the road, and kissed her hand. "I love you too, Amy. And I praise God that He sent me home."

He sighed, pulling her close to him with one arm while the other held the steering wheel. "I want to tell you something else. I've learned a lot from you. You always challenged me in one way or another to be a better person than I wanted to be. I've had girlfriends, I can't deny that. But none of them have ever been as much a part of me as you were and are. I never asked any of them to marry me because I knew none of them measured up to you." He pressed a kiss on her head. "You who were always so worried about being faithful..."

"Not anymore, Paul," she interrupted. "Not since I found out what really happened between my parents."

"I know that. But I want to tell you this, to dispel any doubts you might have." He cleared his throat. "Now look what you did, I have to start over again."

"So, start."

"So, let me."

They laughed, sharing a moment of accord.

"Seriously, Amy. I was thinking about this the other day, as I was reading II Corinthians, chapter five, where it says 'We live by faith, not by sight.' Our faith in Christ is like that. We can't see, but we trust that one day all will be revealed. Sometimes it happens sooner and sometimes later." He paused a moment, tilting his head as he struggled to find the right words. "You always worried about being faithful, and you were. You kept faith with God when I was running around ignoring Him and His love. And the truth is...you have always been faithful to me. That sounds conceited, but I know it's true. And I cling to that. I feel unworthy of your love, much as I feel unworthy of God's love." He turned to her, his expression tinged with sadness. "But I cling to the comfort that as God is faithful, so you have been and will be."

Amy could say nothing. To hear him speak so freely of God showed her even more clearly what she hadn't felt with Tim.

She had never doubted Tim's faith, but the accord she and Paul shared, the faith they had in common, bound them firmly.

"I'm so glad I am able to love you, Paul," she whispered, reaching over to brush a kiss across his cheek. "I thank God for you. And I pray that we can continue to be faithful to Him and each other."

She laid her head on his shoulder and watched the windshield wipers slap back and forth, each beat bringing them both closer to their new life. Closer to home.

* * * * *

Dear Reader,

How many of us have ever made a promise and decided to stick with it to the bitter end? Our friendships can be like that, our business decisions, our other relationships.

When Amy made her promise to marry Tim, she was determined to prove that she could be faithful, that she could show herself to be true to her promises, unlike her mother. However, her determination was misguided and I believe there are times that we make the same mistakes in our lives. We want to be faithful, we want to be true, but sometimes we need to cut ties before we get pulled into a situation that cannot change.

I believe our lives are a balance of keeping promises and changing circumstances and we must prayerfully make every decision. We must never be afraid to change our mind if we know we can't truly glorify God in the path we have taken.

We may be fickle people who make wrong decisions and in all things we must be prayerful and trusting. But we can cling to the promise that in all things, God's love never changes.

Carolyne Aarsen

Love Inspired

presents

THE BENNETT WOMEN

a new series by

Virginia Myers

Introducing Jill, Kate and Beth:
three special women who find the faith and
courage to meet life's toughest tests.

HELPMATE

(August 1998)

The pressures of juggling dual careers and raising
children were taking a toll on Jill Rhys's beloved
family. She could feel her husband, Greg, pulling
away from her—now more than ever. But deep in her
heart Jill truly believed the love they shared could
survive anything, *especially* when the Lord
extended a helping hand....

Watch for the second book in this heartwarming
series in the spring of 1999, only from Love Inspired.

Steeple
Hill™

Available at your favorite retail outlet.

Take 3 inspirational love stories FREE!

PLUS get a FREE surprise gift!

Special Limited-time Offer

Mail to Steeple Hill Reader Service™
3010 Walden Avenue
P.O. Box 1867
Buffalo, N.Y. 14240-1867

YES! Please send me 3 free Love Inspired™ novels and my free surprise gift. Then send me 3 brand-new novels every month, which I will receive months before they appear in bookstores. Bill me at the low price of $3.19 each plus 25¢ delivery and applicable sales tax, if any*. That's the complete price and a saving of over 10% off the cover prices—quite a bargain! I understand that accepting the books and gift places me under no obligation ever to buy any books. I can always return a shipment and cancel at any time. Even if I never buy another book from Steeple Hill, the 3 free books and the surprise gift are mine to keep forever.

103 IEN CFAG

Name	(PLEASE PRINT)	
Address	Apt. No.	
City	State	Zip

This offer is limited to one order per household and not valid to present Love Inspired™ subscribers. *Terms and prices are subject to change without notice. Sales tax applicable in New York.

ULI-198 ©1997 Steeple Hill